Acknowledgements

There are many in my life who helped made this book, and so much more possible. They stayed by me when turning away would have been much easier. They were kind when I didn't deserve their kindness. They were honest when honesty was the last thing I wanted to hear, and at the same time showed me how important it was to be honest with myself.

They also loved me enough to kick me in the ass on the many occasions when my ass needed kicking. And, they did it out of love not anger.

So to my family and friends, thank you for your love, support and companionship along my way through life. The journey would have meant nothing without you.

Preface

Of the millions of individuals and families in this world, each has a unique story. What follows is an account of the lives of a family who pursued their dreams even though those dreams became clouded and hard to find. The characters were created from parts of the men and women who shaped my life, and in so many ways are responsible for who I am today.

As I wrote this account I came to realize how much I failed to appreciate all who faced so much, and sacrificed so greatly to remain true to the beliefs, principles and loved ones they held so dear. I wish I would have taken more time to watch them all more closely, understand them better and value them more while I still had the opportunities. Writing this book helped me capture much of what I allowed to slip by.

Although this is fiction every character is based on someone from my past, and each account is taken from an actual event. I learned that the truth makes me far more creative than my imagination.

Two of the characters are combat veterans who carry the burdens created by conflict. I included many of the things that make post traumatic stress so difficult. This is based on my own experience. I truly hope it gives all who read this a clearer view of war's true cost. But, war is only one part of the story I've told. I tried to include a little of what we all face as we try to follow our own dreams.

Chasing Shadow Covered Dreams

This work is fiction, and although the characters and happenings were gathered from personal experience they are in no way intended to represent any persons or actual events.

Nothing in life

As Precious As Dreams

Ever Comes Easily

Tony slid forward on the bench trying to concentrate on the pitcher and ignore the effects of last night's beer and jalapeño poppers. He was 0 for 2 and due up next inning. The pitcher wasn't overpowering, just nasty. His pitch selection was good, and location nearly perfect.

"Damn, I gotta figure this guy out. There must be something I can pick up." He said to himself as the poppers rolled in his stomach one more time.

Suddenly he heard, "fastball on the inside corner," in a low voice from about half way down the bench. And sure enough, pop, a fast ball caught the inside corner.

"Lucky guess wapp." Tony snapped at Vic Morretto, the cigar smoking Sicilian who joined the team just before last week's road trip.

"Wanna bet paisano?" Vic snapped back.

"Hell man, if you've got this guy figured out, I'll kiss your ass during tomorrow's national anthem." Tony promised.

"Well pucker up, and slide down here next to me." said Vic.

Tony moved down the bench as Vic pointed out "Look at the catcher's ass."

"What"? asked Tony "You want me to kiss his ass too?"

"Just look at his butt when he calls the next pitch you dumb northern dago." Vic insisted.

"Damn, the dummy is dropping his hand half way to his ankle. I can see every pitch he calls." Tony observed.

"Sure is. He does it every time." Vic added.

Tony leaned back and smiled. That's what he was looking for, all the edge he needed. Now he just had to figure out how to set it up so that they could relay the catcher's signals to him in the batter's box.

"Vic, can you pass the signals onto the first base coach next inning?" Tony asked.

A chipped front tooth appeared as Vic smiled and said "What's in it for me northern boy?"

"A chance to help the team you selfish ginni ass hole." Tony replied as a smile crossed his face.

"Hey, wow, you mean I get to help a bunch of shit heads I barely know from a town I never heard of until a few weeks ago? Man, and to think I almost passed this up to shovel shit on my uncle's chicken farm." Vic added.

3

Tony reminded Vic "I said I'd kiss your ass."

"How about introducing me to your long haired cousin?" Vic negotiated.

"Thanks to my northern Italian grandfather, the last Sicilian who tried to date my long haired cousin is part of the footings of the Centennial Bridge." Tony pointed out.

"Then, how about lending me your convertible for the week end?" Vic pressed.

"No, on second thought, take my cousin." Tony agreed.

The Old Man

The old man's form fit the worn easy chair as if it was part of him. He slumped a little as he slept with his head tilted to the side, resting on the old wrinkled pillow.

Tony looked at the huge hands that covered the ends of the arm rests. The scars on the knuckles showed up against the tan skin like lines on a road map showing passage through mountain passes. These hands that had shoveled coal, split rails, driven railroad spikes, and broken jaw bones were now wrinkled and weathered. But, even after all the years still commanded great respect and even a little fear. They were the hands of his grandfather, the senior male member of the Frisano family, the "Old Man", Fred Frisano, the boss.

Along side the chair was an empty Falstaff beer bottle lying on its side where the "Old Man" dropped it. Tony had seen him drop hundreds of them over the years, and was always amazed that no left over brew ever spilled on the shag carpet. It was as if the beer knew it wasn't allowed out of the bottle and onto *Nona's carpet. If the "Old Man" decided beer wasn't allowed on the carpet then there was no beer on the carpet. Not even warm beer crossed "The Old Man."

Fred's most dominating feature was his smile. It was almost always there in one form or another, sometimes broad and wide as it lit up a room, and sometimes subtle as if he knew what no one else did. Tony, like all the second generation Frisano kids, grew up knowing that as long as the smile was there everything was alright.

When the smile went away it was replaced by a cold, deadly stare. When locked in the stare, Fred's dark, deep-set eyes could cut through boiler plate, and stop wild beasts in their tracks. In his entire life Tony had never heard the "Old Man" raise his voice. He never had to, and never said anything more than once when the smile went away. He never threatened or gave ultimatums. He never had to say "do it or else" because no one wanted to know what "or else" was. The eyes said. "You don't want to know."

This cold, deadly side of Fred Frisano came from a past that began in northern Italy before the turn of the century. His roots were in the mountains where his family scratched out a living as best it could.

6

Once off the ship and through customs on Ellis Island, Fred Frisano's life was no easier. The young immigrant's American dream started in the coal mines in Ohio and Illinois where, at age fourteen, he shoveled the black rocks and breathed the deadly dust along side men who were old at age thirty. The thought of asking for help or sympathy from the men who struggled at his side never occurred to Fred. Neither did the idea of not doing his share, or backing down from anyone, old or young, big or small. He never asked for anything but respect. The only way to make him back down was kill him, and no one was able to do that. Several men tried.

After years bending his back and using his huge hands to shovel coal he moved onto a new job as a mule skinner in the same Illinois mine. The key to making these pig headed, incredibly powerful mules manageable was dominating them, never giving them a chance to do anything but what he demanded of them.

Each mule had a string of cars to move from deep in the mine where the cars were filled to the unloading station near the entrance. This meant dragging them up a long grade many times each day. Every muscle, bone, and tendon in the huge animal's body was conditioned to that task. It was their sole purpose in life. There was nothing else for them all the years that they lived.

Fred handled the task of managing these difficult beasts the same as he did all matters that were his to accomplish with total concentration and complete commitment. Any thought of failure, any analysis of the scope of the task, any method to cover his mistakes were never a part of his approach. It was something that had to be done, and he simply set about doing it. He never took the approach that failure was not an option. With Fred it was never a consideration.

One huge mule proved a match for every mule skinner in the mine. He was powerful, had tremendous stamina, and was meaner than a junk yard dog. Fred bore the scars of many kicks and bites delivered by this massive knot head. The animal would wait for days for Fred or one of the other mule skinners to relax or turn their back just long enough for him to deliver a kick to the thigh or bite to the cheek of the ass. One man walked with a permanent limp because of a kick to the knee.

This mule, like all the others, had a routine burned into his mind after countless trips in and out of the mine. As he topped the grade with a load of filled cars the mule skinner would set the brake and he and the mule would relax. The signal to the mule that it was OK to ease his pressure on the harness was the metallic click of the brake.

One late afternoon as Fred set the brake at the top of the grade and turned away from the string of cars the big mule struck again. The bite he delivered to the back of Fred's mid section was unusually damaging. As Fred reached behind to examine the wound he could feel the warm blood and a section of loose skin that was torn away from the muscle.

Fred spun on his left foot, and with his right kicked the brake lever to release the cars. The mule had no chance to react. Before he could lean into the harness the cars dragged him backward, down into the mine. By the time he reached the bottom most of the bones in his body, including his neck were broken. Fred didn't act out of anger or vengeance. He calmly and coldly killed the beast that intended to kill or cripple him.

Fred's smile was never brighter than the day he took his new bride, Virginia, to the three-room house he'd built behind the store and dance hall that, later in his life, he ran with his Uncle Dominic. By age twenty-six he'd left the mine and became a store keeper by day, dance hall bouncer by night, and bootlegger on the week-ends.

The wine that he and Dominic made was very good, very popular, and very dangerous. There were several other Italian families making wine, and they didn't like competition. To add to their problems the local Sheriff wanted a much bigger cut of total sales than the Frisano family was willing to pay. The local Klu-Klux-Klan hated the Italians the same as they did all non-Klan groups, and the county was full of armed detectives who were originally brought to the area to break miner's strikes, but would hire out to anyone for anything as long as the price was right.

The Frisano family with Dominic as the brains and Fred as the muscle, stood alone in a time and place where there was no law and no rules. They'd have had little chance for survival except for a deal made with a local gangster named Tommy Thornton. The alliance gave the Frisanos and Thorntons just enough power and money to make any serious effort against either too costly to be worth while. However, the alliance didn't mean that any of them was immune to attack.

There was always trouble at the dance hall. It was located above the store with only one way in and one way out. The entrance was at the end of a long flight a stairs, ascending from a large vacant lot. In more recent times it would have been called a parking lot. But in rural Illinois in the 1920s most people walked. So, there was nothing to park.

Fred's toughest job when trouble broke out was deciding if it was a simple Saturday night brawl, or someone setting him up to be killed. Developing a sense for the difference was his means for survival. If he handled trouble as an attempt on his life and was wrong, he'd kill innocent paying customers. If he handled it as a fight and was wrong, he would surely be killed.

To make things simpler Fred made it a policy to control the dance hall and everyone in it. This was his only chance to stop trouble before it started. At the first sign of a problem he would ask one, both, or all of the potential combatants to leave. When he did the famous smile was gone, replaced by a stare from the dark, deep set eyes.

Those involved had only the briefest of moments to quietly head for the door. If not they would be carried out. Fred armed himself with weapons to match the situation. His huge hands were lightning fast, but he couldn't risk a one-on-one fist fight. It would make him far too vulnerable to attack from the rear. He ended all hand-to-hand battled with a home made "sap." With a simple flick of the wrist this weapon could break a jaw bone, cave in a rib, or smash a forearm. He used it with surgical precision.

The sap was made of a thin piece of steel about one inch wide, eight inches long, and less than a thirty-second of an inch thick. It was designed to flex a little during impact. The end of the steel, the last two and a half inches, was dipped in molten lead to form a large tear drop, about one half inch thick at its widest point. The whole thing was covered in heavy leather that was soaked so that it would shrink to form tightly around the steel and lead. An extra piece of leather was added to the handle to form a grip and a strap was sewn on to keep it from slipping from his hand.

If the sap wasn't enough he also carried a thirty-eight revolver. It was small enough to be concealed and light enough to be drawn and fired quickly and accurately. If all else failed there was a sawed off twelve gauge shotgun and thirty-thirty rifle hidden under the bar. One of the Frisanos was always in reach of the shot gun and rifle. There were never less than four Frisano men in the dance hall any time it was open. They didn't play fair. They couldn't afford to. No one else did.

There were times that the store was no safer than the dance hall. The women took care of most of the day-to-day tasks, but at least two of the men were there at all times to take care of heavy lifting and provide security. They were always armed.

One quiet summer afternoon Mary Farenzano, Fred's sister-in-law, was stocking shelves with dry goods that Dominic had unloaded from a truck at the back of the store. Fred was behind the counter installing a new cash register, a much heavier lockable model. As he bolted the register to the counter he saw two men slowly walking up the steps at the front of the store. Neither had been there before. One was familiar, but Fred couldn't place him. He couldn't ignore the fact that they were moving too slowly and being too careful to be shopping.

Fred turned slightly and said in Italian "Mary, see how much more Uncle Dom has to unload."

Mary was surprised at the request to check on the unloading operation. She looked up at Fred and saw that there was no smile on his face, and his dark eyes sent a chill up her back. Without a word she headed for the back of the store. As she went through the door into the store room she passed Dominic standing just inside the doorway, shotgun in hand.

Fred slowly reached under the counter and slipped the rifle off the hooks where it hung. As he did he released the safety, and took a quarter step back to give himself room to swing the weapon.

The men quickly crossed the porch and pushed through the door. Both raised revolvers, and pointed them at Fred. The one to his right said, "Open the register you ginni bast....."

The roar of the shotgun that Dominic fired interrupted his demand. The blast hit him full in the chest, and slammed him into the wall. Fred dropped to a half crouch as the other man fired. The bullet passed over his head and ripped through the wall of the store room.

The second man ran back through the front door of the store, and jumped from the porch to the ground. He turned to his left and ran toward the back of the vacant lot. As he passed bye the side window Fred fired, hitting him in the head.

Both men lay twitching and bleeding as Sheriff Starkey's car pulled up in front of the store. The Sheriff and two deputies jumped from the car and ran up the stairs into the store, guns drawn.

As the officers raised their pistols Dominic screamed "Freeze, all you bastards." He had reloaded the shotgun and had it leveled at the sheriff.

The sheriff's voice cracked a little as he said. "Put it down Dom."

11

Bye this time five more Frisano men were entering the store, two with shotguns and three with pistols. The sheriff and his deputies were surrounded.

The sheriff's voice got higher and louder as he said, "Fred is coming with me God damn it." Now it clicked, Fred remembered the second man. He was the sheriff's brother.

No one spoke for about five seconds. It seamed like five hours. Finally Dominic said, "Here's what you're gonna do, pick those two up and get them outta here. If anything else happens Starkey, you're a dead man. Understand me? Any more shooting and I'm gonna blow your God damned head off."

Sheriff Starkey said, "I'm taking Fred with me, understand?"

Dominic spoke slowly as he said, "I'm gonna kill ya Starkey, right now."

The sheriff handed his revolver to the deputy to his right, and slowly walked out of the store, down the steps, and around the corner to where his brother was lying. The deputies turned to follow him, but Fred stopped them as he said, "Take that son-of-a-bitch with you, he's one of you."

The deputies paused, and looked at him for a moment. Fred screamed, "Get him outta here God damn you."

The deputies lifted the now lifeless body, and carried it to the sheriff's car. Before they could load him in the back seat Sheriff Starkey hollered "Drop that piece of shit and help me with Bud." In a few moments all five were in Starkey's patrol car and headed down the highway.

Fred turned toward Dominic who was standing with Fred's brother-in-law Louie and said, "The second guy, the one I shot was Bud Starkey."

12

"That ties it up then, All five of them came after us. Starkey was back up for the first two. If you hadn't spotted them they could have hurt us bad." Dominic said.

Louie asked, "Why now? We've been saying no to Starkey for years. What's different?"

Dominic said, "I'll talk to Tommy, and see what he knows."

*Nona

Virginia Frisano waited inside the front door of the little house behind the store. Her sister Mary was sitting at the small table in the living room. Young, four year old Paul, Fred and Virginia's oldest was at his mother's side. Mary held their newborn daughter Rose in her lap.

"Who were the men who came in when the shooting started?" Virginia asked.

"I didn't see them. When I saw Uncle Dominic with the shotgun I just kept going through the storeroom. When I heard the shooting I ran here." Mary said.

"I gotta go over there and see what happened. I have to know if Fred and the rest of the men are OK." Virginia insisted.

"Sweet Mary, Mother of God, you stay right here with these babies Gin. You got no business there until we know it's safe. The men are OK.

14

They ran Starkey and his deputies off. So, they have to be alright." Mary said adamantly.

"That son-a-ma-bitch Starkey can't leave anyone alone. Maurine Thornton said Tommy told her Starkey and his brother Bud were going through houses looking for wine last week. They went into Nick and Francine Silvio's house while they were asleep, kicked them out of their own bed, hit Nick across the head, and tore their place apart. I don't know where this will all end." Virginia said in a low, concerned voice.

"We just have to wait and pray." Mary insisted as she turned the Rosary beads in her fingers.

Mary's husband Sam was delivering wine to Tommy Thornton's warehouse in Mill City. He and Tommy's cousin Sean would be back by dinner. Sean loved Virginia's polenta and Mary's antiposto. He always pushed hard to be back by suppertime. It made the women feel better when the Thorntons and Frisanos were together on the weekend when the dance hall was open.

"I wish Sam was here. I pray he's alright." Mary said softly.

Virginia reassured her. "He's with Sean and the Starkey's were busy here. He'll be fine. You'll see him at supper."

Then she shouted. "Thank God, oh thank God," as she rushed through the front door and across the lot to meet Fred half way to the house. She threw he arms around her husband as the tears ran down her face and soaked tiny spots on the front of his shirt. Fred smiled a smile that lit up half the county as he held his wife and watched his son toddle after his mother.

"I'm fine. Let's take Paul back inside. Common Poulo, you and your Papa will have a beer." Fred said as he scooped his son up in one arm and held his wife with the other.

15

Once back in the house Virginia asked Fred. "Who were those men, and how did the sheriff get here so fast?"

"Don't worry. It's over now, and everyone is fine." Fred said as he tried to comfort his wife and sister-in-law. He always held back as much as he could about the violence that was too big a part of this world. But, his wife was not the kind of women to ignore loose ends. She had to know, and would find a way to know more.

Virginia Frisano was a true Italian woman, raised in a tradition that dictated her key roll in the structure of the family. She, like her mother, sisters, and countless women before them, was the foundation of the family unit.

The children looked to her as the ever-present source of comfort, guidance, companionship, and limitless love. The bond between them was incredible. It was a force that overshadowed all others. It allowed for flexibility, individuality, and even disagreement. But these freedoms were always accompanied by love, and deep respect. The children held her in high regard because she was the center of their universe, around which all other things revolved.

Virginia held her husband in the same kind of high regard. He was her security, companion, lover, and best friend. But, there was much more to the relationship. Fred made her life whole and gave it purpose. Each of them filled their part of the relationship, one that made the family unit complete. It was the basis of their lives.

Fred returned the respect and honor that his wife extended to him in many ways each day. He would begin his day early, long before dawn, by starting the morning coffee and having a cigarette. Then before the rest of the family was up he would bring his wife fresh coffee in bed. They would spend a half an hour or so talking or just sitting together and watching the sun come up. They often disagreed as strong willed people often do, but they never argued. Each gave the other the latitude and respect that allowed them to agree to disagree.

In her later years she became Nona *(Italian for Grandmother) to all who knew her, and she touched the lives of countless people. Sunday afternoon at the Frisano house was an event with family and friends stopping by through the afternoon and early evening. There was always a huge pot of polenta on the stove that provided for all the dinner guests and plenty of leftovers for anyone who stopped later.

Tony knew Nona, his Grandmother, in her later years. She was forty-six when he was born. By then she had left the violence of southern Illinois behind her many years before. Tony and her son Paul, Tony's father, came home on many occasions with cuts over their eyes and bloody knuckles as a result of fights in the bars that surrounded the factories where they worked. But, those healed much quicker than the gun shot wounds and knife cuts she'd cleaned and dressed before the depression forced her family to move from the mining town in the south.

Nona kept a special place in her heart for her Tony. Each family member had their individual spot there, but Tony's was a particularly warm place. When he would stop by late on a summer evening after a double-header at Andrews Park, she would be waiting with a steak, home-made bread, and a cold beer.

She'd say. "Take off that dirty uniform and mangia (eat in Italian). I'll have it clean for you tomorrow morning."

"It's OK Nona, It's fine for tomorrow's game." He'd protest, knowing what the final outcome would be.

"Mangia-e-zitto (eat and shut-up in Italian)." She'd snap as a little smile crossed her face. "No boy of mine is going to play in dirty pants."

On these evenings Tony would sit at the old kitchen table eating his steak and sipping his beer in his gym shorts and t-shirt as Nona headed for the basement, sweat soaked uniform in hand. She'd soon return and join him

17

for a little conversation about the game, and who had stopped to see her that day.

Sometime during the evening Tony's Grandfather would wake from his nap, and join him for a detailed description of the game. Fred, in his early years, was an excellent catcher, and always had tips on the fine points of baseball. It was the only recreation available to the Frisano men during the years in southern Illinois. It was the "Old Man's" passion through out his life, and Tony listened to every word of advice.

While they talked Nona would quietly do the dishes and clean up the kitchen. She loved to listen to the two of them talk, and reveled in the bonds that kept them so close. Tony would always offer to help, and she would always scold him for even thinking of it while baseball was being discussed. But, she loved the fact that he offered. They repeated this ritual countless times during Tony's teens and early twenties.

The third man in her life was her son, Paul, the original wild child. He'd won a huge spot in her heart thirty years before Tony found his place there. It's hard to imagine what would have become of him without his mother's love and father's no nonsense control.

While under Fred and Virginia's roof Paul was subject to the same rules as all other family members, and he suffered under the control that was always difficult for his free spirit to accept. Every Sunday morning he would here his mother say, "It's time for Mass, alzati (get up in Italian)."

He'd roll over and softly moan, "Oh God no, please Ma, not this morning," as he tried to fight off the effects of the hangover that caused his head to throb and his stomach roll. But, there was no mercy and no comfort. Sunday belonged to Nona, and it started with Mass for everyone, bright and shiny or hung over and tired. So, Paul would roll out of bed, slip into some clean cloths, and climb behind the wheel of the car, waiting on the rest of the Frisanos to gather for the trip to St. Mary's and early Mass.

18

Each and every day Nona included prayers in her busy routine. While Fred made coffee and had his morning cigarette she would say a Rosary. Every meal started with a prayer, and every day ended with prayers that lasted about forty-five minutes. Every family member remembered hearing her softly do her beads after the lights were out.

This deeply religious, loving woman was full on contrast. This same sweet thing would head for the chicken coop on Saturday morning, butcher knife in hand, and pick out a nice fat bird. With a few smooth moves she would snatch the foul of her choice, swing it over the chopping block, and part its head from its body. Later in the day she would tenderly water her house plants as she softly whispered. "If you don't grow I gonna cut you God damned head off."

Tough as she was the violence of southern Illinois, the depression, and the years of hard work and worry took their toll. Nona leaned on her faith to help her through the hardest of times, but even with God's help she couldn't sleep on nights when Fred was at the dance hall breaking up fight. Every day that Paul served in the Air Corps during World War Two she suffered quietly with no relief from the thought that he might never return. And, when her Tony went to Vietnam with the First Marine Division it was even worse. She hated to read the paper or watch the evening news because it was full of information about what she knew her grandson was facing. But every day she would read the war news, and every evening she would watch the combat footage as Walter Cronkite described the day's action.

When Tony came home from Viet Nam in 1967 he found his Nona in the basement doing laundry as she always did when the whether outside was bad. As he greeted her she dropped to her knees and began to cry. Nothing he said or did could stop her weeping for several minutes. Then, she gathered herself up, and took him into the kitchen for a cold beer and polenta. As he ate she tried to busy herself around the kitchen as she had done after the baseball games, but it wasn't the same, and would never be again. Her Tony had changed, and all the love in her huge heart couldn't bring back the young man who came to her house on those

19

warm summer evenings. The loss of the innocent young man that she loved so deeply broke her heart. Many times during her remaining years family members saw her shake her head and whisper. "What did they do to my boy?"

It wasn't that Tony didn't care. He loved her as deeply then as he ever did. But, the war left him empty inside. In Viet Nam he learned to cover the emotions that would have torn him apart, So, when he returned to Nona, and the rest of his family the cold, hard side that he developed kept him from the ones he loved. Even with all the violence that Nona had seen in her own life, she could never understand the change in Tony.

Paul

"Hey Buddy." Paul said as he greeted his son who had just come through the back door after school.

"Hey Pop." Tony replied as he returned his father's greeting.

"How's school," Paul inquired as his son hung up his jacket and pulled two baseball gloves and a ball from the top shelf of the closet.

"Fine. Pete Morello and Dan Riley have to serve detention for fighting in the cafeteria again. Pete's still got a big chip on his shoulder and Danny doesn't know when to shut up and leave him alone. They're both gonna get expelled next time." Tony explained.

"Who won?" Paul asked as a small smile began to appear.

"Nobody. Mr. Taylor broke it up before it really got started." Tony explained.

"You staying out of trouble?" Paul inquired half heartedly. "Your mother is concerned about you. She says one crooked nose in the family is enough."

"I know." Tony said as he slowly shook his head. "I got the walk-away talk again last week. I actually tried that once, and damn near got the shit kicked outa me by every ass hole in the park."

"Watch you mouth." Paul snapped.

"Sorry Pop." Tony said, allowing himself a little smile. "You ready?"

"Right now?" Paul complained.

"Come on Pop. I need a little infield practice before supper." Tony insisted.

"OK then, get a bat and a few more balls." Paul instructed.

Paul flipped a ball in the air with his right hand, slid that hand back onto the bat handle, and popped a sharp ground ball to his son's right side. Tony made a quick shuffle step and turned as he backhanded the grounder.

"Bend you knees and be loose. You look like you have a cob up your ass." Paul snapped. "Soft hands damn it, handle the ball like an egg."

"Sorry Pop." Tony said half heartedly. He listened closely to all his father's instructions, but took the "cob up your ass" type remarks in the spirit they were intended. Paul was not the kind to brow beat his son or anyone else, but where baseball was concerned, he was a perfectionist. He'd have made it to the Majors if World War II hadn't ended his chances at a serious pro career.

Paul picked up the pace as he snapped a half dozen hard ground shots at his son. He took great pleasure from watching Tony slide into a groove that turned him into a cat. Once he settled into that special rhythm Paul no longer criticized or gave advice. Instead he allowed his son to find that special place where thought gave way to instinct and balance and timing came naturally. He had watched Tony raise his game to higher levels countless times since the first time he tossed his only son a ball. This understanding and training was his legacy to his son, a special gift that few saw and fewer understood. It went far beyond anything that words could describe. Tony and Paul communicated without words in an almost extrasensory way that none but the very fortunate ever experienced.

Paul passed his nickname, Tony, onto his son. During Paul's younger days in the minor leagues the stands in the ball parks in both southern and northern Illinois were filled with Frisano family and friends who made a week end of watching Paul play. His Uncle Louis was an avid fan who also loved a Major Leaguer named Tony Lazarri. Each time Paul came to the plate Uncle Louis would scream "Push em up Tony", and Paul would wave in the direction of the screams. Everyone knew Uncle Louis from the boot legging days in southern Illinois, and the name stuck. In fact, no one in the bars and night clubs in northern Illinois new him as anything else, and the elder Tony spent considerable time in all of them.

One of his favorites was a small neighborhood bar owned and operated by his close friend Walt Buckner. The two grew up together after the Frisano family left southern Illinois during the depression. Those lean times made it necessary for young people to make their own fun, and none were more creative than the crew that Paul "Tony" Frisano and Walt Buckner ran with. The chemistry that the group's imaginations created was incredible.

This creativity coupled with some special physical ability opened up many opportunities for mayhem at the Catholic schools they attended. Young Paul, like all the Frisano men had the unusual ability to produce great quantities of gas in his lower digestive systems, and store it for long periods of time. It could be expelled in a thunderous roar, or quietly dispersed with nauseous effects.

The favorite target of the later attack mode was Sister Mary Margaret, the terror of St Mary's. There was no defense against her twelve inch ruler that she wielded with the skill of Zorro and the brutality of an executioner. There was seldom a day when at least one of the boys didn't fall victim to red, swollen knuckles due to the good Sisters discipline.

There was nothing for "the guys" to do but take it, and retaliate later. The favorite time for a counter attack was during the weekly spelling or math tests. But, the attack had to be planned carefully, and executed without sound or warning. If the good Sister, or any of her informants anticipated the gas bombardment, then the attacker was at serious risk.

Paul's timing was nothing short of brilliant. He often let one or two tests go by, allowing the Sister and her snitches to relax. He usually chose a math test for a bombardment because the girls loyal to Sister Terror would be deep in thought over each math problem. Sister Margaret would also regularly become engrossed in correcting papers during the test session, and that was Paul, "Thunder Ass", Frisano's time to strike.

Walt Buckner was in charge of preparations for the attack. He'd stop at his father's tavern the night before and steel three pickled eggs and a bottle of beer that he'd allow to warm up over night. That was Paul's breakfast the morning of the bombing raid. The effects of three pickled eggs and a warm beer processed in Paul's incredible digestive system were devastating. They were actually known to bring tears to the eyes of many in the class who never learned how to appreciate a classic fart.

The source of the atomic farts was a closely guarded secret, given the same high level security as other ultimate weapons systems. Only a select few in the entire city knew of the incredible power that was centered in Paul Frisano's thunderous ass.

In all the years at St. Mary's he was never caught although there was no doubt in Sister Terror's mind that Paul was the culprit. She confronted him a number of times, but could never make him admit his guilt. This was quite an accomplishment considering the Sister's questioning methods. But Paul never cracked. He could look directly into her dagger eyes and deny anything and everything.

The only eyes that could make him flinch were those of the senior Frisano, his father Fred. He was the only man to ever make Paul back down. It only happened once, but Paul remembered it and related the incident to family members all the rest of his life.

It happened one Saturday night after Paul had been drinking heavily at Walt's bar. The night ended in a fight as many evenings did at Walt's place. During the may lay he lost his watch, one of his prized possessions. He didn't realize it was gone until he returned home.

At the time Paul and his wife Olga were living with his parents in a huge old house just outside of town. When he realized that the heirloom was gone he put on clean cloths and headed down the stairs, through the kitchen, and toward the back door. As he walked through the kitchen Fred was waiting.

"Where ya goin?" Fred asked in a slow, deep voice.

"I gotta get my watch Pa." Paul said quickly as he headed toward the door.

"You can get the watch tomorrow. Walt will take care of it for you." Fred said in the same low, quite tone.

"How'd you know I was at Walt's?" Paul inquired. Some how Fred always knew where Paul had been, what he was doing, and how things turned out.

Fred said nothing, but moved over between Paul and the back door. His hands were at his sides. He was relaxed, and the smile was gone.

"I gotta go Pa. I gotta get that watch. Someone will find it, and it'll be gone forever." Paul insisted.

"Go to bed son. Your Mother and Wife have been worried about you all night. The watch will be fine." The words from Fred's low, deep voice seemed to bounce off each wall like an echo.

"No damn it, I gotta get my watch." Paul insisted as the took a half step toward his father and the door. After all, he was a full grown, married man who never allowed anyone to run any part of his life.

Fred's voice got lower and deeper as the said slowly, "Go to bed."

Paul watched the fingers of his father's huge right hand slowly roll into his palm to form a massive fist. In all his years Paul had never backed down from such a challenge. In all those same years, through countless bar room brawls he'd never been beaten. He was in his prime. His hands were lightning fast, and he'd been know to take out many larger men with one blow.

For a brief moment Paul stared into his father's eyes. For that same brief moment he allowed himself to wonder what the outcome would be. Then, suddenly it didn't matter. This was his father. There was no one in the world that he respected more. This was the man who cared for, loved, and protected the family through the back breaking coal mine years, the dangerous boot legging years, and the desperate depression years. This was the "Old Man", the senior Frisano who had earned every bit of respect through years of blood, sweat, and back breaking work. He was a man of great honor.

"Good night Pa." Paul said as he turned toward the stairs.

"Good night Son." Fred said, still standing in front of the door.

Olga

Olga was one of the few non-Italians in the Frisano family. Her people came from Germany and Russia just a few years before she was born. Her mother was a tiny, soft spoken, deeply religious German lady. Her father was a huge, bull necked Russian with a quick temper and junk yard dog disposition. Olga's two older brothers were terrified of him for good reason.

Olga, on the other hand, wasn't afraid of him or anyone else. She was as high spirited and fearless as she was beautiful. Her brown hair and dark eyes were in sharp contrast to her light skin. She was tall, just over 5'7", and slender like her mother. The first time Paul saw her he couldn't take his eyes off her.

When they met Paul was engaged to a night club singer named Jenny Slone (shortened from Sulvanno at the advice of her manager). Jenny and Paul had been lovers for two years, but Jenny's career kept them apart for long periods, a situation that fit Paul's love of freedom and a good time.

Olga and Paul's mother, Virginia struggled through the first few years after Paul and Olga were married. These two strong willed women had a very difficult time sharing Paul and Tony. The cement that held the family together during those turbulent years was Olga's relationship with her sister-in-law Rose. They became best friends the very first day they met.

One early autumn evening the two young women decided to take a ride into town, and add a little spice to what had been a very dull afternoon. Olga was pregnant, and having a difficult time adjusting to the limits that her condition placed on her normally active life style. The outing also gave her a chance to have a cigarette, a habit that she told the family she was trying to give up while she was waiting for the baby to be born.

The young women were the center of attention on the bus as they rode through town laughing about the cigarette ashes that fell on Olga's protruding belly. No matter what she did there was no way to hide the huge bulge that was so out of place on her slender frame.

As the bus stopped for a red light in a section of town lined by night clubs and restraints Rose glanced out the window, then focused on the door way of one of the night clubs and softly said. "Son-of-a-bitch."

Olga looked in the same direction in time to see Paul casually leaning against the building talking with Jenny Slone. Neither Paul nor Jenny noticed the bus, the two women staring out the window, or anything else for that matter.

Rose reached across Olga and grabbed the cord that signaled the driver to stop the bus as she screamed. "Stop this fucking bus and let me out so I can kill that canary bitch."

Rose jumped to her feet, sprinted down the aisle, and jumped through the open door. Olga struggled out of her seat, pushed the man in front of her out of the way as she said. "Move it fat boy, I want a piece of her too and I can't move very fast."

Olga waddled down the steps of the bus and out onto the side walk followed by every other passenger. The bus driver cursed the green light that meant he had to drive away and miss what he believed would be the best action sense Gene Tunney beat Jack Dempsey.

"He's married and you know it God-damn-you." Rose screeched as she sprinted across the side walk toward Paul and Jenny.

Jenny fumbled for the door knob, not taking her eyes off the attacking, wild eyed, Rose coming at her at top speed. As she stumbled through the door she hollered at the bouncer just inside "Stop that dago bitch, she's crazy."

"Damn it Rose, settle down." Paul hollered after his blood thirsty sister. But, his mind was on his wife, now half way across the side walk. He didn't have to look in her direction. He could feel the stare from her eyes as they cut into his back.

Rose was more than willing to blame Jenny because it let her brother off the hook. But, Olga wasn't buying it. Her uncanny bullshit sensor had sorted out the situation immediately, and she wasn't willing to shift the blame to Jenny no matter how convenient it made things.

"You asshole." She said as Paul turned slowly away from the door. "Is she what you want?"

"Come on Og, we were talking on a public street in broad day light. Don't go crazy over nothing. It's bad enough that Rose is in a night club trying to kill the entertainment." Smooth talking Paul argued as he tried to settle things down.

The small crowd from the bus split into two groups. The men headed into the night club to watch Rose kill Jenny, and the women stayed outside to see if Olga would let Paul off the hook. The only ones putting their money on Paul were the ones who didn't know Olga. Once she locked in there was no turning her around. She would forgive this as she had so many other incidents, but she would never forget.

She used this uncanny ability to remember on everyone in her life, and coupled it with her own version of right and wrong. Olga classified things in black and white. There was little room for gray. As much as she loved her son, Tony, she cut him no slack. Both her son and husband were expected to live their lives to her very high standards, and both regularly failed in her eyes. She never stopped loving them, but often fought back her disappointment.

Tony tried hard to keep his weaknesses from his mother. He regularly gave her advice a try, but seldom was able to make her philosophy work in his world. It didn't fit in the bars and on the street corners where he found himself on most week ends. In those places there was very little "black and white." Grey was the color that dominated. Yesterday's assholes could be tomorrow's allies. So, Tony made it a policy not to judge. This was the greatest difference between his mother and him.

Rose

She got her smile from her father along with his ability to light up a room by just walking in. Her warmth, tenderness, and capacity to love deeply came from her mother. She truly captured the best of both her parents. She represented the phrase "To know her is to love her" more closely than anyone ever did.

Tony won a place in the heart of his Aunt Rose the day he was born. He had the same ability to communicate silently with her as he had with his father. All through her life she stayed close to Tony, and would spend many hours at her kitchen table talking over everything from the old days before he was born to items in the daily news.

Many members of the family bounced problems and ideas off her just to gauge the gravity of the situation by her reaction. She could pass on her approval or disapproval, agreement or disagreement, encouragement or reservations with just a look or gesture. Her unwavering honesty was the key to this rare ability to influence others. She never tried to "bullshit" anyone, and never tolerated anyone's "bullshit."

During one warm Sunday afternoon in Paul's huge back yard, the older kids organized a game of croquet. It was a typical Frisano gathering with no less than twenty-five family members and friends sitting around in lawn chairs and at picnic tables with bellies stuffed with polenta, red wine and beer. The younger members of the family who didn't intend to be left out of the croquet match constantly interrupted the older kids play to a point where tempers began to flare.

Rose grabbed the last two croquet mallets, handed one to her Uncle Louis, and they both headed to the playing field. Together they reorganized the game with Rose as the coordinator and Uncle Louis as the enforcer. Each teamed up with one of the youngest Frisano s and together challenged the field to a winner-take-all world croquet championship. Rose kicked balls, played out of turn, and generally cheated her way to the title to the delight of everyone watching including the older Frisano kids who, just minutes earlier were not willing to tolerate any funny business.

Her most precious asset was the ability to bring the best out in others. She somehow enabled those around her to make the most of their own best qualities. In spite of her exceptional people skills, her down fall was in her choice of men, and the relationships that resulted from her choices. She spent her life trying to adjust to men who seemed to change for the worst as time passed. It was as if they became blind to the person she was and all she had to offer.

At first things went well. Rose and her man would begin a relationship with a love of life and a genuine taste for the good times that simple pleasures could bring. But, after a few years her partner would loose his taste for those things that brought them together in the beginning, and she'd find herself in a relationship where there was little left in common between them. Her answer to the break down was to make the best of the rest of the people in her life.

Annie In His Life

"OK, OK, Frisano, there are dozens of fans who wanna see you has-beens and wanna-bees play football, or whatever it is you call that shit you do out there. So, go earn your money." Henry Barber snapped loud enough for all the dozens in the stands to hear. He loved the game, but hated semi-pro ball. His pro career ended as fast as it began several years earlier, and cheap scotch kept him from any real coaching jobs.

"You betcha Hank. Two more payments, and I'll have my jock paid for. Then I can go to the pawn shop and claim my socks." Tony called back as he ran onto the field.

"Socks and jocks my ass, block and catch the damned ball." Barber snorted as Tony joined the huddle.

"He's drunk again isn't he Tony?" Dave Murphy asked. He'd been at the top of every scout's list because of his million dollar arm and blinding speed. But, his inability to read defenses, play books or anything else made him worthless to anyone after his high school career was over.

"I've never seen him sober. OK, play action right on two. Look for me or Jake over the middle, or somebody on the outside if you have time." Tony ordered.

"What do you mean if he has time?" The big right tackle, Butch May growled.

"You'll see." Tony smiled broadly.

"Did Hank send that in?" Dave asked.

"He doesn't even know what it is. Break." Tony told him as the huddle broke, and the offence headed for the line of scrimmage.

As Dave barked the second snap count Tony broke past the strong safety, and slid behind the linebacker. When he turned back expecting the ball he saw the defensive end roll over Dave Murphy taking Butch May with him.

As they huddled again, about twelve yards farther back than the last time Tony asked Butch. "Need some help."

"Who the hell is that guy?" Butch asked, shaking his head.

"He was with the Bears for two years. OK, right at Mr. Chicago Bears. Butch and I got him. Jake, you got the outside backer on a draw to Woody." Tony ordered.

"Hey, I'm the quarterback." Dave protested.

"OK, what the fuck you wanna do?" Tony asked.

"Just what you said, on three. Break." Dave said as he watched Tony shake his head.

Woody Thatcher made up the twelve yards they lost and forty-five more for a touchdown. He too was high on the scout's list until drugs, women, sports cars and just about every other vice known to man found their way into his life.

As Tony reached the side lines he said to Hank. "See the block Butch threw to spring Woody?"

"Ya, I saw the first one too. Lucky Dave is still alive. Bye the way, nice call." Hank returned with a knowing smile.

"I learned it all from you coach". Tony laughed.

"Fuck you Frisano." Was his reply.

When Tony reached the tables where the water bottles were kept he glanced past the fence in front of the bleachers as he'd done hundreds of times before when he actually care who was watching. There he saw her in a jogging suit and baseball cap, leaning on the fence like she owned it. "Nice block." She hollered.

Tony just stood there staring. There were always girls at the games, and parties after. But, none of those girls wore jogging suits or complimented him on his blocking. But it wasn't even jogging suits or blocking that caught his attention. He wasn't sure exactly what it was.

"Frisano, we still got a game here." Hank's voice roared.

Tony kept one eye on the game and the other on the stands. She was there during half time, but gone by the end of the third quarter. He took one more long look at the end of the game, but she was nowhere to be found.

As the locker room cleared Tony stepped into Hanks office. "Well, so much for another season. You gonna be here next year?" Tony asked.

"No. Lombardi offered me the head coaching job with the Packers." Hank growled. "How about you?"

"I have a feeling I'll be playing for Uncle Sam next year". Tony replied. "See you around."

"Honestly Tony, thanks for everything. I couldn't have done it without you." Hank admitted.

"No problem. But, don't change. I like you mean and nasty." Tony smiled as he turned toward the door.

"Get the fuck outta here." Hank roared.

As he stepped out of the locker room he found his dad, mom and Aunt Rose waiting. "Can you take your mom home? Rose and I have a couple of stops to make on the way?" Paul asked.

"Sure. Be my pleasure." Tony smiled at the three of them. After all these years they still came to the games.

While walking to the car Olga said. "Her name is Ann Riley. She plays softball and basketball, and is in nurses training."

Tony laughed out loud. "You don't miss much do you ma?"

"You spent half the game staring into the stands. She's a very nice girl, and her eyes never left you as long as she was here. Her mom is a nurse, and works at the same office where we take Nona......."

"Wait a minute." Tony broke in. "How in the hell do you know all this?"

"Watch your language. I'm your mother." Olga went on. "Rose and I talked with her during half time."

"You didn't happen to break out the album with my naked baby pictures did you?" Tony asked.

"No. But, thanks for mentioning it. I'll bring them next time." His mother added.

"You're incredible. And together, you and Aunt Rose are dangerous." Tony said. "You didn't happen to get her phone number did you?"

"No, but she'll be at Gino's later on tonight. You owe me big time boy." Olga said through a laugh.

"Incredible." Tony finished.

As he walked into Gino's he saw his dad and Vic Moretto sitting at the bar and joined them. Before sitting down Tony scanned the room. And sure enough, there she was in a booth with another young lady about the same age.

"Vic, ya gotta help me." Tony insisted. "There's two girls sitting in the booth behind us. Ask the one in the green dress to dance."

"What's in it for me northern boy?" Vic asked.

"Do we have to do this every time?" Tony asked as he looked at Vic. Then added. "What the fuck happened to you?"

"I picked up a few extra bucks last night fighting Burzinski." Vic informed him.

"Hope it covered the cost of medical treatment." Tony added. "But shit, the girl in green isn't gonna dance with someone who looks like a train wreck."

"You looked in the mirror lately. You got a few bumps Miss Jogging Suit will have to look past." Vic observed.

"You two don't know jack shit. The lumps make you interesting. These guys are dumb as stumps Rocko." Paul said to the smiling bar tender. "Get over there Vic or I'll go myself, and Rocko will dance with the lady in the baseball cap."

"Like to dance? I'm Vic." Tony's battered friend asked.

"Sure. I'm Ginger." The girl in green said.

"Would you like to dance?" Tony asked as he followed behind his friend to the girl's table.

"Yes. But, I'd rather sit and talk if that's OK." She replied. "I'm Ann."

"I'm Tony, and that's great. Can I buy you a drink?" He asked as he sat down.

"I have one, but I'll take a rain check." She said with a smile.

"So, how do you know about rain checks and blocking? I never had a lady compliment me on my blocking before." Tony added as he returned her smile.

Ann's face lit up as she half looked at Tony and half looked away. "Hank Barber is my uncle. I grew up around ball parks and football fields. He thinks a great deal of you. And, it was a good block that helped spring Woody. Butch had his hands full all day long."

"Butch is a great guy. Just a little more size and speed and he'd have made the big time." Football talk was fine, but he wanted to know more about her. "So, do you play ball?"

"I played softball and basketball. But, study and work take up most of my time now. I want to graduate as soon as I can." She added.

"Nursing school, right?" Tony thought it would be a good time for a little honesty.

"You must have seen your mother and Aunt Rose after the game." Her smile was back.

"Mom moves fast. She's too quick for me. I'm amazed that they all still come to the games. My family must have spent more time at games than your Uncle Hank." Tony said as he returned another smile.

"My uncle loves football. It's been his life for as long as I can remember. If he wasn't coaching he was playing. If he wasn't playing he was working out, or training some promising rookie. I wish he could find someone or something else." Ann said in a more serious tone.

"It gets into your blood. Once it's there, it's there forever. But, you're right. There has to be more or things don't balance." Tony added.

"So, what keeps you balanced." Ann decided to press a little more.

"Work, school part time and family, we're Italian. The place is always full of family and old friends. I can't remember a week end or holiday that I spent alone. It's crazy, but a comfortable kind of crazy." Tony was surprised at how easy it was to talk to her.

"Lucky you all get along so well with everyone so close." Ann said.

"The funny part is we don't. The women are mad at the men cause they drink too much. The men are mad at each other just because. Big brothers pick on little brother cause they can. And, little sisters drive their big sisters and mothers nuts. It's a zoo with no cages." Tony shook his head as he finished.

"So, that's what comfortable crazy is?" She wanted to hear more.

"It's funny but no matter how insane things get, I'm always sure of the family. There are plenty of times they don't like one another. But, they never drift apart." Tony had never been this open and comfortable with any of the girls he'd known in the past, and he'd only just met her.

"Hi, pretty lady. I'm Paul, Tony's dad." He said as he broke into the conversation. "Vic would like me to take him and Ginger over to his car. Will that work for you?"

"Hi, Paul. I'm Ann. That's fine. I have my own transportation." She said.

Before anyone else could talk Gino came over with an order of antipasto and two fresh drinks. "This is on the house. We're ball player friendly here. Let me know what else you'd like." Thank you came from all directions as Paul slapped Gino on the back.

"Would you like something else Ann?" Tony asked.

"No thanks. I'm fine. This is a whole meal." She pointed to the plate of appetizers.

After things settled down, and Tony and Ann were left alone, she took a minute for a close look. Her uncle told her about the many opportunities offered to him. Yet, he chose to stay in this factory town where there were so few chances to take advantage of what age and injury would soon take away. "Can I ask you something?"

"Wow, you look so serious." Tony knew what was coming. He could read it in her eyes. This wouldn't be the first time someone asked him why he was still here.

"Why not college football, or minor league baseball? You certainly have all the tools." She found herself hoping he'd understand that she was interested in him, and didn't intend to pass judgment.

"I don't mind at all. In fact, it's a good question. And I'll give you an honest answer. There were offers, and scouts talked to me for quite a while. But, when I looked at the teams they represented I didn't see the games I loved. What I saw was big money, foolish young athletes and big disappointments. The guys who play for Hank are there because they love the game, and no other reason. That's what athletics is all about." Tony watched her closely to catch the reaction to his honesty.

"The sad part is the nature of the game. One bad hit, one soft spot on the field and it's all over. There goes a knee, and it's done forever." Ann watched him even closer.

"And, if it happened tomorrow I wouldn't have a single regret. Those fields are where I found out who I was, and what I could overcome. That's worth more than any scout could offer." Tony was amazed at how good it felt to talk to her about things that never were a part of most of the conversations with those he knew. This lady was different.

"So, what's happening with school? What are you taking?" Ann asked.

"Engineering is my major, but I'm bouncing between electrical and mechanical. I love to take things apart, and find out what makes them work. But, electrical is the wave of the future. Computers and electronic controls are gonna be more a part of everything." Tony cut himself off to check her reaction.

"I see that too, in medicine. I just hope they invent a computer to handle bed pans and changing dressings. Diaper duty would be nice too." She wanted to lighten things up.

"I'll work on that for my mid-term project. Let's call it the Frisano diaper dunk. OK, OK, work with me on this. We'll dip the kid in a harness into an oversized toilet filled with warm, soapy water. Jets will shoot at his, or her butt just like in a whirlpool. Then a rinse cycle will finish the job, and we'll lift and blow dry at the end. What do ya think?" Tony could play this game.

"What about the diaper?" She asked.

"Disposable, we'll make um out of paper with tape to hold them on." He was on a roll.

"Won't that hurt when the jets pull the tape off?" Ann pressed.

"Hey, if they're gonna play football they gotta learn to take it." He replied.

"What about the girls?" Was the next question.

"They need to learn to play football." He was still rolling.

"You better have sons." She was watching him again.

"Sons would be great. But, daughters are special." He watched back.

"OK, you're moving too fast for me now. Besides, I have an early class tomorrow. I should get home. But, I'd like to hear more about the Frisano flusher." Ann was definitely fishing.

"How about tomorrow night, dinner and a movie?" Tony was a very willing catch.

"I'd like that very much." She meant every word.

"Pick you up at six. Can I give you a ride home tonight?" He asked.

"I'd like that too. My mom is here with friends. She can take my car home. I'll talk with her, and be right back." Ann disappeared into the dining room, and was back in just a few minutes.

The drive home was filled with lighter conversation. Both were having fun talking about nothing at all.

As Tony walked her to her back door he couldn't help noticing how graceful she was, very athletic, but very much a lady. When they reached the door she turned and said. "Thank you for a very enjoyable conversation. But, I guess I owe you a dance."

Tony stood looking at her for as long as he could, and then said. "Can I kiss you goodnight?"

Ann looked back for just as long, and said. "I'd like that too."

The kiss was as special as everything else had been that night. It was warm and tender, but also passionate in a way he'd never know before. She was definitely a lady, but also every inch a woman.

As Tony drove himself home his mind raced through the events of that afternoon and evening. The whole thing made no sense. This certainly wasn't the first woman in his life. Many of the others had lots to offer, passion, intelligence, looks, charm, the things that every man wanted. Why was this different? He asked himself the question over and over again. The only consistency that continued through the drive home was the incredibly strong urge to see her again.

The next day seemed endless. The more he tried to busy himself the more he yearned for six o'clock. Early on he gave up on trying to understand his feelings as he reach the conclusion that logic couldn't provide answers to what he felt. He didn't care why. He just knew he had to see her again.

When evening finally came, and he found himself walking to her door he was surprised that he felt none of the apprehension that comes with new relationships. He usually hated first dates with all the gamesmanship that normally made up a huge part of the evening. Somehow he knew that this evening would be different.

Tony couldn't believe his eyes as the door swung open. There in front of him stood the one he'd been dreaming of with one large curler still hanging from her hair. She was in her stocking feet with a robe wrapped around her.

Before he could say anything Ann blurted. "God Tony, I'm so sorry. I just got home, and haven't had time to get ready. Can you wait a few minutes? I promise I'll be ready soon."

"I think you look great. Just slip on your shoes, and we can head out." He replied through a broad smile.

"Oh please give me a break, and a few more minutes." She begged.

"Relax, we have the whole evening. Gino will save a table for us. He's like family." Tony assured her.

"Oh thank you." Ann said as she turned and headed down the hall way. Then he heard her say. "Thanks mom. You could have answered the door."

"And miss watching you ramble and scramble? Not a chance." Tony heard from a much deeper voice as Ann reappeared with a stately woman at her side.

"This is my mom Tony. Be nice mom. I can hear everything." Ann growled through the introduction.

"Hi Tony. I'm Helen Riley." She said as she extended her hand.

"Good evening Mrs. Riley." He returned.

"Call me Helen." As Tony shook her hand and looked closely he realized that a first name basis was not appropriate, and Helen Riley knew it. This was a test, and there would be many more.

45

"How about Mrs. R? I'd be more comfortable with that?" He said slowly.

"So would I." Was her reply. And, Tony knew he passed the first test.

"Should I call you Anthony?" She continued.

"Only if you're angry." That's the name my mother uses as a first warning." Tony said through a smile.

"Does she say it often?" Came the quick reply.

"Probably more than she should have to." Tony admitted.

He normally hated the kind of probing that mothers do as they try to determine what kind of man their daughters spend time with. But, this was different. Helen Riley made it fun. He knew she was gathering information, but did it in a way that allowed him to feel comfortable.

In a short time Ann appeared, and the wait was worth every moment. She was beautiful. The skirt and blouse she wore were simple, but fit perfectly. They made her look relaxed and confident. Tony couldn't help staring.

"I think he likes this better than the robe and stocking feet." Helen said through a quiet laugh.

Tony smiled and nodded. "We'll be at Gino's for dinner, and then a movie at the Orpheum."

"Have fun." Helen said as Ann and Tony headed for the door. She liked Ann's new friend immediately. And, she wasn't easy to please.

"I hope mom wasn't too tough on you." Ann said as Tony opened the car door.

"She's an interesting lady. She kept me on my toes, but I never felt uncomfortable." Tony assured her.

"Sometimes she goes a little too far, and pushes too hard." Ann went on.

"Do you like Italian food?" Tony asked.

"Yes, and Gino's is a great place for it. Mom and I go there probably once a week. The bar tender hits on mom, and she loves it." Ann confided through a quiet laugh.

"Rocko?" Tony blurted.

"I think so. Is he the big guy who looks like a wrestler?" She asked.

"That's the guy. The old fart is a real kick, but also a good guy. He and my dad go way back to the days in high school." Tony went on.

"Do you think he's serious, or just fooling around?" She asked.

"I'd say if Rocko acts interested, he's interested," He informed her.

"I think that Italian guys like acting interested. They do it very well, very smooth and very charming." Ann looked quickly at him waiting for a reaction. Her smile was subtle, but definitely a smile.

"I think Irish girls know how to be interesting, very smooth and very charming." Tony said through his own smile.

"I'm an Irish girl. Is it working?" She said as she punched him in the arm.

"I'm an Italian guy, and definitely interested. Was that the right answer, or are you gonna hit me again?" He flashed his own subtle smile.

Ann slid across the seat next to him. "You're doing fine Italian boy."

Dinner at Gino's went bye in a flash in spite of the four courses and two bottles of wine. And they talked between each sip and bite. Two drinks into the second bottle Tony said. "We should go if we're gonna make the last show."

Ann said through a warm and tender look. "How about a dance? I owe you one, and the band just started."

They were doing a cover of a Jerry Vale song, Inamorata. As Tony and Ann began to dance she moved close, and followed each move and step as if she was part of him. Her hair brushed the side of his face as she moved her hand softly to the back of his neck. They danced through the band's first set, and barely noticed when the music stopped.

Once back at the table Tony sat quietly looking into her eyes. She smiles softly and said. "You're staring."

Tony sat back in his chair and said in a mildly embarrassed tone. "I'm sorry." Then he paused for a long moment and said. "No I'm not," as he continued to look into her eyes.

Ann returned his gaze and confessed. "I'm having a wonderful time."

At that moment the words burst from Tony's mouth. "I want to see you again, tomorrow, next week end, as often as I can. I've never felt like this before. I'm serious Annie."

"Annie, no one's ever called me that." She paused for a moment, and then said. "I like it."

"How bout a dance sweet thing?" Came a deep, slurred voice alongside their table.

They both turned quickly to see a large, and very drunk young man staring down at Ann. "She's dancing with me tonight." Tony said in a calm, deliberate tone.

"I'm not talking to you pal. I asked her, and I'm waiting for an answer." The drunk's voice was now loud enough for people at the nearby tables to turn and notice.

Tony's voice broke the momentary silence. "If you make me stand up, I'll put you in the hospital."

It wasn't what Tony said, or even how he said it. It was the cold, dark look in his eyes. It was his impersonal way he described the violence and injury he was about to inflict.

The rude young drunk looked at him closely, and said nothing.

"I'm not going to tell you again." Tony's voice was still calm and forceful, and the cold dark eyed look hadn't changed.

As the young man turned to leave Rocko's huge hand grabbed him by the collar, and half pushed and half carried him to the door. But, the people nearby weren't looking at Rocko. They were all staring at Tony, including Ann.

There was another long pause as Tony watched Rocko toss the drunk into the street. As he turned back to her the look in her eyes disturbed him. It was filled with surprise and confusion. Tony gave a long, deep sigh, and said slowly. "I'm sorry. I guess I didn't handle that very well."

"Oh no, you definitely handled it. You scared the hell out of the guy, and half the people in the restaurant." She said in a light hearted voice.

"Are you upset?" He asked in a very sincere voice.

"No Tony, I'm not upset, just a little surprised. You changed so quickly. I didn't expect that reaction. It's OK, really." Ann reassured him.

"Can we get out of here?" He asked.

"Sure." She replied.

They were out of Gino's quickly, and crossed the parking lot to Tony's car. As he got in she slid over close to him, and kissed him softly on the cheek. "My hero. Tarzan save Jane from bad gorilla." She grabbed his right arm with both hands. "Tarzan big strong guy. He swing from trees, and shit in bushes."

The laughter exploded as she continued to squeeze his arm. "You're not going to let this go are you?" He asked.

"Not a chance big boy." She replied.

Tony drove to the baseball park along the river. He jumped out in front of the locked gate at the entrance to the parking lot, kicked the gate, and the lock assembly swung to the side allowing the gate to open. He drove through, and closed the gate behind him. "I gotta show you this. It's my favorite spot". He drove across the lot to a place where the trees opened up to provide a clear view of the river.

"It's beautiful". Then through a smile Ann added. "Do you come here often?"

"I sit here at night when things don't work, or I just want to be in a quiet spot for a while." He told her.

Just then the beam from a flash light came through the window. "Is that you Tony?" The voice behind the light asked. "Did you close the gate?"

"Ya, we're all locked in." He assured the security guard.

"You got time to work with my kid next Sunday? He couldn't hit anything last year." The voice asked.

"You bet. Same time, same place." Tony answered.

He turned back to see Ann her staring at him. "You're full of surprises Anthony Frisano."

Tony shook his head and said very softly. "His kid is a great little guy, and loves baseball. But, he couldn't hit is ass with either hand. But, ya just never know. Today's puts could be tomorrow's superstar."

"I have to tell you something". It was now her turn to be serious. "I don't park on the first date. I like you very much, and want to keep seeing you. But, you have to know there are limits."

He reached over and punched her softly on the arm. "Jane keep Tarzan on straight and narrow. Let him know no hanky panky." He loved payback, but wanted her to understand how he felt. It was very important to him.

So, he let himself get serious, and said. "I brought you here because the place is special to me, and I wanted to show it to you. I've never felt like this about anyone Annie. That probably sounds corny, maybe like a line, but it's true."

"I believe you and trust you. That's why I'm parking on the first date." She leaned back against his arm, and laid her head on his shoulder. They sat for a long time, and simply watched the moonlight dance on the water.

Tony finally broke the silence as he said in a very mater-of-fact tone. "So, you wanna fool around?"

This time she hit him in the chest. "I'll knock you out Frisano if you don't behave. "

"Ouch, that actually hurt." He complained.

"It was supposed to." She said as she turned to face him, and settle into his arms. "And, the answer is yes, I'd love to fool around. But, we're not going to. I want to spend lots of time with you, Tony. I want to get to know all I can about you. I've enjoyed every minute of this evening." She kissed him, a long kiss that was both tender and passionate. Then settled back in his arms.

After a few moments he realized she was asleep. He could feel most of her body next to his, and she felt good, very good. He settled back, cradled her in his arms and again watched the moon on the water.

Suddenly he saw the flashlight beam again. This time the security guard pointed it at his watch. Tony rolled the window down slightly and said. "Thanks."

The noise woke Annie, and she said in a sleepy and embarrassed tone. "I'm so sorry. I didn't mean to nod off like that."

"It's OK. You're cute when you're asleep. But, we should go. It's late." He told her.

"All right." She leaned over and kissed him again.

He drove through the gate that the guard had already opened for him. They said nothing during the drive home. Sometime conversation isn't necessary.

Over the next several months they spent most evenings together. Each one brought them closer to one another. Even the disagreements strengthened their relationship. Like Tony's grandparents they learned to agree to disagree. Tony loved to fire up Ann's Irish temper. And, she loved to kick him out of his comfort zone by catching him off guard. Against the Riley women Tony had no chance, and he loved it.

On one particular evening Ann started by saying. "I need some exercise. We could both use a good work out."

Tony replied instantly. "Wanna fool around? They say it's a great way to burn calories."

She hit him in her favorite spot, just below the shoulder on his right arm. "Forget it Frisano. How many times do I have to tell you? We're gonna wait."

"Damn it Annie. Can't you find a new spot. By the time we get to it I'll only have one arm." He complained.

"Suck it up buttercup, and learn to be patient." She replied through her usual satisfied smile.

"I'm tired of waiting." He said as he reached inside his jacket pocket. Ann sat speechless as he opened the small black box that held an engagement ring. She seemed to sit there forever staring at the ring he held in his hand. "Ah, you can't have it until you say yes." He added.

She looked up slowly as tears began to fill her eyes. "Yes." She said as she managed a soft smile through the tears. "Now can I have my ring?"

It was his turn to say. "Yes." As he slipped the ring on her finger.

"It fits." She exclaimed. "How did you know my size?"

"Your mom." He added through his own satisfied smile.

"My mom knew about this?" She exclaimed.

He said nothing, and just sat there with the woman he loved. Like the ride home from the baseball parking lot, sometime words aren't necessary.

The next several days were full of family announcements, dinner parties at Gino's and plenty of time making plans. But, then there was a night that broke the mood. Ann said nothing until the ride home. "What's wrong?" She asked as she touched his arm.

Tony took a deep breath and sighed. "I've been drafted Annie. That's why I was gone the other day. I had to report for my physical. Not only that, but I was picked up by the Marines. I didn't know how to tell you."

Ann sat quietly for a long time trying hard to make some sense of it all, trying to understand how things could change so quickly. She looked at Tony who was intently looking back at her. "They can't, not now. Why now Tony?"

He pulled her close, and held her tight. "Trust me. We're gonna get through this, and we'll have the rest of our lives. We'll tough this out, and then the world is ours."

"I don't want to be tough. I don't want to wait. And, I don't need a Marine, I need you here with me." She said as the tears ran down her face.

He thought of many things to say to comfort her, but said none of them. Ann was a realist. It was one of the qualities he admired most in her. So, a pep talk would not make things easier. "I don't know how to handle this except one day at a time. And, I don't have to report for two weeks. That time is ours, and I want to make the most of every minute."

In the blink of an eye he watched her change. She sat back and placed her hands on either side of his face, looked deeply into his eyes and said softy. "OK my Marine, we're gonna pack lots of living in the next two weeks."

Ann went with him as they told family and friends about their new situation. Olga Frisano took it hardest. But then, like Ann, turned away from the sorrow and concern so that the little time left could be as good as hard times could be.

Fred Frisano was furious. "Why can't the suns-a-bitches who started the God-damned war send their sons?" Although his view seemed narrow and naïve, history would prove him much wiser than most could imagine. When his son, Paul, went off to war he tried to justify America's involvement with the fact that Japan attacked our navy. But, he knew there was far more to the situation than unprovoked aggression. The corruption and ruthlessness he'd seen when he arrived so many years before left him with no trust of confidence in any part of government.

"I have to go Pa. I have no choice. But, I promise I'll be back." Tony assured him.

Fred looked back at his grandson with eyes that spoke volumes. The silent conversation between the two men was something few have seen, and fewer could understand. It came from years of honesty and honor. Neither would allow anything but the truth when maters of importance were the issue.

Paul sat quietly, watching his father and son. What he saw cut deeply into his soul. He too was filled with honesty based on what he'd seen during his time in the service. He knew too well that Tony could not promise he'd return. No one could. He'd seen whole B-29 crews killed in a split second as the plane exploded. The only mistake any of them made was being in the wrong place at the wrong time.

But, more than that he knew how Tony would change. The son he saw in that room on that night would be gone forever once he left for war. And, if he was lucky enough to return the trust and innocence that was still a part of him would be gone forever. He wondered how he and Ann would handle the changes. They had so much to live for. They found so much in that short time together. Would they ever have a chance to build on what was now so beautiful?

55

The Worst of Times

Tony could hear his heart pounding in his chest as he peered into the darkness, trying to pick up any sign of movement. Rain on the surrounding foliage drowned out any other sound. The rest of the Marine Corps platoon was spread out in defensive positions across the hill top they'd taken late that afternoon. Since sun down they'd been probed several times by the V.C. and N.V.A. Everyone on that hill knew they'd be hit in force before day break.

Just before midnight the ground around Tony's position shook with the explosions of enemy mortar shells. Within a few minutes the surrounding jungle erupted with small arms fire. Tony and Jack Heart, the Marine sharing the position began returning fire, trying to pinpoint targets by the muzzle flashes from the N.V.A.'s AK-47s. Soon target selection became easier as the Vietnamese rushed the hill top.

Illumination rounds and flashes from high explosive shells fired by the Marine artillery battery at the near bye fire base lit the area with an eerie half light, good only for making the killing process more effective. "God-damn-it there right on top of us man." Jack shouted.

In the next moment a force hit Tony, the like of which he'd never known before. In all the years of playing football and fighting on street corners he'd never absorbed that kind of energy. He struggled desperately to re-orient himself, but his vision was badly blurred and a roaring in his ears made it difficult to hear anything. He knew if he couldn't pull himself together he would die. He felt a sickening terror as he urgently tried to clear his eyes. As his hearing returned all he heard were Vietnamese voices. He knew that his life was about to end. He would never see Annie again. He was about to die in a place that meant nothing to him, and in that place he would loose everything.

Suddenly the terror he felt subsided as he dedicated all his concentration to his remaining senses. He lost every other instinct and emotion as survival took over as his only purpose. There was nothing else for him now except the reaction of the animal inside. In that terrible moment he became a killer, as brutal and heatless as any animal in any jungle.

His vision began to clear as he searched the area around him for his M-16. The riffle was no where to be found, but he located the remains of Jack Heart. He was blown nearly in half. His left side was completely gone.

Tony turned toward the Vietnamese voices in time to see a figure appear directly in front of him. Its silhouette was clear enough against the night sky for him to know the N.V.A. soldier he was looking at was only an arms length away. Tony's movement exploded in one smooth motion. As

57

he sprang forward he pulled the K-bar (jungle knife) from its sheath on his back pack strap. As he slammed into his foe he spun him to the ground and with all the force at his command rammed the knife under the young man's ribs. He repeated stabbing him several times, and could feel the knife blade slide along his ribs.

Tony was amazed at how light and fragile the Vietnamese soldier felt in his grasp. It was almost like a child's body. He pushed the still twitching soldier aside and quickly moved into the surrounding brush. There he waited for the next Vietnamese to come close enough. The next man he killed was even easier than the first. As he drove the knife home he lifted his victim off his feet. The force of the knife thrust allowed part of Tony's hand to slide part way into the wound cavity the wide knife blade made. Warm blood shot half way up his arm. He pulled away and allowed the man to drop in front of him. Instantly, he move back into the brush and crouched close to the ground.

Tracers from a Marine M-60 machine gun ripped through the brush around him. Tony dropped flat and pressed his body as close to the ground as he could. An N.V.A. soldier fell at his side, and the young man's now lifeless eyes looked directly into Tony's in a cold, blank stare. His head was twisted back in an unnatural position and blood ran from his mouth.

Tony began to move slowly toward the machine gun fire. There were Marines there, and he had to get back to them. For now, their fire would have the attention of the Vietnamese, and limit their movement. He moved like a cat stalking prey, one slow, calculated motion at a time.

He'd gone about thirty yards when the firing stopped. Tony froze. His still ringing ears strained, trying to pick up the slightest sound. His eyes scanned the darkness for any movement. Suddenly, off to his left the brush rustled, and he heard someone say in a deep, low voice. "Grab his other arm, I'm loosing him."

"Hay Marines, I'm coming out." Tony said in the same low voice.

"Come ahead, and stay down." The voice returned.

Tony raised himself to one knee, and took another quick look around, then moved quickly toward the voices. As he broke into a small clearing he saw four Marines. Three of them were carrying the forth on a poncho they'd rigged as a litter. The Marine in the front, closest to Tony, had an M-16 in one hand and another slung on his shoulder. Tony pointed to the rifle in the Marine's hand. "Give me your spare."

As Tony took the rifle he replaced the existing ammo clip with a fresh one from his belt, then jacked a fresh round into the chamber. He turned to the group and said. "We gotta get some cover. The gooks are all over."

"He's hurt bad. We can't drag him through the brush." One of the guys pointed out as he tried to fill Tony in on the injured man's condition.

The words were barely out of his mouth when a blast rocked all of them. Tony and two of the Marines snapped up to a firing position and sprayed the surrounding brush with rounds from their rifles. The third check his buddy that they'd been carrying on the homemade stretcher.

"Damn it, we gotta get some fucking cover." Tony ordered. He grabbed the front of the poncho and a part of the wounded Marine's shirt and single handedly dragged him into the undergrowth. The other three followed.

As they stopped Tony noticed one of the guys staring at the side of his head as he said. "How bad you hurt?"

Tony reached up, and as his fingers passed along the side of his head, one slid under a loose piece of scalp. He looked at his hand, and it was covered with blood. Instantly, he pulled the bandage pack from the first aid kit on his backpack strap and pressed a bandage against to open wound. He then pulled his service cap down tightly over the dressing to keep it in position.

As Tony finished his do-it-yourself first aid job an aerial flair popped overhead. Its light dimly illuminated the small clearing to expose a half-dozen Vietnamese moving toward them. As one of the Marines raised his riffle Tony grabbed his arm and showed him a grenade. All three men tossed grenades simultaneously, and then opened fire on the survivors.

A single Vietnamese lived through the attack. He stood nearly motionless about thirty yards away at the edge of the clearing. He wobbled slightly as he tried to regain his senses. Tony raised to a kneeling position and pumped three rounds into his chest. Killing was second nature now, a part of him that would haunt his life forever.

As Tony turned back toward the group who were now getting ready to move their injured buddy he felt a dull ache on the side of his right leg. When he ran his hand across it something scratched his finger. There was a dime size hole in his pant leg and more blood on his hand. "Damn it, I'm hit in the leg too." A small piece of shrapnel was buried in his flesh just above, and to the right of his knee cap. "Son-of-a-fucking-bitch." He cursed under his breath as he hooked the piece of steel between his finger nail and thumb and pulled it out. He could feel a trickle of blood run down his leg.

"You OK man?" One of the Marines questioned.

"Ya, lets get the fuck outta here, and back to the top of the hill." Tony replied.

The four men carried the fifth injured Marine as best they could through the undergrowth. It was difficult for the wounded Marine to breath, and he'd lost a lot of blood. The best they could do was get him to a landing zone a soon as possible so that he could be airlifted to proper medical attention. But, darkness, the terrain, and the Vietnamese were making that very difficult.

Tony and the others were guessing at their position and the direction they needed to go. They knew they should move up hill, but the hill top was large and it would be easy to miss the spot where the rest of the Marines were dug in. Vietnamese were still between them and the landing zone. So, they had to fight their way up the hill, and there were only four of them able to engage the enemy. If the hill top had been overrun then they were all dead men.

As they stopped for a short break one of the guys whispered to Tony. "What if there's nobody left up there?"

"No, if that was true the artillery would be tearing the hill top apart." Tony assured him.

Within seconds the hill top erupted with heavy artillery fire. Then Puff (An Air Force transport converted to a gun ship) strafed the area. "Oh fuck me. Now what?" The Marine closest to Tony whispered.

"We gotta keep moving up hill." Tony told them. "It's our only chance. If we stay here we're gonna be hit with more gooks than we can handle. There may be someone left up there we can hook up with. There's sure as hell nobody here."

"OK, let's do it." One of them said.

It took half an hour to reach the hill top. Before they got there they engaged four more Vietnamese and killed all four. All were encouraged to hear helicopters coming and going in the direction they were headed. They used the sound as a homing beacon. As the ground in front of them leveled out they stopped the get their bearings. "Is that the L.Z.?" Tony heard one of the guys ask.

"Must be. It's the only open spot up here." Someone else added.

As they scanned their surroundings an aerial flare popped overhead. Tony's heart lifted as he saw familiar figures moving in the dim light. He slapped the arm of the guy next to him and pointed to the moving figures. "Hay Marines. We're coming in." Tony said in a loud whisper.

Three of the figures turned their way and returned. "Come ahead." They watched closely as the four men carried the litter out of the brush and quickly crossed the L.Z.

"We need a corpsman." The guy next to Tony said.

"Hay Doc, get over here." Someone else ordered, and a stocky Navy medic rushed to the litter that was now on the ground at the edge of the landing zone.

In a few seconds the medic said. "He's dead. Sorry, but he has been for a long time."

All four men looked at the litter and the young man they'd carried for so long. Why couldn't he hold on till they got back?

"Hay man, you should have the Doc look at you." One of the guys reminded Tony.

As the medic lifted Tony's do-it-yourself dressing he said. "We need to get you on a chopper."

"It's not that bad." Tony returned.

"Well hard ass, don't take your hat off because part of your head will come with it." The medic snapped.

"Sit down over here until the next flight comes in." The corpsman took a large, fresh bandage from his bag, and re-wrapped Tony's head wound. "Anything else?"

"Ya, my right leg above the knee." Tony returned.

"Well one piece is out but there's another one a few inches away." The medic observed.

Suddenly Tony felt light headed, and a little sick at the same time. He looked up at the men he'd been with and asked. "Who are you guys?"

"We're Hotel Company, sent up here to reinforce you. The rest of your platoon was moved off just before you got here." Someone explained.

"Who called in the artillery?" Tony inquired.

"Your guys called it in on themselves. It was the only way to get the gooks off them." The closest Marine explained.

"How many of our guys made it." Tony asked, afraid of what the answer would be.

"About half, but everyone got hit, some not as bad as others. How the hell did you make it?" The same guy went on.

"I killed Vietnamese faster than they could kill me. Ya know, there like rats, hard to find, but once they're out in the open they're easy to kill." Tony hissed in a low, hateful voice.

"Ya man, you get some." Another Marine growled from the darkness.

Tony sat back and gathered his thoughts. He was amazed at his own comment about the men he'd killed. They were human beings. No, no, no, they were gooks, little bastards trying to take his life. He'd kill them by the hundreds if it meant seeing Annie again. Annie, God how he wanted to hold her and tell her how much he loved her. How would he ever explain a day like this to her? How would he make it through the next months without her? No, God-damn-it, no, he couldn't think of Annie, or his folks, or home. The pain of being twelve thousand miles from them was too hard to bear. He had to stay sharp. He had to stay cool. He had to kill gooks. "One of you guys got a cigarette?" He asked.

The medic tossed him a half empty pack. "Keep um."

"Thanks Doc. Got a light?" Tony asked.

"Fucking Foxtrot Company guys, you got anything but the habit?" The young corpsman snapped.

"Are all you navy guys on the rag?" Tony chuckled.

"Fuck you grunt. I hope your head falls off." Doc chuckled through his reply.

"I'm Italian. Nothing can penetrate this skull." Tony answered back.

"No wonder you're still alive. That greasy hair helped plug the hole in your head." Doc snapped again.

"Kiss my greasy ass sailor boy." Was Tony's reply

"I'll kick you ass grunt." Doc growled.

"Gee thanks Doc. I could use a good ass kickin. But, I think I'll pass and smoke your cigarettes." Tony chuckled again.

The whole group laughed quietly. "OK, enjoy." Doc finished.

Tony had barely finished his smoke when the chopper touched down within easy walking distance of him. As he got to his feet the light headed feeling came back. His legs felt week and his hands shook slightly as he gathered his gear.

Once on board he made himself as comfortable as possible. The pain in his head was much worse and the wounds in his leg produced a dull ache. As they lifted off he wished he'd have asked Doc for a shot of morphine. "Well," He told himself. "The flight won't be that long." He knew they'd give him something at the aid station.

As the helicopter blades pounded the air above him he struggled with the increasing pain from his wounds. Tony took a deep breath, then exhaled and closed his eyes. This time he let his mind wander back to Annie. He thought about the look in her eyes when he gave her the engagement ring. He remembered looking for her in the stands during a game. He could almost feel her next to him, could almost smell her long dark hair, and could almost hear her laughter. "God." He whispered. "Please let me get back to her. Just give me a chance to make a life with this woman I love."

He felt a sharp pain in his head as the helicopter touched down. Then he heard a voice say. "Can you walk?"

He looked in the direction of the voice and saw a tall, young nurse just outside the chopper door backed by two large navy corpsmen. "Ya, I can make it on my own." Tony replied.

As he slid to the open door and dropped his legs to the ground the light headedness returned more intensely than ever. When he rose to his feet his legs buckled. Before he collapsed the two corpsmen were along side him, one at each arm. They didn't try to hold him up, but rather supported him as he sank to one knee. "Hang on Marine." One said in a low, deep voice.

"Shit." Tony snapped. "An hour ago I was carrying a guy through the jungle, and now I can't even carry myself."

"Relax and we'll get a stretcher." The nurse ordered.

"I don't need a fucking stretcher." Tony growled, and pushed himself back to a standing position. That was the last thing he remembered before waking in the hospital bed.

His first reaction was to check all his body parts to make sure everything was still there. As he found his right leg he discovered a large bandage that extended from his thigh to his calf. There was a large dressing around his head centered over the spot where he found the large scalp wound the night of the battle. "Ya, everything is still there." It was the same nurse that greeted him at the helicopter.

"Where the hell am I, and how long have I been here?" Tony snapped.

"Da Nang." The nurse snapped back. "You came in last night. They finished patching you up this morning. The doctor will be in soon to talk with you."

"How bad was I shot up? Hell, I killed gooks for hours after I was hit." Tony pointed out.

"You lost a lot of blood. Everyone was amazed that you stayed conscious as long as you did." The young nurse went on to explain.

"What's your name?" Tony asked. "You were there last night when I got off the chopper."

"My name's lieutenant." The nurse said as she pointed to the bars on her uniform. "And I don't give my name or anything else to enlisted men."

"Well don't worry about your name or anything else sister, I have a nurse of my own back in the real world. And, how does the line go, why would I go out for hamburger when I have steak at home?" Tony snapped again.

"You're talking to a Navy Officer, grunt. Watch it." She snapped back.

Tony began to laugh. It started below his chest and worked its way to the top of his head. "I'm not trying to be a jerk, but ya gotta know I've had my ass chewed by professionals. For several months the VC and NVA have done their best to kill me, and last night they just about got the job done. There's a woman I love more than I thought possible half way around the world that I may never see again cause I'm gonna die in this shit hole of a country that I couldn't care less about. So, with all due respect lieutenant, I really don't give a continental fuck who in the hell I'm talking to."

"Well excuse me ass hole. I didn't know I was talking to the only one in Vietnam who was far away from someone they loved. And as far as what the NVA did to you, I've been watching men die for the last six months. So, you're in good company." The young nurse growled.

They went silent for several seconds, locked in a cold stare. Then Tony began to smile a smile he couldn't hold back. The smile turned to more laughter. He held out his hand. "I'm Tony Frisano."

By this time the nurse's own smile turned to laughter. "She took Tony's hand. "Rose DeAngello."

"God damn it, I knew you had to be either Italian or Irish." Tony blurted. "I gotta write my Annie and let her know my nurse got the last word."

"Annie's a nurse?" Rose asked.

"Ya, a nurse, softball player, my fiancé, my best friend, and the only woman who ever kept me in line." Tony went on.

"My guy's name is Frank. He just finished a tour as a Navy pilot. He's getting out before he has to come back for another tour. He loves to fly." Rose explained.

"Talk to your man Rose. Tell him this place isn't worth his life or anyone else's." Tony said in a slow, deep voice.

Rose smiled softly as she walked away. "The doctor will be here soon. Keep your head down. Annie needs you back home."

Homecoming

Snow fell softly across the seemingly endless fields of northern Illinois. The train was only a short way from the suburbs of Chicago and yet it was if the huge city no longer existed. In fact it was as if nothing existed except the emptiness that surrounded Tony as he made his way back home after so many terrible months in Vietnam. He was lucky to have caught the last train out that night. Nothing else was moving due to the early winter storm that paralyzed the mid-west.

How could things change so fast he asked himself as he gazed into the darkness? Just three days before he was in the jungle where snow had never fallen, where rain, daytime suffocating heat, and damp, penetrating night time cold were what made up his environment for the past year, an environment that was filled with so much blood, pain and death.

His mind was blank as he stared out the window of the unlit train. Only the night lights along the aisle broke the darkness just enough to show the pathway to the next car. He was completely alone there with not even his own thought to keep him company. It was the first peace he'd felt in over a year.

The snow seamed to catch light where there was none as it drifted to the ground. It shut out the rest of the world, a world that brought him so much confusion and despair for so long. He was lost in it, and comforted by it, a comfort that he recognized, but could not remember. He let the feeling take over and cover him with relief. It was the first time in as long as he could remember that he felt he could rest.

His surroundings were like a nineteen-forties movie. Through the window in the doorway he could see the dining car just behind the one he was in. The small tables were dimly lit with just a single lamp. At the far end of the car were overstuffed chairs that had seen more than their share of use. The train was clean, but the faint smell of tobacco was everywhere.

He reached into his inside coat pocket and pulled out a fresh pack of cigarettes. He pulled the coat back up to his chin as he tried to get used to the chill of a winter season he'd forgotten. He lit his cigarette and slowly inhaled, then let the smoke pass slowly out his mouth and nose as he began to think of home and Ann. He closed his eyes and tried to remember her face as she looked when he said goodbye to her a year before.

Her letters kept him going through that terrible year, but there were times he wouldn't allow himself to think of her. The realization that she was so far away was too much for him to bear. He felt guilty about shutting her out when she meant so much to him. What would she be like? How would she react to him? He'd changed so much, and shut out so many things in order to survive, good things and bad.

"No, God damn it, don't make this into a soap opera" he told himself. Suddenly he felt the peace slipping away. Reality was back, and driving away the comfort he'd found on that lonely train. He took another drag on his smoke, and let the night close in. He had to have faith in himself, in Ann, and believe that they could continue from where they'd left off so long ago.

"The bar is closed, but I can find you a drink if you like." The deep voice came from behind, just over his left shoulder. It snapped Tony around, and brought him to his feet.

"Take it easy Marine. No problem here." The conductor spoke slowly and softly, but there was authority in his voice that Tony recognized even though he'd never met the man before.

"Man, I'd love a drink." Tony said.

"Relax, I'll be right back." The conductor said as he headed toward the dining car.

In a few moments he returned with two water glasses and a pint of Jack Daniels. "This OK?" he asked.

"You kidding?" Tony said. "I can't remember my last decent drink. That's great."

"Ya, I remember" the conductor reflected as he sat down and poured a couple of fingers of bourbon in each glass.

"Remember what?" Tony inquired as he looked more closely at the older man now sitting across from him.

"Times from half a lifetime ago, and also yesterday. Never mind. It's a long story." The conductor reflected.

Now Tony looked even more closely at the old man. It was like seeing a close friend and stranger at the same time. Did he know this guy, and from where? Why was he so willing to share his booze? What did he want?

70

"Do I know you from somewhere, baseball, football maybe? " Do you know my family?" Tony inquired.

"No, but I know you, and not from baseball or football. You're my brother. That Bronze Star and Purple Heart on your chest make it so." The conductor said in a low powerful voice.

Tony felt anger welling up inside him, a dangerous, overpowering anger. He stared deeply into the eyes of his new companion. He could take this asshole out with one punch, and the guy would never see it coming. Their eyes were locked. The old man didn't flinch. His cold, dark gaze reminded Tony of his grandfather.

Finally the young Marine broke the silence by snapping "Look man, if you're planning on swapping war stories I'm the wrong guy. That shit's behind me and I'm going back to my life in the real world."

"Slow down Marine. I don't give a damn about your war stories. After two years in the South Pacific I have plenty of my own. I live with them every day of my life." The old man said firmly. "And you'll live with yours. Take a drink and relax."

"I don't want a fucking drink if it means wallowing in the past with you or anyone else. I told you, that part of my life is over." Tony growled.

The old man didn't snap back. Still lock in the same dark eyed stare he said in the voice of an ex-drill sergeant. "Shut the fuck up and listen grunt. Understand that you have to adjust to what will never go away." He stopped for a minute to let his remark sink in.

Tony was tense and confused. Why was he still sitting there listening to this old bastard. In a few weeks he'd be discharged, and the war would be out of his life forever. But, somehow he knew he should hear the old man out. He couldn't understand why this might be important until he remembered his concern about Ann, and how much they'd both changed. What did this old man know?

"You went to war a laid back guy with not much more on your mind other than the next ball game, a cold beer, and the hope of getting lucky in the back seat of your hot rod." The old man began. "The Corps turned you into a killer, no different than a hit man except your training and equipment were much better. You've changed, and you can never go back to the way it was. Take time my young brother to rebuild your life. You have to work on it every day." The old Marine, a veteran of some of the bloodiest fighting the world had ever seen got up slowly, put his hand on Tony's shoulder and finished with "Semper Fi my young brother."

He picked up the half empty bottle of bourbon and headed back the way he'd come. Tony switched seats and watched the conductor disappear through the doors into the next car. He was alone again with the snow, the darkness, and the quiet that he'd come to cherish so much in the short time on this train from Chicago. But, now he had new thoughts for company. The old Marine had struck a nerve and Tony couldn't shake what he said. He found that he really didn't want to.

He took a slow sip of the whisky left in his glass and felt its warm effects slide gently down his throat. "Adjust every day huh, but to what? " he asked himself. Then he remembered the anger that instantly came over him when the old man began to talk about war. He realized how close he came to punching that old man in the mouth and slowly began to understand. He'd changed, more than he believed possible. So much of him was reflex and instinct now. "My God, I'm bringing the jungle back home with me." He thought.

He took another long slow drink from what was left in the glass. "No, God damn it, that's not how it is. The guy just took me by surprise, caught me in a bad mood. DON'T MAKE A SOAP OPRA OUT OF YOUR LIFE" He told himself again. He pulled his coat back up around his neck and watched the beautiful white snow flash by the window and then fall silently to the ground.

It was 2:00 am when the train pulled into the old terminal in Rock Island, Illinois. The once busy station was now all but deserted except for the crews that still manned the switching yard. Tony saw the conductor pass back through the door into Tony's car with the same slow, steady gate with which he had moved a few short hours before.

"Yah done with that?" he asked as he pointed at the empty glass at Tony's side.

"Ya, thanks for the drink." Tony replied. "Be happy to buy you one some time."

"I'll take a rain check." The conductor said as a faint smile crossed his lips. "You have a ride waiting for you?"

"No, no one knows I'm back. I spent so much time running from planes to cabs to trains that I didn't have a chance to call." Tony responded.

"How far do you have to go?" The conductor inquired.

"Too far to walk." Tony replied. "But I'll be able to get someone down here. I'll try a cab first."

"I'll make sure the terminal is open. There's a phone inside." The conductor reassured him.

"Thanks" Tony replied. He stood up, stretched the kinks out of his back and legs, and swung his sea bag up on his shoulder.

As they stepped off the train the conductor pointed through the terminal windows and said. "You're in luck. There's a cab sitting out front. They must have got word that the train would be in tonight." The conductor said as he extended a hand to Tony.

Tony stopped, turned slowly and grasped the old man's hand in a firm hand shake. He looked deeply into the Ex-Marines eyes and asked. "Every day huh?"

"Every God-damned day." The old man said.

The cab driver stepped out into the deepening snow to open the trunk. Tony tossed the bag inside, stepped around the cab and tried to kick the snow off his shoes as he asked the driver. "Can you give me a minute to make a quick call? I need to find out who's home."

"Sure Marine, I'll be right here." The driver said as he looked past Tony, and waved at the conductor standing at to corner of the terminal.

Tony knew his Dad and Mom would be home, but he had to see Ann first. Her phone rang five times before a sleepy voice he hadn't heard in over a years said. "Hello."

"Annie, it's me. Sorry……." He started.

"Tony, my God is that you. Where are you?" Ann's normally deep voice was now high pitched and shaky.

"I'm at the station in Rock Island. Trains were the only thing running. I've got a cab. Can I come to your place? I want to see you."

"Oh God yes. I'll be waiting for you." She said. Tony could tell she was crying.

"The roads are bad, but I'll be there as soon as I can." Tony felt a lump in his throat as he spoke.

"Be careful. I love you." Ann said in a trembling voice.

Tony began to smile as he said to her softly. "A little snow won't stop me. I've waited a year to see you again. I love you too."

The driver took down Ann's address and said. "This may take a while, but I'll get you there."

"Man, it's been a year since I've seen her. So hurry every chance you get." Tony replied.

The old cab's tires spun a little before the chains bit into the fresh snow. Tony could feel the back of the cab sway slightly as they pulled away from the curb. It was snowing heavier now, but that was a good thing. The fresh snow gave the chains something to bite into. It wasn't deep enough to build up in front of the tires yet, but soon would be.

"Want a drink to chase the cold?" The driver asked.

Tony laughed out loud. "Hell, I wasn't surprised that they had booze on the train, but never expected bar service in a cab. No thanks, I'm good."

"My brother keeps a private stash on his train. It's always ready, but he's selective about who he drinks with, railroad regulation ya know." The driver commented.

"Your brother, no shit?" Tony exclaimed. "Wait a minute, brother by blood or another grunt?"

The driver laughed. "Just another old grunt. We were in the South Pacific in forty-four and forty-five."

Tony laughed again and said. "You crusty old bastards are all over the place."

"We always were. You just never noticed before." The old Marine said.

Tony could see the old man's eyes in the mirror. He smiled and said. "Every God-damned day huh?"

The driver looked back and said. "Every God-damned day."

The cab rattled and shuddered as the tire chains rolled over the fresh snow. There was no other traffic and the old driver / Ex-Marine made good advantage of having the whole road to himself. He stayed in the center, and used the extra maneuvering room to compensate for the slippery conditions. He kept his speed up and plowed through the deepening snow. The extra speed was fine with Tony. It was getting him closer to Ann.

Ann put down the phone, fell back into the chair and sobbed deeply. News of the war had been bad for the last several months. Casualty numbers were increasing, and, for a time, she wondered if she'd ever see her man again. Each night she went to sleep saying her Rosary and praying for his return. Before Tony left, Ann's mother had to drag her to Mass. Now she went to church several times a week. Tonight there would be another prayer for his trip through the snow. She cried more quietly now, and asked God for his help one more time.

"Ann, what's wrong?" Her mother called from the back bed room. She'd taken a sleeping pill before bed to help control the pain of her worsening arthritis. But, even the strong drugs couldn't cover the sound of the phone and Ann's weeping.

From the day that Tony and Ann began dating, Helen Riley tried not to like him. The reputation of the Frisano family was well known, and word was Tony was no different than the rest. But, he won her over one step at a time with his grandfather's smile, his father's line of bull shit, and his mother's capacity for unconditional love.

Ann paused for a moment as she finished her snow prayer. "Tony's home mom. He's on the way over."

Helen looked over at the clock and protested. "At 2:30 in the morning?"

"Yes mom, at 2:30 in the morning." Ann said firmly.

"And where's he going to sleep?" Helen protested more firmly.

A broad smile crossed Ann's face as she stopped in the open door way of her mother's room. "What makes you think we're going to sleep?"

Helen smiled at her daughter's silhouette in the bedroom doorway. "I'm too young to be a grandmother, understand?"

Ann laughed out loud. "Then we'll have to be very careful."

Helen tried to muffle her laughter behind a deep, stern voice as she said. "Well at least try to keep the noise down."

"OK, I promise if we need to moan or cry out we'll head for the garage." Ann said as she fell into another laugh filled outburst. She crossed the room to her mother's bed side, leaned over and kissed her on the forehead. "I missed him so much, mom."

"I know. I remember what it felt like when your dad was in France after D-Day. There were times when I'd stay away from home in the afternoon so that I wouldn't be there if a telegram arrived. The days were long, and the nights were endless. You hold your man tight when he gets here, and make all the noise you like." Helen said as a tear ran down her cheek. "Now, go get cleaned up."

"I love you mom." Ann said as she wiped a tear from her own cheek.

The cab fought its way up the long hill past Augustana College. Now there was nothing but flat, open road between them and Ann's front door. "Nice job." Tony said.

"Hey, me and this old rust bucket have a few moves left." The driver smiled and said.

"Never had a doubt." Tony replied.

As they continued on the snow fell more heavily. Suddenly they saw the lights of the plow ahead straining to keep the main roads clear. As they approached the light at the last turn to the subdivision where Ann lived the driver said." We've got a problem brother."

The snow on the side roads was well over a foot deep. "I'll never make it through that. Sorry."

"No problem." Tony said. It's only a few more blocks. You better get home yourself."

Tony leaned over the seat to pass a twenty to the driver. "Keep the change."

"Your money's no good tonight Marine. Semper Fi" The driver said with a subtle smile.

"Semper Fi." Tony said. "And don't forget, Every God-damned day"

"Ya, Every God-damned day." The driver said as he opened the trunk.

Tony grabbed the bag, swung it up on his shoulder and headed through the snow. The new powder was nearly half way to his knees as he trudged along. All he could think about was Ann's trembling voice on the phone. Now he ignored the winter scene around him that was his silent companion on the train. Now there was nothing in the world but Ann. Suddenly he was on the porch where he'd first kissed her good night so long ago.

Before he could ring the bell the door swing open and she flew into his arms, knocking the sea bag to the ground. Her feet were a full six inches off the porch as she clung tightly to his six foot three inch frame. She sobbed and laughed at the same time as the tears ran down her face. He held her closely, almost afraid to let go.

"For God sake, bring him inside before we all freeze" Helen Riley said to her weeping daughter. After another moment she hollered, "Damn it, get him inside before he dies of pneumonia. I'm a nurse and know about that stuff."

Tony opened his own eyes and saw his future mother-in-law leaning on her cane at the end of the living room couch. "Hi Mrs. R."

"Carry her in Tony. It's the only way you're going to get through the door." Helen said as a broad smile crossed her face.

Tony half dragged and half carried Ann and the sea bag through the front door and into the living room trailed by much of the snow that had piled up on the front porch. Helen made her way across the room to the couple still clinging to one another. "Any room for me in there?" she asked.

"All the room in the world." Tony returned, as he hugged them both, one on each arm.

"Come on, get that wet coat off and sit down for a minute." Helen ordered in her best head nurse tone. "I'll make some coffee."

"Let me help mom. Just give me a minute." Ann said.

"Well that's not going to work unless Tony carries you into the kitchen. Come on, let him go long enough to take his overcoat off." Helen said, still wearing the same smile.

Tony pulled off the wet overcoat and hung it on the coat tree beside the front door. As he began to unbutton his uniform jacket Helen saw the combat ribbons above his left pocket and a chill went down her spine. The decorations reminded her of her husband's return over twenty years before. Her memory flashed back to his sleepless nights and bouts with depression and rage that followed him for the rest of his life. God, why did this have to touch so many in her life? She shook off the memories and headed for the kitchen.

When she returned she found Ann and Tony on the couch quietly watching the snow fall past the living room window. Ann's head was resting on Tony's shoulder, and her tear were replaced by a soft smile. Helen set the tray with two steaming cups of brew down in front of them as she leaned on her cane with her other hand. "Tony's is on the right. I doctored it up a bit."

"Thanks Mrs. R." Tony said as he reached for the cup. As he did all three watch as his right hand began to shake. No one was more surprised than Tony. He released the cup, made a fist, relaxed his hand and shook it. As Ann reached for his hand Tony pulled away.

Ann said in the nurse's voice that she inherited from her mother. "How far did you have to walk in the snow?"

Tony felt anger and frustration well up inside. Then he remembered the conductor. The old man was right and it was starting already. After staying in control in hell for over a year was he loosing it on his first night back with the woman he loved?

"Tony, how long were you out in the snow?" Ann insisted.

He took a deep breath and fought back his driving urge to be in complete control. "I walked about three blocks, just the distance from the light."

Ann put her hand on his forehead as he leaned back on the couch. Now he felt the rest of his body start to tremble. "Annie, this is not right. I'm not sick. I can't be sick. God damn it, this is my first night back with you."

"You listen to me Anthony Frisano, I'll take you sick, well, or anywhere in between. Now shut up and let me look at you." Ann snapped.

As she loosened his shirt and tie Helen returned from the bathroom with a thermometer. "Open." She ordered.

"Mrs. R., right now?" Tony pleaded and then began to laugh. The quiet living room had turned into a hospital examining room and two registered nurses were all over him, one looking down his shirt and taking his pulse, and the other shoving a thermometer under his tongue.

"Can I have sip of the coffee and brandy?" Tony pleaded. The thermometer bounced up and down as he spoke.

"No, and stop talking." Helen snapped her second set of orders.

Tony looked at Ann. "I love you." He said as the thermometer wiggled again.

'Sssssshhhhhhhh" Ann hissed.

"He has a fever, just over one-hundred. How's his pulse?" Helen asked.

"Elevated," Ann added. "We need to get him to bed."

"Now you're talking." Tony said as he laughed out loud.

"Forget it." Ann and Helen said simultaneously.

He felt a little light headed as he walked to Ann's room. What the hell was going on he asked himself. "Annie, I can't believe this. I don't get sick. Hell, I walked a few blocks in the snow, that's all."

"Take off your shirt and pants and crawl into bed." Ann snapped another set of orders.

"I thought you said forget it." Tony said with a broad smile. "This is so sudden, so unexpected. Will you respect me in the morning?"

All three burst into laughter, Helen Riley most of all. Thank God he has a sense of humor she thought. After satisfying herself that the necessary tests and precautions were taken she said. "I'm going to bed. Good night Tony. I'll leave you in good hands. And remember, no noise. I'm a light sleeper."

"Good night Mrs. R. and thanks for everything." Tony said sincerely.

"You make my daughter happy. That's all the thanks I need." Helen said in return.

Ann slipped into bed next to Tony who was now shivering heavily. "Slide over next to me sweet heart."

"I can't believe this. I'm here with you after all this time and I'm shaking like a leaf. What in the hell is wrong with me?" Tony asked in frustration.

"Whatever it is we'll take care of it. You went from a jungle to a blizzard in less than forty-eight hours. That's too big an adjustment for anyone. Remember how long it took you to adjust to the jungle.' Ann said softly. "Just lay here next to me and rest."

"Some lover you have. Here we are........." Tony started.

"Anthony, shut up and relax. I have you back. Being here close to you is all I want right now. I love you, you hard headed Dago." She ran her fingers through his hair along his temple and felt some of the tension drain out of him.

"God Annie, you feel so good. I want to make love to you now, all night long, all morning." Tony whispered.

"Shhhh, we have plenty of time, all the rest of our lives." Ann reassured him.

Tony pulled her close and lost himself in her touch, As the snow fell outside the window he drifted off to sleep. Ann lay next to him and watched as he slept. Every twenty minutes or so she'd checked his temperature and pulse. Just before dawn her mother came in and asked. "How's he doing?"

"He still feels warm, but is resting. God, he looks like he needs it mom." Ann reported.

"He does Ann, rest and lots of love. You're going to see changes in Tony that will be hard to understand. We'll talk later." Helen said in a half whisper.

Shortly after sunup Ann slipped out of bed and went to the kitchen. Her mother was already there sipping a fresh cup of coffee. "Good morning mom."

"Good morning. How's he doing?" Helen inquired.

"The fever broke just a little while ago. He was so concerned about spoiling his first night back. All I wanted to do was hold him and never let go." Ann told her mother.

"I know. It's like you will never let the world have him again. I remember the feeling when your dad came home. You and I never talked about that, but we need to." Helen said.

"I remember you mentioning that last night. I know he's been through a lot, but he's home now, and we can begin where we left off." Ann replied.

"It's not that easy sweetheart. Tony still loves you, in fact more now than ever. But, he has things to work out, terrible dark things. It will take time, but he's a very good man. I saw that last night when he drew away from you as he started to get sick, then allowed you to take over when he needed you. Do you know how hard that is for someone who's been under the pressure he's endured for the last year?" Helen tried to explain to her daughter.

"But mom, he must know he can trust me." Ann insisted.

"He does Ann, but he's come from a world where instinct and reflexes were what he depended on. The only ones he trusted were the guys fighting along side him." Helen explained further. "It took years for me to understand that about your dad. It nearly ruined our marriage. I was ready to divorce him when he finally opened up and talked to me. It was very hard for him."

"God mom, where do I start?" Ann asked in an almost panicky voice.

"You already have sweetheart. You were there for him last night. You stayed with him and took the time to work through it. Just take it one day at a time. I have all the faith in both of you." Helen reassured her.

"Thanks mom, I wish that I understood more of what was happening." Ann said as she sipped her own coffee.

"You will. Stay close to him and give it some time" Her mother added.

Just before midnight on the following evening Tony sat up in bed. His eyes darted back and forth in the darkness as his mind raced to identify his surroundings. Suddenly a light came on to his left and he snapped toward it. "Honey, what's wrong." Ann said in a startled voice.

Tony blinked as he adjusted to the light. "I'm sorry. I didn't mean to scare you. What time is it." He asked.

"Just a little before midnight." She told him. "Are you OK?"

"How long have I been asleep?" Tony asked.

"All day and half the night. Your fever broke this morning." Ann informed him.

"God Annie, I'm sorry I wanted........" He started to explain.

"Honey, please don't feel bad about anything. I have you home now. Come over here next to me." Ann said as she turned out the light.

Tony put his arms around her and pulled her close. "You feel so good Annie. I thought I'd never get to hold you again."

She stroked his hair and said softly. "Would you like to make love to me?"

"Right now, all night, and all morning" He answered softly as a smile crossed his face.

Tony'd been with many women before he met Ann, but none came close to making him feel the way she did. It was as if she gave herself completely to him in a way that made him feel whole and complete. She was very attractive, but so were many of the others. She was passionate, but there was more to it than that. She was a lady in every sense of the word, but at the same time all women.

She slipped out of the jogging suit that was her answer to pajamas and pulled herself close to him. As she kissed him softly she ran her fingers through his thick, soft hair, then drew his cheek close to hers and whispered "I love you" softly in his ear.

Now Tony left the rest of the world behind. Ann was in his arms and nothing else mattered. In those precious moments the world was at his feet, and it was perfect. His senses were full of every part of her, her soft warm skin, her firm athletic muscles, her long slender legs, the smell of her hair as it spread across the pillow, her long slender fingers as they dug into his back. That night he was true to his word, "Right now, all night, and all morning."

The next morning as Helen Riley passed her daughter's bed room door she said in her deepest head nurse voice. "So much for being quiet."

Tony looked at his fiancé who buried her face in the pillow as she tried to muffle her laughter. "We're busted." He said. "She sounds furious."

Ann lifted the covers exposing her naked body in the morning light. She threw a leg over Tony's waist and slid on top of him, then pulled the covers over their heads. She leaned forward allowing her body to rest on his as she kissed his forehead. "Good morning." She giggled. Then she slid down his torso pressing her hips on top of his. "Oh something tells me you're happy to see me Anthony Frisano." She said as a soft satisfied smile came over her face. "You're so full of energy sense your fever broke."

"God Annie I........" He tried to say as Ann began to make love to him again. He opened his eyes and watched her smile broaden as she closed her own eyes. He grabbed her waist, pulled her close, and lost himself in her again.

Ann lay still for a moment with her head resting on his chest. Suddenly her face popped up as she sighed. "God I'm hungry. Want some pancakes? I need pancakes." She jumped out of bed and slipped her jogging suit back on. Come on Marine, give me a hand.

"Your mom's in the kitchen isn't she?" Tony asked.

"Of course. She'd probably like some pancakes too." Ann said smiling from ear to ear.

"She's going to give me more than pancakes this morning." Tony said shaking his head.

"Mom loves you. But, you're right. You'll take the heat this morning." Ann said without mercy.

"Can I have breakfast in bed?" Tony pleaded.

"Sure. Mom does room service." Ann said laughing out loud. "Better get some clothes on unless you plan to go skinny-eating.

Tony did his best to look presentable as they walked to the kitchen. As they entered Ann said in her most cheerful voice. "Good morning mom."

Helen let her gaze pass Ann and drop directly onto Tony. "Good morning Anthony. Somehow I think that you're feeling better."

"Yes Mrs. R. I feel lots better thank you." Tony said knowing what was coming.

"A little tired though I'll bet. Sounded like you were up most of the night." Helen said in a mater-of-fact tone. "Did your fever come back?"

"Boy did it ever. Talk about a fever. This guy was burning up." Ann said with her back turned as she poured Bisquick into a large mixing bowl.

"Well you don't look feverish now." Helen observed.

"No, the fever came and went, came and went, came and went." Ann said, still with her back turned as she mixed the batter.

"Must be some kind of Asian thing." Helen suggested.

"No, I think it's an Irish / Italian thing actually." Ann observed.

This wasn't the first time Tony had been at the mercy of the Riley women. When he proposed to Ann she said yes, but he would have to talk to her mother sense her father had passed away and wasn't available for the blessing. The whole thing was a set up and Helen Riley was brutal. But, it wasn't all in fun. She was testing his patience, resolve, and sense of humor and Tony passed with flying colors. That was the day he won Helen's heart.

"Well, while Ann finishes breakfast I'm going to strip the beds and do the laundry." Helen stood up, slipped on a pair of rubber gloves, rubber apron, and face mask. Then with a bottle of Clorox bleach in one hand and her cane in the other she headed for the hall. She stopped at the door, turned and said. "Bye."

The site of her standing there in her biohazard suit was more than either of them could stand. Tony and Ann burst into laughter simultaneously. It was the kind of laughter that grows with the moment. Tony felt the tears run down his face as he held his sides. Ann knocked over the bowl of batter, slipped in the mess and wound up on the floor covered in tears and pancake batter. Helen turned and walked out of the room swinging the Clorox at her side.

In a while Tony was able to gather himself enough to say. "Let me help you." He pulled the still laughing Ann to her feet, grabbed a towel and went after the mess on the floor.

Ann was out of action. She pulled a box of Wheaties from the cupboard and milk from the refrigerator and said. "That's the best I can do."

Helen returned with a satisfied smile on her face, gave Tony a hug and said. "Welcome home. We love you."

"I love you too Mrs. R. You're priceless." Tony said as he hugged this very special woman.

"I talked to your folks the morning you arrived, and promised them you'd call as soon as you could. I talked with your mom a few time during the day to let her know you were OK." Helen reassured him. "You need to call them right away."

"I'll take care of it right now. I know they want to hear from me." Tony said gratefully.

The phone didn't ring one full time before Olga Frisano snatched it from the receiver. "Hello."

"Hi mom. It's me." Tony said with a broad smile.

"Are you alright? Helen said you had some kind of flu or something." Olga asked frantically.

"I'm fine now. We don't know what it was, probably some kind of twenty-four hour thing because of the climate change. That's the best the Riley Clinic could come up with." Tony explained. "They were all over me with thermometers, blood pressure machines. Helen was thinking about exploratory surgery. They took great care of me mom."

"Tell them both I said thank you. When do we get to see you?" Olga asked.

"What's the weather like? I haven't looked outside in a while." Tony inquired.

"It's awful, still snowing with no relief in site." His mom told him. "They're concerned about power losses all over town."

"There's no way to get to your place then. I had to walk the last three blocks when I arrived because of snow on the side streets." Tony remembered. "We'll have to wait it out. Are you and Pop OK, and how about Nona and Grandpa?"

"We're fine. Your dad is thawing out. He had to go out and shovel the walk between our place and your Grandpa's. It'll only stay clear for a few hours and then pile up again. But, he had to get it done. You know how he is.? She explained.

"I know. Is he there?" Tony asked.

"Sure, hang on." Olga set the phone down and hollered. "Paul."

"Jesus woman, I'm right behind you." Tony could hear in the idle receiver. He smiled as he heard his father say. "Hi Buddy, how ya doin?"

"Fine Pop. I was a little rough yesterday, but the Riley nurses got me back in shape. Thought I'd come over for a game of catch. You up for it?" Tony asked.

"Sure head on over. We can go fishing afterwards." Paul suggested.

"Hold it old man. That's too much for me. I nearly froze my fucking balls off walking three blocks to Ann's place." Tony could feel the eyes from Ann and Helen on the back of his neck.

"Are you there with Ann and Helen?" Tony heard his father ask.

"Hang on Pop." Tony said.

He turned, but before he could udder a word of apology Helen jumped in with. "Ann he nearly froze his fucking balls off. That would have certainly changed things." She said in a voice loud enough for Paul to here, and the laughter began all over again.

"They're killin' me, Pop. It's brutal over here." Tony said through the uproar. "Mrs. R. is in her best form and I'm on the receiving end."

"Then you deserve it. Welcome home son. I love you." Paul said as he choked back the tears. "Here's your mom."

"OK, give us a call and get over here as soon as you can. I need a hug." Olga's hand was shaking as she put the phone down. She slumped into the chair and burst into tears.

Vic's Return

Three days later Vic Morretto boarded a 707 out of the DaNang airfield for his long hide home. He tried several times to contact Tony while still in country without success. He'd cheated death for a full year in the Vietnam hell hole, the same as he had on the streets of Chicago. Now he was headed home for a cold beer, rare steak, and safe piece of ass he told himself.

As with all service men leaving Nam, Vic was processed through stations where he turned in his field gear and drew fresh uniforms for the trip home. At one station everyone was asked to leave all weapons, both legal issue and illegal contraband, no questions asked. This included knives, guns, explosives, drugs, alcohol, enemy body parts, and anything else not issued by Uncle Sam. Even street-wise Vic was amazed at the variety of items that had been dropped off. There was enough deadly ordinances to supply a third world revolution. "Man, if there was only some way to get even a sample of that firepower to the streets of the old neighborhood." He thought. But, the officer in charge was very clear on the policy, leave it voluntarily with no problem, but God help you if you're caught with it later.

Vic's wife, Ginger had only written once in the past two months, and the last letter was notice that she would meet him at the air port because they had things to discuss. She said it was important that she talk to him alone. So, in spite of his long standing policy not to allow anyone to dictate terms concerning his personal life, he agreed. It meant lying to his family about his arrival, but he wanted to size Ginger up without distractions. If divorce was on her mind, and he was sure it was, then he would hear her out, looking for some chink in her armor.

As the truck full of departing GIs and Marines rolled to a stop at the airbase, Vic tossed his duffle bag out and swung his now wirey frame over the tail gate, dropping to the airfield tarmac for the last time. A faint sense of satisfaction came over him as he thought about how he had cheated death and the system. It was soon replaced by an overpowering feeling of guilt because so many he knew and served with were flying back to homes they would never see again. He was amazed that a hard ass like him could be so attached to guys he wouldn't have given the time of day before the war.

Vic had two soft spots, the guys in his unit and Ginger. He would deal with her the way he had so many others who turned on him, but the thought of loosing her cut him to the core. He honestly tried to make things work. He never once cheated on her or took a cheap shot at her, physical or otherwise. These weren't sacrifices on his part. He honestly cared deeply for her from the moment they first met. But, she was slipping away and somehow he knew he couldn't stop it.

In the beginning the relationship was very special. They talked, laughed, made love, and found ways of communicating without saying a word. But, it felt like day-to-day things, little things, chipped away at what started out so perfect. Maybe that was it. What they once had was too good to last in this all too often, rotten world.

"Well fuck it." Vic thought. "If that's the way it has to be, then bring it on. None of the other crap in my life could bring me down. This won't either." This go-to-hell attitude was his only way to deal with a loss that was tearing him apart.

The 707 touched down at SeaTac airport outside Seattle just before noon. It had been an incredibly long trip with one stop in Hawaii for fuel. Vic felt uneasy and at the same time almost numb. It was as if home was now foreign soil, a place where nothing fit. In fact, he couldn't shake the feeling that home no longer existed.

Then things got military again. The Army veterans were escorted to waiting bussed for the trip to Fort Lewis where they would be either processed out or be given leave orders before their next assignment. Vic's feelings were now even more confused. The Army routine that he hated so much was almost comforting now. "God" he thought, "I gotta get out of this man's army before I turn into a lifer."

When the busses arrived at Ft. Lewis the greeting was much different than the one given new recruits and draftees as they process in. First, the young combat veterans were taken to a small mess hall. As Vic went in with the others they were politely seated at tables with table cloth and silver ware arranged in individual setting. Each was asked how he would like his steak prepared, what each wanted on his baked potato, and what kind of vegetable each would prefer. Vic was astounded. The food was delicious, but none of the men could eat much more than a small portion of the outstanding meal. After a full year on mostly C-rations their stomachs could only handle small portions.

After the meal they were taken to a barracks for their last overnight stay before final processing. Then it was back to SeaTac and a flight home. However, even this red carpet treatment and thoughts of home couldn't keep Vic's mind off Ginger. "What did it take," he asked himself over and over again, "to make a relationship last. Maybe he wasn't capable of piece and happiness considering his past. Well fuck it. If the sunny side was out of his reach then he'd learn to enjoy the shit side."

As the plane touched down at Chicago's OHare International Airport Vic peered out the window, hoping to see something that would make him feel at home, but the out of place feeling lingered. This was his home town, his turf. Yet, he still felt foreign. As he left the plane filled with the first mix of civilians he'd been around in over a year things got worse. People seemed to step back as if afraid of catching something. Even the flight crew avoided direct eye contact. "What the hell is with these ass holes? " He asked himself.

As he exited the ramp onto the concourse he passed a group of young people dressed in beads, tie died shirts, and bell bottom pants. "These ass holes would stand out in a crowd of ass holes." He thought.

As he passed the last male member of the group the guy raised two fingers in the shape of a V and said. "Peace brother."

Vic snapped. "I'm not your brother." He felt rage and contempt building from deep inside.

With his back now to the group he heard some one else say. "No, you're a baby killer."

Vic stopped. He felt the bag drop from his hand. He turned slowly and asked. "Which one of you said it?"

No one said a word. In fact, everyone at the gate was quiet. All had their eyes on the Vic. "Now that I'm facing you, say it again." Vic insisted.

His cold, black eyes cut through each member of the group, one bye one. No one moved.

Suddenly a voice behind him said. "Let me buy you a drink sergeant." Vic didn't move. His eyes were still locked onto the young people at the gate.

"Come on." The voice came again. "I could use one myself and the company in this airport sucks."

He allowed himself a glance over his shoulder, and saw a tall army officer in a special-forces uniform standing behind him. "It's not worth it. It'd be like kicking over a garbage can."

The tall Green Beret picked up Vic's bag and also began to stare at the group. He kept his gaze fixed on them until Vic finally turned slowly and walked into the main aisle of the concourse.

"Here." The young captain said as he handed Vic his duffle bag. "There's a bar in the main terminal that has good gin and tonic."

"I'm scotch and water." Vic pointed out.

"First round's on me." The captain offered.

As they seated themselves at the bar and ordered drinks Vic asked. "You just get back too?"

"No, I'm headed back over. It'll be my second tour." The captain corrected.

Vic turned slowly and looked deeply at the man seated next to him. "Why?"

The captain returned Vic's eye contact and said. "You know the feeling you had when you boarded the plane as you left Nam, that deep survivor guilt because you made it and so many others didn't? Well, I can't shake it. It's with me all the time. I left a lot of good people in Vietnam, people who depended on me. I can't let them down. I have to go back."

Vic continued to look deeply into the captain's eyes. "The more time you spend there the closer you come to getting your ass shot off. Are you willing to pay that price?"

"If I stay long enough they'll kill me. I'm sure of it. Some day the odds will catch up with me. But, I have to see this through." The captain explained.

"Man, even if you come back your life will be over. After one tour I don't even know who I am anymore. My wife wants a divorce. I feel like a stranger in my own home town. What the hell is it all for anyway?" Vic shook his head. "Ya know, I don't even care. It just doesn't matter any more."

"Lots of things matter sergeant. You'll find them. Just don't stop looking. If you do then you'll truly die inside. That's when it's not worth it anymore. We have to adjust, every God-damned-day. Let go of the things that don't really matter." The captain advised. "The reason you feel the way you do is because you've seen the world from a different perspective, one full of pain and death. Of course your world has changed. Of course you don't feel the same way about your home town. That town is gone forever. Find a new one. If it's with your wife, great. If not, then look alone, or with someone new."

"It's just that I feel so empty inside, that is until I run into ass holes like the ones back at the gate. I was ready to kill one of them." Vic added.

"Killing's easy once you've done it. Living is what's tough." The captain added. "If going back meant nothing but killing more V.C. then I might as well kill myself and save the grief and aggravation. I'm going back to those I'm close to, those who still need me. Each day will be a difficult adjustment, but that's what makes it worth while. There's great satisfaction in every new thing you find. Start over my brother, and make every day count."

"God damn it, I don't even know where to start." Vic said in frustration.

"You already have. The first step was getting off the plane, the second, not killing anyone." The Green Beret added in detail. "Don't even try to figure out the big picture. There's too much for you to see right now. Don't expect to find peace or any kind of satisfaction. They will take time. Light up a smoke, have a drink, close your eyes and listen to the radio. Tell the world and everyone in it to kiss your ass. There's nothing for you to do right now but get right with yourself."

The captain bought another round and several more after that. Then the bar tender who had been listening intently to the conversation bought a few more on the house. That's the last that Vic remembers of his short stay at O'Hare Airport. He suddenly awoke at the small terminal in Moline, Illinois, his final destination, the place he was to meet Ginger.

He slowly opened his eyes, gave himself a long moment to look around, and then began to wonder what angel, or more likely team of angels had delivered him over the last one hundred and eighty miles from Chicago. He sure as hell didn't get himself or his bag on and off the plane and into the terminal. This must be step five or six. The angels will get credit for three and four along with the captain. "Shit," He thought. "I don't even like officers."

As he looked at those passing by he caught the same reception he'd received in Chicago. It was like he had some disease that could be transmitted by eye contact. Vic felt the contempt and deep rage coming over him again, just as intense as it had been at the terminal in Chicago. "Well fuck every God-damned one of them." He thought. "I'll get this damned green suit off, blend in with the crowd, and throw a king sized fucking into as many of these ass holes as I can, as fast as I can. But first, I'll deal with Ginger."

The phone rang twice before Vic heard her say. "Hello."

"Ginger, it's me, Vic. I'm at the air port." He said slowly.

"Why didn't you let me know you were coming?" Ginger replied.

"The flights were a mess. I was lucky to get the last seat. I didn't have a chance." Lie or not, this explanation fit better than angels loading his drunken ass onto and off the plane.

"I'll be there as soon as I can." Ginger agreed.

"Want me to call someone else?" Vic asked.

"No, I want to talk to you first, remember?" Ginger insisted.

"I'll be here." Vic said as he hung up the phone. "Love you too you miserable bitch." He thought to himself. He normally didn't hold back, but he wasn't going to give her a reason to fight back at him right away. That would be too easy. He was going to play this slow and force her to make the first moves.

He went back to the waiting area closest to the main entrance, lit a cigarette, and settled into one of the chairs. He thought about the incident at the Chicago terminal and the captain who'd given him the advice. Then, suddenly he had visions of body bags lined up on one of the landing zones where he'd helped load them onto helicopters. He saw the faces of all the guys he knew who would never see home again. He took another look around the airport at those who past him by, and suddenly they didn't matter anymore. He remembered the captain saying. "Of course you don't feel the same way about your home town. That town is gone forever. Find a new one. If it's with your wife, great. If not, then look alone, or with someone new."

Vic began to feel a great calm. Those who passed didn't care, and could never understand. Suddenly he saw them in a new way. They looked small and insignificant. They had no idea how lucky they were to have never seen the death and despair that had been his life for the past year. Their cold indifference no longer mattered to him because they no longer mattered. He put out his smoke, closed his eyes, and drifted off to sleep. "Fuck em all." That was his last conscious thought.

"Vic!" He heard the voice say over several times.

"Hi Gin." He said as he slowly stood up and hugged his wife. She half heartedly returned the embrace.

"God, you're skin and bones." Ginger said as she stepped back and looked at him.

It was true. His once stocky frame was reduced to one hundred and fifty-five pounds with little or no body fat. "It's the U.S. Army diet and death plan. Works great. More people should try it." Vic snapped sarcastically.

"We heard about the death part in your letters. Why did you do that? Do you know how hard it was on your family? You never should have written about that." Ginger insisted.

"Ya, that was heartless of me. I should have just written about the fun stuff. Only problem with that was there wasn't a lot of fun stuff happening. On the other hand death was all around. Maybe we can have a happy war sometime so that everyone can enjoy it." Vic snapped again.

"God damn it, you know what I mean. Besides, it's been three weeks sense your last letter. I didn't even know if you were alive." Ginger pointed out.

"And it was eight weeks sense I heard from you." Vic paused for a moment. "Gin, let's give it a rest for now. I just want to slip into a pair of jeans and sweat shirt, and relax with a cold beer."

"Well, if you think you're just going to sit around in old cloths and drink beer, you're wrong." Ginger wasn't ready for a rest.

"Let it go for a while. We can pick at one another later. You can tell me all about what you think is right and wrong, and I'll act like I really care. It'll be great. But, for right now, just give it a fucking rest." Vic knew if she didn't back off it would get ugly.

"I told you we had things to discuss, and I need to get them off my chest right now." Ginger insisted.

"So far all you've done is bitch, and if you plan to keep it up, that's your choice. But, understand that I'm not going to tuck my tail between my legs like some puppy while you work me over. If you want to talk we'll talk. If you want to fight then bring it on." Vic had enough. He was ready to play this out no matter what the outcome.

"Do you think you were the only one who suffered for the past year? Do you know what I've been through? Ginger asked as she slid behind the wheel of the car.

"I thought that bad stuff was off limits, or is that just for me. But, to answer your question, no I don't know what you've been through. Although, I think I'm about to find out." Vic replied as he got in on the passenger side.

Things were quiet for a while as Ginger headed for the freeway. Then, suddenly she began again. "I sat at home every night while you and the boys were chasing Vietnamese whores. How do you think that made me feel?" Ginger exploded.

"That's what you think I was doing for the past year?" Vic stared at her in amazement. "Tell me something Ginger sense we're talking about the bad stuff, have you ever watched a friend die as he puked blood? Have you ever looked into a bloody hole that used to be a man's face? Have you ever shoved a jungle knife under a man's ribs and felt the warm blood squirt up your arm? That's what the boys and I were doing for the past year you stupid bitch. Take the first exit and let me out. I don't need this shit. If this is what's in store I want no part of it. Stop the car and let me out."

They both fell silent as Ginger continued driving down the freeway. The next exit was several miles ahead, and she had no intention of letting Vic out. She tried hard to fight back the tears, but they began to run down her cheeks in spite of her best efforts. She knew that their relationship was doomed. She didn't love Vic anymore, and wondered if she ever really did. She was confused because the conflict hurt so much. Or maybe it was guilt because she hadn't been faithful while he was gone. Part of her wanted the whole thing over and done with and part wanted to hang on. She had no idea why.

The silence lasted longer this time. Ginger broke it by saying. "I don't want to hurt you, Vic. You're a nice guy. But, I can't hold my feelings in. It wouldn't be fair to either of us."

Vic sighed. "I'm not a nice guy, and I'm not asking you to hold back. I know we have problems, and it's not all your fault. I'm tired, beat up, and empty inside. In the past two days I've either been crazy with hate or felt nothing." The words surprised him. He was cutting her more slack than he intended. "I know we have to settle things, but you have to give me room. I can't deal with this all at once. If you pressure me I'll come out fighting, and nothing will be settled."

"I don't see how it's that complicated." Ginger replied. "Just be honest with me and yourself. Do you love me?"

Vic took a deep breath as he choked back the anger. He looked at her and began slowly. "Listen to me. I've been killing men and watching friends die for the past year. It's been so long since I was around anything decent that I don't even know what love is anymore. I'm telling you this so that you can understand why it's not simple, why my view of everything is different than yours."

101

"Then what do we do?" Ginger asked. "I mean, we can't even have a conversation. It's like we're speaking different languages. What's the answer?"

"I'm trying to tell you I don't have the answers. I'm figuring things out as I go. There's nothing else I can do." Vic feelings were beginning to fade. They both fell silent as they continued into town, and the apartment Ginger rented after Vic left.

As they pulled into the parking space adjacent to the front door a light snow began to fall. Much of the buildup left by the blizzard three days before had been cleared away. But, all indications were that another storm was on the way.

Vic lifted his duffle bag from the back seat and followed Ginger inside. He walked past her toward the bedroom to unpack and change. "Do I have any cloths here?" He asked.

"Your stuff is in the top dresser drawer and the right side of the closet. Your car keys are on the night stand." Ginger answered. "There are towels and the usual stuff in the bathroom if you want to clean up." There was a short pause and then she added. "Leave the door open and I'll wash you back."

"First she's a mile up my ass about everything and now she wants to wash my back." Vic thought. "She's crazier than ever."

He tossed his uniform on the bed and headed for the bathroom. He didn't wait for the tub to fill, but instead, jumped in and let the warm water run over his feet and legs. It was incredible, the first time in over a year that he'd actually bathed in clean, warm water.

True to her word Ginger came in as soon as he shut off the water. "Lean forward a little and hand me the soap." She said softly. As he did she began to wash his back and shoulders. Suddenly she stood up and tossed the soap back into the tub. "So, if you were hit in the back why don't I see any scars you fucking liar? Shrapnel leaves big ugly scars and you don't have any. And, where's the Purple Heart?"

"The scars are under water, on the back of my legs and left arm. The Purple Heart and Bronze Star are on the uniform that's lying on the bed. There's some shrapnel that's still in my back that the doctors said wasn't worth going after. Wanna dig around and see if you can find it you cold blooded bitch?" Vic said as he stood up and walked past her toward the bedroom. He put his uniform back on only because it was conveniently lying on the bed where he'd left it. He didn't take the time to dry off. He just wanted out the there and away from Ginger. When he was dressed he pulled the case from his duffel bag that held the full dress version of his Purple Heart and threw it through the open bed room door. He watched it hit the wall in the hall and fly open dumping the medal and ribbons on the floor. He grabbed his Keys from the night stand and headed for the front door. Ginger was no where to be seen.

He blew through the door and headed for his car parked in the visitor's area. His Malibu Super Sport had been his pride and joy before he left a year before. As he turned the key the engine fired immediately. He'd given his father responsibility of keeping it in running condition while he was gone and the old man had done a great job. It was clean, full of gas, and ready to go. As Vic pulled away he saw Ginger standing in the door of the apartment. It was too dark to see tears, but he could tell she was crying. It made no difference now. He'd taken all he could, and knew there was no point in any more contact with her tonight.

His first thought was seeing his family, but first he needed a little time to shake the thoughts of killing Ginger. He had real images of choking the life out of her, and he had to shake them and get back into control.

There was a popular bar, The Jolly Roger, not far away where he, Tony and many baseball players hung out before the war. He headed there to have a drink, and pull himself together. As he drove he noticed his hands cramping up and looked down to see his knuckles turning white from his intense grip on the steering wheel. He also felt his neck and shoulders tighten. "Come on Vic, get a grip." He told himself. "You're home and have a chance at life again. Don't let some worthless bitch screw you up."

As Vic walked into the Jolly Roger he noticed that the bar was nearly empty, but it was still very early. The evening crowd wouldn't be in for several hours. Nothing in the place looked the way he remembered it. Even the bartenders were new. Then he noticed a familiar silhouette on a stool at the end of the bar. As he approached the friendly form he said slowly. "Hay you northern ginny bastard. How ya doin?"

"Vic." Tony replied. "Welcome back. Have you been home yet?" He was surprised to see his old friend still in uniform.

Vic paused for a moment and then replied. "Ya,Ginger picked me up at the airport. I decided to leave before I killed her. I didn't take time to change cloths."

"I'm sorry man. That sucks. Let me buy the first round. Bring my friend a scotch and water." Tony signaled to the bartender at the other end of the bar.

"We don't serve service men in uniform." The bartender snapped.

Both Tony and Vic stared at the man for a long moment, not ready to believe what they heard. Suddenly Tony stood up, walked around the bar, grabbed a bottle of scotch and glass, and poured Vic a drink. He then pulled a twenty-dollar bill from his pocket and threw it on the bar.

By the time the glass was full the bartender was along side Tony and reached for the glass and bottle. "I said we don't serve service men."

At the same time Tony reached for him and replied. "You didn't serve him you chicken necked cock sucker, I did. That's my fucking scotch and I'll decide who drinks it."

Tony was between the bartender and Vic and the scotch. The bartender backed off a couple of steps and picked up the twenty. He had no intention of dealing with Tony or Vic on his own. "I don't want any trouble." He said as he stared into Tony's wild eyes.

"Then leave us alone. We're not bothering you or anyone else. All we want is to have a drink and talk for a while." Tony said in a slow deep voice.

The bartender didn't say another word. He walked back down the length of the bar and disappeared into the store room at the rear of the building.

"I can't even get a drink without a hassle." Vic said as he slowly shook his head. "What the hell happened while we were gone?"

"I don't know, but I've had enough shit to last forever. If it wasn't for Annie I don't know where I'd be now." Tony admitted.

"You're one lucky bastard to have her. She's one in a million. Hang on tight to that one brother." Vic advised.

"Things not good with Ginger?" Tony asked.

"If I stay with her I'll kill her Tony. I can't deal with it anymore." Vic admitted. "I'm serious. I'm afraid I'll actually kill her."

"Then get the hell out while you can Vic." Tony said in a concerned voice. "You have plenty to live for, and don't need to waste your life on something if it can't work. You deserve better."

"I'm gonna have better, and if Ginger gets in the way it'll be her problem." Vic mood was changing. Suddenly the violence he'd avoided at both the airports began to sound good to him, as if it would make things right.

Tony picked up on the change in his old friend as if he could head his mind. "Listen to me Vic. You have to let it go. Don't ruin your life. You have another chance, one that lots of guys will never have. You owe it to them, and most of all yourself to make the most of it. Going after Ginger would be like kicking over a garbage can. You have more important things to do. Make your adjustments brother, every fucking day."

Vic put down his drink and looked at Tony in amazement. Then he began to laugh softly. "Garbage cans and adjustments every fucking day. Are all vets singing the same song about garbage cans and adjustments? Well, what the hell, maybe it really doesn't matter. Fuck-em all."

"Maybe not all, but definitely most of them." Tony also began to laugh softly.

"You boys having a good time?" The voice came from directly behind Tony and Vic. As they turned they saw four uniformed policemen with night sticks in hand, all within arms length.

Tony gave himself a short moment to size up the situation, then said. "As a matter of fact we're enjoying each others company over drinks that I paid for, and not bothering anyone. Is there a problem that I missed?"

Vic began to laugh out loud. "Garbage cans and adjustments brother, garbage cans and adjustments."

"Ya, I'll tell you about the problem you missed. The bartender threw you out of here, but you decided not to leave. That's a problem." The biggest and ugliest cop said.

"No, the bartender said that he didn't want to serve us, but he took the money for the drinks, and, as a matter of fact, kept change from a twenty that I never intended as a tip." Tony said, locked in a stare with the big, ugly cop.

"That's not the way the bartender tells it." The cop insisted.

"Funny, I don't see the bartender. He must be on break." Tony said with a smile.

"You think this is funny?" The policeman asked.

"No, I think it's ridiculous. We paid for the drinks. There's no one else in the place for us to bother, and the bartender isn't ever here." Tony said slowly.

"Come on boys. You're under arrest." The cop informed them.

"Welcome home Tony." Vic said, still laughing. "God, this makes me proud to be an American."

"You should behave. You're in uniform." One of the other policemen said to Vic.

"Kiss my ass doughnut eater. I've been dodging bullets for the past year while you and your buddies were rousting drunks." Vic snapped.

"Don't push it G.I." The ugly cop said.

"Save your threats for the winos." Vic replied. "I have to do a lot of things to get through the day, but taking crap from you is not one of them. I'm not resisting. So, back off. But understand, if you use that stick you'd better kill me cause that's what it'll take if we get started."

All four policemen had their eyes on Vic and Tony. They moved slowly through the front door of the tavern toward the two patrol cars parked at the curb. Nothing more was said as they got in for the ride to the police station.

Tony was loaded into one car and Vic the other. The ride was also quiet. No words were spoken until they were inside precinct headquarters and the desk sergeant on duty gave them a chance at a phone call. Tony made his first. The phone rang just once before his mother answered. "Hi Mom, can I talk to Pop?"

"Is everything all right?" His mother asked.

"Ya, I'm fine. I just need to talk to Pop for a minute." He replied.

"Hold on, he's right here." Olga said.

"Hi buddy. What's up?" Paul asked.

"I'm in jail Pop. They arrested Vic and me at the Roger."

"Are you OK?" What happened?" Paul tried to stay calm and not upset his wife who he knew would not understand.

"They wouldn't serve Vic because he was in uniform. He just got back. Anyway, they said we were out of line and called the cops." Tony explained.

"What the hell? It all started just because Vic wanted a drink?" Paul shouted, forgetting his wife and his earlier concerns.

"I swear Pop, all we were doing was having a drink and talking. There have been times I deserved to be arrested, but honestly we weren't bothering anyone. In fact, I paid for the drinks with a twenty and the ass hole of a bartender left with my change." Tony added.

"Give me twenty minutes and I'll be there. Just relax and take it easy. Tell Vic to do the same." Paul reassured his son.

"What's going on?" Olga demanded.

"Tony and Vic were arrested at the Jolly Roger. I heard the guys talking the other day over some new policy they have about not serving service

108

men there. Vic was in uniform and Tony tried to buy him a drink." Paul explained. "I'm going to call Max Schiller before I head for the station."

Paul dialed the number of his old friend, Chief of Police Schiller. Max was one of the few men Paul honestly never wanted to fight. He'd been a pro football player and heavyweight boxer before the war, and made his own rules about how to keep the piece. Paul watched in amazement one night as Max and his friend Tim Callahan clean out a bar, arresting everyone inside, but not before sending six to the hospital. It happened soon after Max became chief of police. Before the fight started Tim gave Paul his night stick and said. "Just make sure none of them get out."

"Max, your cops arrested my kid and Vic Moretto at the Jolly Roger because Tony tried to buy Vic a drink while he was in uniform. Can you give the station a call before I get there?" Paul explained to Max.

"Was there a fight? Were they raising hell?" Max asked.

"Not according to Tony. In fact Tony gave the bartender a twenty for the drink and didn't even get his change." Paul added.

"I'll do better than call, I'll meet you there. Give me about fifteen minutes." Max said as he hung up the phone.

As Paul pulled up in front of the station he saw Max heading up the steps to the front door. He hurried to catch up and they walked in together.

"Good evening Chief Schiller." The desk sergeant said.

"Good evening my ass. Who's locked up back there and why?" Max snapped.

"A couple of vets who were raising hell at the Roger Chief. The bar tender tried to throw them out, but they wouldn't leave." The sergeant tried to explain.

"Did he serve them?" Max pressed for details.

"What do you mean?" The sergeant asked.

"Did the fucking bartender take money from them." Max exploded.

"According to one of the vets, yes he did." The sergeant admitted.

"Find out who made the arrest, and if he checked on weather or not the bartender served them. In the mean time let the guys out until this is cleared up." Max ordered.

Then he turned to Paul and said under his breath. "Callahan is headed for the Roger. Wanna come along and watch? Give the boys your car and you can ride with me."

"I wouldn't miss it for the world." Paul said with a broad smile.

As Tony and Vic walked out of the holding area Paul tossed Tony his keys. "Take my car. Max will give me a ride. We have some business to take care of."

"Vic and I would love to come along." Tony said with a smile.

"I'll let you know how it turns out." Paul told his son.

"Thanks Pop. Thanks Mr. Schiller." Tony said gratefully. He and Vic had the greatest respect for the two older men.

"You boys call it a night. We'll set things right." Max added.

As Paul and Max approached the front door of the Jolly Roger. Paul saw a smile form on Max's lips. He turned slowly to Paul and said. "Kind of like old times."

"You and Callahan gonna let me join in this time or do I just watch the door?" Paul asked, now smiling himself.

"These pussies won't fight. They just make phone calls. But, maybe if we push a little someone will get stupid." Max explained. "Paul, I'm glad your boy made it back. I hope things go well for him."

"Thanks Max. He's a good man." Paul told his old friend.

As they walked in they saw Tim Callahan already seated at the bar. He was in his police lieutenant's uniform sipping a Coke. The owner of the Jolly Roger, Woody Sutton, was behind the bar just a few feet from Tim.

Max hollered at Woody as the leaned on the bar. "I'd like to buy Officer Callahan a drink now that he's off duty."

"First round's on me." Woody said through a crooked smile.

"No, lets do it this way. Why don't you take the price of his drink out of the twenty that Tony and Vic left before you had them arrested." Max said as his eyes locked onto Woody. "Oh wait a minute. Officer Callahan is in uniform. I guess that means he's not allowed to drink in your fucking shit hole."

Woody froze where he stood. His mind races for the right thing to say, knowing that there was none. "Come on Max. You know what would happen if I let the college kids and vets mix in my bar. There'd be trouble every night."

"Sure, I understand. You make a ton of money off the college crowd. Apparently, you don't think that Lieutenant Callahan and I can handle our jobs and keep the peace. I'm really sorry to hear that Woody."

"Wait a minute Max." Woody interrupted.

"Shut up. I'm not finished." Max snapped. "Tell you what we're going to do. I'm going to put a cop in here every night for the next week. He's going to spend his time checking IDs and sniffing for pot. He'll also make sure that the band doesn't play loud enough to bother the neighbors. What do you think Tim? You see any problems in here?"

Tim Callahan smiled a broad Irish smile and slowly stood, turned, and headed for the nearest table. Once there he grabbed a big, long haired young man sitting with his back to the band stand, shuffled him across the floor and threw him against the bar. "Hands on the rail ass hole." Tim shouted.

He began unloading the contents of the guy's pockets on the bar. Out came a switch blade, two packs of Trojans, a bag of marijuana, and two driver's licenses, neither of which were his. "Damn Max, you were right. We gotta spend lots more time in this place."

Woody shook his head and looked at Paul. "You're loving every minute of this aren't you?"

"Only way it could be better is if Tony and Vic were here." Paul said through a broad smile.

Max grabbed the young man still leaning against the bar and said loud enough for everyone inside the hear. "You have a problem drinking with veterans in uniform?"

"No Sir, Mr. Schiller, I love every one of them. In fact, I'd love to buy one a drink right now." The young man said quickly.

"Tell ya what son, grab your stuff, and finish your drink. Leave the blade, fake I.D. and dope on the bar. We'll consider this a lesson in understanding." Max said.

He turned to Woody as he collected the items left on the bar. "See, there's no problem with vets, just with you. I'm going to send Vic and

Tony back over and let you buy them a drink. I'm sure there won't be any more problems. If there are, I'm going to stuff your sorry ass in that gogo girl cage while Tim and Paul take this place apart."

Paul and Tim followed Max out of the now, totally silent bar.

Max

The Best of Times

Tony

It was after 6:00 pm by the time Tony and Vic returned Paul's car to his home, explained as best they could to Olga about what happened at the bar, and picked up their own vehicles outside the Jolly Roger. Vic told Tony that he was headed for his family's home, and would give him a call later. He'd made more than his share of adjustments in the past few days. The Morretto family was more than a little eccentric, but Tony knew they would welcome Vic unconditionally, and give him love that Ginger could never provide.

Before leaving his Mom's home Tony called Ann to explain why their dinner date would be a little late. He assured her he'd be there as soon as he could, knowing she had lots to tell him about their upcoming wedding. He was amazed at how she seamed to always understand even when he was delayed because of things like being thrown in jail. As Ann answered the door he said. "I'm so sorry for being late. I know we have a lot to talk about."

"What happened?' Ann asked.

"I stopped for a beer at the Jolly Roger after my interview and ran into Vic Morretto. He just got back today." Tony explained.

"Is he OK?" Ann interrupted.

"No, not really. He and Ginger had a blow up at the airport that lasted all the way home. He walked out before things got out of hand." Tony added.

"My God, he just got home and they're fighting already?" Ann inquired.

"Ya, I think they both know it's over, but just won't let go. The way Vic described it they tour one another up badly." Tony went on.

"So, what happened at the Roger?" Ann asked.

"I tried to buy Vic a drink, and they wouldn't serve him because he was still in uniform. He walked out on Ginger before he took time to change." Tony said as his voice became irritated.

"They wouldn't serve him in uniform?" Ann blurted in amazement.

"That's right. It's some kind of knew rule Woody game up with. Anyway, instead of just going somewhere else, I got mad and poured Vic a drink myself. I paid for it and the bartender took the money. I thought he'd let things go; but instead, he called the cops. They locked us up." Tony finished.

"How'd you get out so quickly?" Helen Riley asked as she entered the room.

"My Dad and Max Schiller are old friends. Max let us go and headed for the Jolly Roger to get Woody's side of the story." Tony added.

"I'll bet old Max went after more than a story." Helen added with a knowing smile.

"You know Max Mrs. R.?" Tony asked.

"I helped patch him up a few times before he became police chief and a couple of time after now that I think about it." Helen explained. "He's one tough old German, but I can't help liking him."

"He's a good man with his own way of handling trouble. He always treated me right even when I was way out of line." Tony added.

"You still want to go out, or we can have something here?" Ann asked.

"How about I take you both out? What do ya say Mrs. R.?" Tony proposed.

"No, you kids go ahead. I'm going to take a pill and call it a day, but thanks." Helen said gracefully.

"Well we'll get you a rain check then." Tony announced.

Ann was ready in minutes, and by eight o'clock they walked into Gino's Place, their favorite restaurant. Gino Vertoli greeted them with his broad smile as he hugged them both. "What's a beautiful girl like you doing with a broken down old ball player like him?" He asked.

"Hay, you have a whole restaurant full of women, leave mine alone." Tony protested through a faint smile.

Gino leaned forward and whispered. "Ya, but yours is the prettiest, much too good for a mug like you." As Ann walked ahead toward their table he added so that just Tony could hear. "Stay away from Woody's shit hole and have a drink in my place. You're family here."

"You heard already?" Tony whispered back.

"It's all over town. I'll talk to you later." Gino hugged Ann again and reassured her. "If he's not nice just come see me."

Tony ordered a bottle of wine, some bread and antipasto as they settled in before dinner. As the waiter filled their glasses Ann asked. "How did the interview go?"

"Annie, you won't believe it. They offered me the slot as an apprentice electrician. The program is set up so that some of my classes will transfer toward a degree in electrical engineering. My first two years of college will count so I'll be done with the apprenticeship in three years. Then, two more years of night school and I'll have my degree. And, they'll pay for my tuition and books." Tony blurted so fast that Ann missed much of what he said.

"Wait, slow down." She laughed as she tried to calm her future husband.

"OK, here's the real world stuff. I'll be working Monday through Friday, going to school two to three nights a week, the company will pay for my school, and I'll get money from the G.I. Bill for the whole five years. Things will be busy during the week, but we'll still have week ends; and, best of all we'll be together. Can you handle being with me fulltime? I have my faults." Tony smiled as he finished.

"No, you have faults? I thought every girl's future husband missed dinner because he was in jail." Ann just couldn't let a chance like that slip by.

Tony looked across the table at his fiancé who was now smiling from ear to ear. "That was a cheap shot." He protested.

"Did you think I would let you completely off the hook?" She asked, still smiling.

"No, you're your mother's daughter, and I'm sure I haven't heard the last of the Jolly Roger incident." Tony said through a smile of his own.

Ann reached across the table and took both his hands in hers. "I'm very proud of you Anthony Frisano. Your accomplishments fill me with joy and your faults make me love you that much more. Your heart, your pride, your strength and your love get you into trouble, but it's because of those things that I love you as much as I do."

Tony looked deeply into her eyes. She made him feel complete. She made all the pieces fit. With Ann life was full and satisfying, and everything he ever wanted. "Thank you for understanding; but, most of all thank you for being you."

"You're welcome." Ann replied. "Now let me tell you my news. Mom and I went to the bank today to check on a very special account. My Dad set it up right after I was born and it's grown nicely. There's enough for a very nice wedding and a little something left over for expenses later on. Mom was so pleased. She's been looking forward to this, and is nearly as excited as I am."

Tony's voice changed a little as he asked. "How's she doing? She looks very tired, and seams to be limping more."

"She's had some very bad nights. The arthritis is getting worse and there's not much that can be done to help her. Sometimes I feel so helpless. I know she's hurting and there's nothing I can do." Ann explained.

"Did you talk to her about living with us? I hope she understands that I honestly want her there and I'm not just being noble." Tony insisted.

"She knows, but deep down doesn't want to be a burden. She's a nurse Tony and knows what's coming. Before long she'll need lots of care." Ann began to look concerned and frightened.

"Annie, your Mom is a fighter and will handle each problem as it comes. We'll do the same. There's no way to plan for everything. So, we'll take the problems one at a time. But, she'll be better off with us for as long as we can take care of her. I think I'll have a talk with her and make sure she understands how I feel." Tony tried to reassure her, and at the same time was speaking from his heart.

"What about baseball. It means so much to you, and you're still young enough to play. Don't you want to give it a shot?" Ann asked.

"There's no time for me to play ball. I have to give it up. The deal that they offered me today is a once in a lifetime chance. It won't come again." Tony explained.

"I don't want you to be sorry later. How are you going to feel when spring comes and tryouts open?" Ann pressed.

"I'll feel like a man with a wife who he loves, a job with a future and the luckiest man in the world. Honestly, I'm ready to move on. Baseball and football were great and I loved every minute that I played. But, that part of my life is over and a new part is starting. I'm very excited about the new job and school. I love that kind of work." Tony told her.

"I just want to make sure you're making the choice because it's what you truly want." Ann continued.

"It is Annie. I spent a lot of time thinking about it today before I met Vic. I realized after the interview that I had to make a choice and I make it. I won't look back. There'll be no regrets." Tony continued honestly. "I'm fascinated by what makes the wheels turn. I honestly want to take my shot at building a better mouse trap."

"OK, I believe you." Ann said. "Now we have a wedding to plan. Mom and I will start working on arrangements; but, where would you like to go on our honeymoon?"

119

"I thought about that today too, and came up with the greatest idea. How about moose hunting in Wisconsin? They have great accommodations for couples with a log cabin that has its own private bathroom. We'd be like John Smith and Pocahontas." Tony said as he fought back a smile.

"Wow John, that'd be great. Private bath and all, I'd be the luckiest squaw in Wisconsin. After you returned from the hunt I could skin the moose and make you some moccasins. I'd be sure to chew the leather to make them nice and soft." Ann replied.

"Annie, you're not taking me seriously." Tony was now smiling from ear to ear.

"Gino, I need your help." Ann waved at their old friend across the room.

"What's the matter sweet heart?" Gino asked as he moved toward them.

"He wants to take me hunting in Wisconsin on our honeymoon." Ann protested.

"I'll break both his knee caps. Then he can hunt from a wheel chair." Gino assured her. "Or better yet, I'll marry you myself and take you to Cabo-San-Lukas. We'll get a suite overlooking the ocean, have lunch by the pool and go sailing in the evening."

"Actually, it's sailing in the afternoon and dinner by the pool in the evening." Tony corrected as he passed a brochure across the table to Ann.

"You set me up Tony and you helped him Gino." Ann said, now smiling herself.

"Sorry sweet heart, but he needs all the help he can get." Gino explained.

"Tony, this is wonderful." She said as she thumbed through the pamphlet. "But, it must cost a fortune."

"I had a little of my own tucked away. It's covered." Tony assured her.

"So, what's it a gonna be kids?" Angelo, Gino's younger brother asked as he approached the table.
"Bring us an order of polenta with a side of bonyacolda, the good stuff that you guys keep on the stove in the back." Tony said, smiling again.

"Wow, that's powerful stuff." Angelo waned. "You sure?"

"Absolutely, and when you bring it why don't you and Gino join us for a taste and a glass of wine?"

"Man if we eat that stuff before closing we can't get close enough to the customers to take orders. But, it'd be a pleasure to join you two for a quick glass of wine, and a toast to the new bride and groom." Angelo said gratefully.

"Tony, how will I work tomorrow if I have bonyacolda tonight? Ann said as she shook her head. "If its anything like Nona's the garlic breath won't wear of for days."

"Then let's take a couple of days and head for Chicago. We can take in a Cubs game and see a show. Lou Rawls is in town and I know a guy that can get us great seats." Tony encouraged. "What do you say?"

"God, Honey I'd love to, but they have me scheduled for surgery first thing in the morning, and it's too late to find someone else. We're really short of surgical nurses right now" Ann said as she took Tony's hand. "But, I'd love a rain check."

"OK, Angelo, cancel the bonyacalda and being us a bottle of your best Chianti. Then tell that brother of yours to get his butt over here for a glass of wine." Tony ordered.

Dinner and drinks took nearly three hours. It was more like Sunday at Nona's, rather than an evening at a restaurant. Actually it was Tony's Nona who provided the polenta sauce recipe that helped put Gino's on the map.

Tony took his time driving home. It was after eleven, but he did everything he could to make the evening last. As they walked slowly to Ann's front door she held his arm and leaned on his shoulder. "Wish you could stay tonight. I don't want to sleep alone anymore. It feels too good waking up next to you in the morning."

"I have one more surprise for you that'll make the mornings even better." Tony said softly.

"What?" Ann asked.

"My Uncle Louie owns a bunch of property overlooking Rock River. I bought an acre of it from him. It's a beautiful spot Annie. I'll show you this week end." Tony said as he pulled her close.

"You bought property? Are you going to build us a house?" Ann stopped a few steps from the front porch, not willing to move any farther without more details.

"I was thinking of a log cabin with an inside toilet and everything. Kind of like a moose hunting lodge." Tony couldn't resist making it tough.

"Look Frisano, I don't need Gino to break your knee caps. Tell me about our new house." Ann blurted as she grabbed him by the front of his jacket.

Tony laughed out loud as he pulled her closer. "I made some preliminary drawing that I'll show you tomorrow night. I want to talk to both you and your Mom about the layout. I'd like to use the time to let her know she has a place there. It's important that she knows I want her with us for as long as she wants to stay."

Ann threw her arms around him as tears began to run down her cheeks. "I love you Anthony Frisano."

She stayed in his arms holding him tight and savoring her feelings as things truly began to fall in to place. Tony finally said. "Come on sweetheart, it's time for both of us to call it a night. I'll be over as soon as I can tomorrow with the plans. Let your Mom know, OK?"

They walked the few remaining steps to Ann's front door. As Tony leaned forward to kiss her good night she stopped him and said. "Stay with me tonight. I can't let you go Tony. It broke my heart waiting for you to come home to me. For a while I thought I'd never see you again. I don't want to sleep alone anymore. I want my man next to me where he belongs."

"It won't be long Annie. Then we'll be together for the rest of our lives." Tony said softly.

"No. It's not enough. I'll skip the wedding and marry you tomorrow if that's what it takes. I laid awake, alone all those nights. I watched the news at night and saw them loading coffins onto air planes wondering if that's how you were coming home. No, I won't let you go again." Ann began to quiver in his arms as she sobbed wildly.

Tony pulled her even closer and said. "OK, I'll stay. It's alright sweetheart, I'm here. We made it. You don't have to worry anymore."

"Please Tony; I can't let you go tonight. I need you here." She continued to cry and tremble in his arms.

On that night it was Tony's turn to take care of her the same way she'd been there for him on his first night back. She cried herself to sleep as he held her in his arms.

In the next room Helen Riley also wept as she remembered waiting for her own man's return. She asked herself if there would ever be a generation that would live without that kind of pain and despair.

The next morning Tony was awake before sunrise. He slid quietly out of bed without waking Ann and kissed her softly before heading for the kitchen. He was surprised to see Helen already there sipping coffee as he came in.

"Good morning Anthony". She said in a soft, but firm voice.

"Mrs. R, you're up early. Everything OK?" He asked.

"Everything's fine. I just felt like starting the day with an early cup." She replied.

"I'm glad you're up. I want to talk to you about plans that Ann and I are making. I bought some land near the river, and am going to build a place for us. I want you to know that it's for the three of us, you, Annie and me. Then, in a while maybe some grandkids. What do you say Mrs. R.? Are you interested?" Tony finished with a smile.

"That's very nice Tony, but you two need a place of your own. I'll be fine here. I truly appreciate the offer. It means a lot to me to know you care that much." Helen choked back a tear.

"Please here me out. I'm not being nice or noble or anything like that. You're much more than a mother-in-law to me. I've spent more time here sense Annie and I got engaged than anywhere else. I've made love to your daughter in the next bed room, ate your food, tracked mud on your carpet, and been treated like a son by you. I'm asking you to live with us because that's what I want. If you stay here we'll spend more time in this place than our own, and I'll never get anything done. Honestly Mrs. R., it's what Annie and I want." Tony said with complete sincerity.

"Tell you what, if you start calling me mom I'll go back to bed and think about it. Now, go and wake my daughter, and please try to keep the noise down." Helen said with a little smile.

"Thanks mom." Tony said as he kissed her on the forehead. "If we need to scream we'll go out to the garage."

"My God, I've allowed my house to become Sodom and Gomorra. My poor husband is turning in his grave." Helen shook her head slowly.

Tony stared at her for a moment. "You're the best."

"You're pretty OK too." Helen replied.

Tony shook Ann softly as he sat bye her on the side of the bed. "Annie."

Ann opened her eyes, turned slowly and said with a tender smile. "Good morning."

"How'd you sleep?" Tony inquired.

"Like a baby." She replied.

"I had a chance to talk to your mom this morning over a quick cup of coffee." Tony informed her. "I told her how much we wanted her with us at the new place."

"And?" Ann pressed.

"After some convincing she said she'd sleep on it and get back to us, but only if I'd promise to call her mom from now on. That part was easy. But, you were right, the first thing she said was you and I needed a place of our own. I countered with the fact that I've been making myself at home here sense we were engaged, and want to move the whole set up to a bigger place for all of us." Tony went on to explain.

"I'll stay after her this afternoon when I get home." Ann told him. "Can we set something up so that she has a corner of the house to herself, kind of like a small apartment?"

"Sure can." Tony assured her. "The side of the property that faces the river slopes down hill, and is perfect for a daylight basement. We can set her up there with a little kitchenette and sitting room all her own. I'll even get her an entrance off her kitchenette"

"Perfect." Ann replied with a soft smile. "Tony: please don't misunderstand but, can you really build something like that? I mean it sounds complicated and a lot of work."

"The answer to all three is yes: yes it's complicated, yes it's a lot of work, and yes I can do it." Tony continued his assurance.

"What about the money? That kind of house sounds very expensive." She went on to question further.

"It is. But, I paid cash for the land, and Uncle Louie will give me a course of construction loan using the property as collateral. I worked on lots of projects for him while I was in school, and he knows my work is good. He's a great guy, and is willing to help all he can." Tony continued.

"Wow, Uncle Louie must have done very well. What did he do?" Ann asked.

"He and lots of my uncles were self-employed during the twenties and early thirties in a part of the country where there weren't many rules. Let's just say that the Frisano family was in the entertainment and distribution business." Tony never talked about his family's past, and Ann knew when not to press for more information.

"Tony, this seams all too good to be true. I mean it's all falling into place so quickly and smoothly. I keep looking for something to go wrong." Ann admitted.

"Just think back to what things have been like over the past few years. We paid our dues and then some in order to have things fall into place. Enjoy the moment Annie. We earned it." Tony assured her. "If things go bad we'll deal with each disaster as it comes. Till then, enjoy."

"But don't you ever…?" Ann tried to continue.

"Annie stop." Tony interrupted. "I know things are moving fast. I also know there are dozens of things that can go wrong. So, we have to set some time aside to work out the details. I have all summer to work on the house before my classed start in the fall. The company I'm going to work for is planning a three week shutdown in June to relocate to a new facility. So, I'll have time to work on the house full time. We can live at your place till it's done. Tomorrow we'll sit down and start working on the budget."

"OK. OK." She said with a smile. "You convinced me. I do like the part about sitting down and working out a budget. I feel a lot better when all the little ducks are in a row."

"Then tomorrow we start herding the ducks. We'll make the little suckers line up. But now we'd better get our herding butts to work." Tony kissed her and gave her a quick wink.

Most of their ducks lined up as planned, but a few got loose. The house project was far more than he expected, and caused long hours in both blazing heat and freezing cold. But, it was a labor of love that represented their future. Tony made it happen, and still fit in work and school.

127

Someone to Hold

Ann turned slowly as she woke from her restless half sleep. As she reached for Tony she found his side of the bed empty. The room was dark except for the light from the clock on the night stand that said 4:00 am. As she scanned the room she saw Tony's silhouette against the background of the bedroom window. "Are you alright?" She asked in a deep, sleepy voice.

There was a smallest trace of light on Tony's face as he took a drag from his cigarette. "I'm OK Annie. Go back to sleep." He said in a detached, almost cold voice.

Ann sat up, swung her legs to the floor, stood and crossed to Tony's side of the room. Once there she turned and settled onto his lap. She reached out and touched is face and felt tears on his cheeks. "What is it? What's wrong?" Her voice was much higher now, and full of anxiety.

Tony took a long, deep breath and crushed the cigarette out in the ash tray on the arm of the chair. He said nothing.

Tony, what's wrong?" Her voice still showed anxiety, but now was very insistent.

"I wish I knew. I don't want you to see me like this Annie. It's not me. I'm loosing it and don't know why." His voice was full of frustration and rage.

The only time Ann had seen any sign of weakness in Tony was the night he returned from Vietnam. He always faced life's problems with complete control and optimism. Even in defeat he always kept going, knowing he'd find a way to finally win. Seeing him so confused and uncertain sent a chill deep into her heart. "Tony, talk to me. I'll understand. I love you."

"How am I going to explain what I don't understand myself?" His voice filled with even more anger and frustration.

"Tell me what you know, what you feel. We'll sort it out together. But, for God sake don't shut me out." Ann's voice now showed frustration and deep concern.

"I don't want to put this on you. It's bad enough that I have to go through it. God damn it Annie, it's not fair. We've been through enough without me falling apart. I can't load you up with this fucking shit." Every muscle in his body was tight, and sweat ran down his face and mixed with the tears.

Ann through her arms around his neck and pulled him as close as she could. "Hang onto me sweetheart. We can handle this just like we do everything else."

After a long pause when neither of them said anything, Ann leaned back and ran her hands down the side of his face. "Talk to me now."

Tony took a deep breath and began. "I close my eyes and all I see is blood. My hands are covered with it. My cloths are soaked in it, and it's not mine." His hands began to shake. "I see the guy we carried up the side of the mountain to the L.Z. The medic told us he'd been dead the whole time we carried him." He stopped for a moment, and then said. "You don't want to hear the rest."

Ann's voice was now completely calm. It was the voice of not only a woman deeply concerned about the man she loved, but also a nurse who had spent many hours soaked in blood tending to broken bodies. "Keep going. Don't stop."

"I see the men I killed. They didn't have faces then, but I see them now." He took a moment to look into to her eyes, and then said. "They were between you and me. They were keeping me from coming home, and I went after them like an animal. It changed me Annie in ways I don't understand. Killing became easy, and I was very good at it, too good. It didn't bother me then. In fact it was natural, and made things right. It made me feel like I had a chance to get back home."

Ann took a deep breath. She gave herself a chance to let at least some of what she'd heard settle in. "How long have you felt this way?"

"It all started about a month ago." Tony explained. "I thought it was just a temporary thing, something that would pass in time. It's not like a nightmare; it's like living it all over again. I mean when it happens it's like I'm back there again, and may not make it home. I feel like I'm dying." Suddenly Tony lifted Ann from his lap as he stood. He crossed the bedroom to the bath in just a few lightning steps, and half closed the door behind him.

"Tony." She shouted.

"Give me a minute." Came his reply.

Ann sat down in the chair where Tony had been, and stared at the half closed door. She could see his motionless shadow as he stood in front of the sink. In a few moments he turned on the water, and then stood still again. When she could stand it no longer she went to the bathroom and slowly opened the door. Tony was still at the sink, staring into the mirror, but the reflection from his eyes told her that he saw nothing in the room. He was thousands of miles away. Ann touched his shoulder and felt his muscles as hard as rocks. "Tony?"

He jumped slightly, and looked briefly around the room, then back into the mirror at Ann's reflection. "God damn it Annie, why? Why is this happening? Is this some kind of punishment for staying alive when so many didn't? It's not my fault they died." He suddenly roared. "God damned son-of-a-bitch." The tube of tooth paste in his hand exploded under the force of his grip. "Oh Christ." He gasped in complete frustration, then walked back into the bed room and sat on the side of the bed.

Ann stood in shock, staring at the toothpaste cover mirror and sink. Her mind raced as she tried to find a place to begin to sort out what had just happened. But, nothing from her past or present could help with this. She was at a complete loss. Then Ann simply did the one thing that came naturally to her. She went into the bedroom, sat down next to Tony, put her arms around him and said. "I love you. What ever happens Tony Frisano, you remember that."

"I'm scared Annie, and I'm ashamed of myself for feeling this way. But, I don't know how to fight this." His rage and frustration turned to confusion.

"You have every right to be afraid, but no reason to be ashamed. You're a good man, Tony, and you've been through a lot. It's gonna take some time to work this out. But, we'll make it." Ann's voice was calm, and filled with love.

"You're one in a million." He pulled her close as they sat together in the dark.

Someone to Lose

Vic got to the phone just before the third ring, and answered with an unconcerned "Ya, this is Vic".

"Vic Marretto"? The voice on the other end inquired.

"Yes for the second and last time, this is Vic". He snapped.

"This is a friend, and I have some information for you about your wife. She was cheating on you while you were over seas". The voice on the other end was calm, but a little shaky.

Vic gave himself a few seconds to settle in on the situation, and allow himself to stay in control. Then he said. "OK, I'm listening".

The voice replied. "That's it. I thought you should know".

"Just like that? You call on the phone, drop something like that on me, and then say that's it? Sorry pal, but I need more information, who, when, where, how many times, you know, details". Vic pressed. He also planned to keep the guy on long enough to get all he could about who he was.

"Man, I'm just trying to help you". The still shaky voice replied.

"So, help me. Give me some real information". Vic continued.

"Sorry, I have to go". The shaky voice said as the caller hung up.

As Vic hung up he heard Ginger come through the back door. As he turned he saw her come into the kitchen with an armload of groceries. "You could give me a hand". She complained.

"Sorry, but I've been on the phone with some guy who said you were fucking lots of new friends while I was gone". Vic said in a low, controlled voice.

She looked at him for a moment as she tried to size up the situation. "Is that supposed to be funny"? She asked as she tried to prepare herself for what she knew would eventually come. Question was, would she have to face it now or later.

"It's been a very interesting day Ginger. Just before the phone call I was going through a box of bills in the desk, trying to figure out how much money you'd pissed away. I found some paper work from your doctor. There's a lab test that says you're pregnant". Vic felt his hands begin to shake as he stared at her.

Ginger felt a cold chill run up her spine as she looked into Vic's cold dark eyes. "What do you want me to say?"

"Relax bitch, there's nothing to say. Be thankful you're pregnant. It's the only reason I don't kill you. But gee, I feel a little silly just standing here". Vic picked up the steam iron from the counter and slammed it into the kitchen table. Pieces of the iron flew in all directions as a corner of the table bounced across the floor.

Ginger dropped the groceries and stumbled back against the adjoining counter. They both stood in silence for a long moment. Suddenly there was a knock on the back door, and a man's voice said. "Is everything all right"'?

"Yep, everything is just fine. In case you're one of the guys who was fucking my wife, just give me a minute and I'll be out of the way". Vic turned slowly, grabbed his jacket and walked out the front door.

About an hour later Max Schiller walked into Gino's Place, and signaled to Gino who was already headed in his direction. "Seen Vic Moretto tonight"? Max inquired.

"Glad you asked. He's been here for about half an hour, and something is wrong. He just sits there at the bar staring at his drink. Is he in trouble"? Gino asked.

"Not yet, but he's real close". Max replied as he walked through the dinning room toward the bar. As he approached the old mahogany bar with cigarette burns and glass rings covering its surface he caught the attention of the bar tender, Rocco DeAngello. He and Max went way back, and had trained together when they were both professional heavy weights.

Rocko nodded and tipped his head toward the end of the bar where Vic was sitting. Max returned the nod, walked the length of the bar and settled himself on the stool next to Vic. While both men sat silently Rocco delivered a bottle of Coke to Max that he'd mixed with a double shot of Jack Daniels.

As Max took a long sip Vic said as he continued to stare at his drink. "I never laid a hand on her".

"She said you threatened to kill her". Max replied.

Vic allowed himself a faint smile as he turned to Max. "No, I said the only reason I wouldn't kill her is because she's pregnant. How bout that Max, I've been away for thirteen months, and my wife is five months pregnant. Guess that's what a guy gets for jacking off in his letters home".

There was a long pause, then Vic went on. "Some son-of-a-bitch was humping my wife while I was dodging bullets. Tell me, who do I see about that"?

Max said slowly. "There's nobody to see. I wish there was".

After another long pause Max went on. "There's something you have to know. Even though there's no way the kid can be yours you'll still be considered the father. The court doesn't give a damn about how many guys she was with. They're only concern is that someone provides for the baby."

Vic stare at Max for a short moment and then began to laugh. It started slowly and grew with every breath. When the laughter subsided Vic said. "Sure, why not. Hell, with the action Ginger provides maybe I can support a dozen or more. I could start my own baseball team."

Max pulled a cigar from his inside jacket pocket and signaled to Rocco. "Bring us another round."

Bye now Gino had moved behind the two men and dropped a hand on each ones shoulder. "How bout something from the kitchen"? Before either could answer he ordered. "Bring a plate of antiposto and some fresh bread". Then he was gone as fast as he appeared. But, before he left he leaned over Vic's shoulder and said. "You're family here."

Vic downed the first drink and started on the second as the food arrived. He reached in his pocket, pulled out a twenty, and dropped it on the bar. "Your money's no good here pizzon." Rocco announced as he pushed the bill back at Vic.

As Max finished the first juiced up Coke and puffed his cigar he said. "What're you plans. Where are you gonna work?"

"Someplace where I can make lots of money. I have a baseball team to support." Vic replied.

"I need a deputy. Interested?" Max offered. "There are fringe benefits".

"I'm listening." Vic said, very much surprised at the offer.

Max turned on the stool and looked deeply into his young companion's eyes. "I need guys who can handle situations without going too far. I have to have people who can stay in control, and control what's around them. There are some differences between being a soldier and being a cop. Guys like Tim Callahan will show you how it works."

Vic stared back. He locked eyes with the older man, trying to gather as much as they would provide. He remembered his grandfather saying to him in Italian. "Watch the eyes, they never lie. But, you gotta look close."

"Why do you think I could handle the job?" He was still watching Max closely.

"Two things right off, after your tour you're still alive; and most important, you didn't kill Ginger." Max explained.

"Anything else?" Vic pressed.

"Ya, the way you're sizing me up right now. You do it naturally, and it gives you a big edge over most people. Then there's the thing with the busted iron and broken table. You let go, but never lost control. Ginger thought you'd lost your mind, and she was terrified. But, that's what you wanted her to think." As Max finished a faint smile crossed his face.

"And the fringe benefits?" Vic continued to push.

Max's smile got broader. "Think it over, and take a day or two to get your head on straight. We'll talk more then." He consumed the last of the super Coke in one gulp, grabbed a piece of garlic soaked vegetables from the antipasto plate and walked away.

A cop Vic thought, my old man and the family in Chicago would shit. That alone makes it worth while.

As Ginger passed the living room window she heard a car pull up. She pulled the corner of the drapes back to see the driver's side door open as Max Schiller climbed out. He didn't have time to knock before she opened the door. "Chief Schiller, come in. Did someone talk to Vic already?"

"Ya, I just left him a few minutes ago." Max replied in a low, almost threatening voice.

"And did you straighten his sorry ass out?" Ginger snapped.

Max took a long pause as he stared at Ginger. "I talked with Vic, and he and I will talk again. But first, I'm going to straighten your sorry ass out. So, sit down, shut up and listen."

Ginger was stunned. She backed up slowly and dropped down on the couch. "Why are you growling? Vic's the one who attacked me."

"I said shut up and listen." Max wasn't giving her any latitude. "He didn't attack you he attacked a table. So don't start by trying to bullshit me. If he'd have come after you you'd be dead. The guys been killing people for a living for the last year. Then, he comes home and finds out you've been humping God knows how many while he was dodging bullets. I give him all the credit in the world for only breaking a table."

"I'm afraid of him." Ginger began to cry.

"You have reason to be." Max replied.

"I can't live with him and be afraid all the time." Ginger continued to cry.

"Here's what we're gonna do. There's a lady cop who is going to come see you, and sit down with you and Vic. You're both gonna be honest with her. She will work you both through what has to be done." Max gave Ginger a chance to settle down, and then went on. "Listen to me Ginger. If you don't cooperate with her we're gonna have problems. I'm not going to waste my officer's time running out here because of your stupidity."

"It's not all my fault. You don't know what it's like to live with Vic. He can be a beast." Ginger protested.

Max paused for what seemed like forever. As he sat quietly he continued to stare at Ginger. Finally he said. "If I know anything about Vic, and I'm paid to know such things, he won't be back. You ripped his heart out and shit in the hole. He won't waste his time on you anymore. You two have some things to work out, and the lady I told you about is gonna help. But, Vic is through with you because he's smart enough to know you're nothing but trouble. It's over, and before long he'll be out of your life forever."

Max's words cut her to the bone. If he was right she was alone with a baby on the way. Her mind began to race with a thousand thoughts of how her life was about to change. "You don't know everything. Vic will be back."

Max smiled as he rose from the chair and headed for the door. "Good luck. The lady I told you about will be in touch."

"I don't want to talk to your fucking lady. So, save your time and leave me alone." Ginger snapped.

Max spun around and was nose to nose with her in the blink of an eye. "I'm only gonna say this one time you little shit. You have a baby to take care of, and Vic's gonna help. The law says that child comes first, and I'm just the man to make that law stick. You're gonna start acting like a responsible mother or I'll God-damned sure make you wish you would have."

Ginger stood motionless as Max turned again for the door. This time she said nothing.

Early the next morning she awoke to the sound of rattling in the kitchen. She climbed out of bed and headed for the sound. As she came to the end of the hall she saw Vic pulling an old pair of tennis shoes out of the pantry. "What are you doing?"

"Packing." Was his answer. "I'll be out of here by the end of the day."

"We need to talk." Ginger's mind was racing again.

"We will. Max Schiller arranged for a councilor to work us through all the details." Vic said without turning around.

"I don't want to talk to a councilor. I want to talk to you. You can't just pack up and leave like this." She protested.

Vic stood up slowly, crossed the kitchen and sat down. He looked at Ginger who was leaning against the counter with her arms folded. "Let's don't make this any tougher than it has to be. We have a lot to work out, and I just want to get it over with."

"Just like that?" She couldn't stop the tears from running down her cheeks.

Vic looked at her for a long moment, and was surprised that he felt absolutely nothing. "It's over Gin. I don't feel anything. I'm just empty inside, no anger, not even disappointment anymore. Yesterday it was like the whole world came down on me. But, today I'm numb."

"You loved me once, and I loved you. What happened?" She asked.

"I can't do this. Tell you what. I'll just grab a few things for now. You tell me when I can pick up the rest." Vic couldn't take any more.

"No, we have to talk." She insisted.

Vic sat there for a minute, and then said. "I just fought a war and came home to find you five months pregnant with someone else's kid. I'm gonna help with the baby because it's sure not the kid's fault. But where you're concerned here's the deal. I don't wanna see ya. I don't wanna know about ya. I don't want to hear the sound of your voice as long as I live. Do you get it Gin? I can't make it any clearer than that."

He got up slowly, quietly walked to the bed room and stuffed all he could into the duffle bag he'd brought along. As he came back into the kitchen he tossed the apartment key on the table and said. "I'll make it easy on both of us. I'm traveling light. You can throw the rest out. I'll be in touch when Max's lady cop contacts me." He threw the duffle bag on his shoulder and walked out.

Ginger stood there for a long time, looking at the empty door way. Then she grabbed the phone, dialed a familiar number, and waited for an answer. "Dr. Springer's office."

"Janet, this is Ginger. Let me talk to Ben." Ginger replied.

"He just finished with a patient. Hold on and I'll see if he can come to the phone." The young receptionist told her.

After a short pause Dr. Ben Springer answered saying. "Hi Gin. Are you OK?"

"Vic just moved out. I don't think he's coming back." Ginger waited for Ben's reply.

He moved quickly across his inner office and closed the door. "Wow, just like that. No muss, no fuss, he just moved out?" He was surprised and very relived. "After the table thing I was afraid he'd do something foolish."

"Then why the fuck did you leave me alone with him?" Ginger felt anger welling up inside.

"Well, what did you expect me to do, move in and sleep on the couch?" Ben snapped. "Or, maybe you could move in with me, my wife and kids."

"Don't talk like a fool. We have some things to work out. What about your wife, Stacy? Have you talked with her yet?" Ginger pressed.

"I need some time. This is going to be tough. I have to talk to my lawyer. Stacy will come after me for everything. We have to do this right." There was a small fortune at stake, and Ben Springer wasn't a man to walk away from money.

"Well you better hurry. In four months you're going to be a daddy. Ask your lawyer about that." Ginger slammed the receiver down.

"Shit". Ben muttered as he hung up.

Starting Over

Tony walked through the breeze way between the kitchen and garage. As he passed by the pile of tools he took a quick moment to arrange them so that they were no longer a tripping hazard. No sense putting them away now, he'd need them again first thing in the morning.

In another day he'd have the Riley place ready for spring. The timing was perfect because day after tomorrow he'd be ready to pour the foundation for the new house. The project was on schedule, although a little over budget. But, Uncle Louie assured him that he'd handle the course of construction finances until the place was done. Tony owned the land, and Louie was more than willing to accept it as collateral.

As he walked into Helen Riley's kitchen he saw Ann at the table looking through their wedding album. "That was one great party Annie." Tony said as he slipped off his boots.

"The best." Ann replied as she continued to slowly turn the pages. Tony took great satisfaction in the faint smile on his wife's face as she allowed herself to go back to the day they were married. "Your Dad was certainly the life of the party."

"Pop definitely knows how to party." Tony added.

"Your Mom was furious at him by the end of the night." Ann remembered.

"It wasn't the first time, but that's gonna change before long." Tony had been waiting for the best time to break the bad news.

Ann looked up from the album, and turned to face Tony. "What do you mean?"

"My folks are splitting up Annie." Tony leaned back against the counter waiting for her reply.

"What?" She exclaimed.

"They're getting a divorce." He went on. "Pop called me last week and asked me to come over and talk to Mom. That's when he told me that she said she'd had enough and wanted out."

"What in the world happened?" Ann couldn't believe what she was hearing.

"The same kind of thing that's been happening for as long as I can remember. He came home drunk. They had a fight. He went to bed." Tony explained. "I can't remember a week end or holiday when I was growing up that it didn't happen. She finally had enough."

"But, he never took a drink while you were over seas. I honestly thought he'd changed." Ann went on.

"This has been building for years. The only reason she didn't leave long ago was because of me." He paused for a moment. "Crazy thing is, she still loves him."

"Then he's the one who doesn't care. Can't he see what he's loosing. Your Mom is a great woman, one of the best I've ever known." Ann went on more confused than before.

"Pop needs the week ends to hang onto the guy he became a long time ago. When he walks into a bar everybody knows him. He and his buddies relive the old days, the ball games, the fights...." Tony tried to explain.

Ann jumped in. "Ball games and fights? My God, he's loosing his marriage so he can hold onto the old days?" She was more confused than ever.

"I know it doesn't make sense. The best way I can explain it is that it's a matter of self respect with him. Without baseball and the scars on his knuckles he's just another guy, and Pop can't be just another guy. As long as I've known him he had to go the extra mile, work just a little harder than the hardest working guy, find a way to get to a pitcher that no one else could hit, and gain the respect of the toughest guys in town. It's who he is." Tony truly wanted her to understand.

Ann could see how hard he was trying, but knew there was no sense in asking more. "I'm sorry. This will be tough on both of them. How are you holding up?"

"I can't struggle with things I can't control. There's nothing that I can do to straighten this mess out. And, Mom has made up her mind. That's it, end of story." Tony shook his head slowly, walked into the living room and settled into his favorite spot on the couch.

Ann settled in along side him, and they found comfort just sitting together. He looked at her and thought how lucky he was. She brought him peace, warmth, and a place where he could shut out the rest of the world. Tony wondered how hard it must be for Vic to go through life without anyone to sit with on quiet evenings when the rest of the world was a piece of shit.

Old Crowd, New Job

The Jolly Roger was filled with the usual Friday night crowd. As Vic walked in he saw all eyes turn his way. A cop in uniform was not only bad for business, but made all the regulars nervous. There were drugs and cash to be exchanged under the table and tricks to be tuned up stairs. Vic's presence meant all business stopped. He wasn't on the take, and couldn't be trusted.

Woody Sutton had tried many times sense Vic joined the force. But, so far Vic stayed clean. It wasn't that he was above shady business. And, he could certainly use the big bucks that the place offered. But, he couldn't trust Woody, and loved hassling him after the incident a couple of years earlier when he and Tony wound up in jail. Most important, he didn't know if Max would allow it, and he would never do anything to interfere with his relationship with a man for whom he had such great respect.

Vic slowly walked the length of the bar to a spot at the end where a tall blond sat sipping a Coke. As he sat down on the bar stool next to her he smiled that predator's smile that fit perfectly in this sleazy place.

"Hi Tammy. You look good girl." Vic said softly.

"Good enough to eat?" She replied with a subtle smile.

"Slow down. I'm on duty." Vic returned.

"You could call it your lunch break. I'm running a special this week for guys in uniform." Her smile was much wider now.

"How about a rain check sweet heart?" His smile was now bigger too.

"Any time, and the special is always on." Tammy assured him.

Vic reached out his hand and pushed back the hair from over her left eye. Makeup covered the bruises, but not the swelling. "You're wearing lots of extra cover up tonight."

"Leave it alone Vic. You'll just make things worse." She insisted.

"I'll guarantee they're gonna get worse." He snapped as he slid off the chair.

"Damn it Vic, let it go." She ordered.

Vic neither spoke nor gestured as he made his way to the table in the very back of the bar. Three men sat in the smoke filled area, two in jeans and sweat shirts and the third in a sport coat and tie.

"Hey Moretto". The well dressed member said as Vic approached. This was Bruno Silva, a local pimp, small time dealer and self-proclaimed bad-ass.

Vic said nothing as he reached across the table and smacked Silva along side the head with his best right cross. The punch drove his victim backwards and onto the filthy floor.

As Bruno's two companions jumped to their feet Vic drew the 1911, mill spec. 45 from his belt and yelled. "Sit down ass holes."

From behind the bar Woody hollered. "God damn you Moretto, have you lost your mind? I'll have your badge and your ass."

As Silva's companions helped him back into his chair and sat down themselves, Vic headed for the bar. "You got a complaint Woody? Hell, we can take care of that for you."

When he reached the place where Woody was standing he leaned over the bar, grabbed the phone and dialed the police station. "Callahan here." the voice on the other end replied.

"Evenin. It's Vic. I'm at Woody's place, and he's pissed because I just knocked Silva on his ass. He's been beating the girls again". Vic announced loud enough for the whole place to hear.

"You keep rousting that place on your own Vic, and somebody's gonna take you out." Callahan warned.

Vic moved the phone a few inches away from his face and hollered. "Callahan is concerned that one of you limp dick ass holes is gonna try to kill me. Any of you chicken-shit sons-a-bitches want to take a chance?"

As Vic pulled the phone back to his ear all he could hear on the other end was laughter. "Nope, nobody here wants to kill me. Guess they're all too busy. You want to talk to Callahan Woody? No? Guess he's busy too. Good night."

"Not so fast. Let me talk to Woody." Callahan insisted.

"Callahan wants to talk to you." Vic said as he passed the phone".

"Ya, this is Woody."

"Just so we understand one another, anything happens to Moretto, my Irish eyes are gonna be the last thing you ever see. Understand?"

"Damn it, the guy's out of control. He's in here slapping my customers around." Woody complained.

"You mean that piece of shit, Silva? Is that the customer you're talking about? Tell ya what. Give the same message to him I just gave to you. Then, tell him instead of beating the girls maybe he'd like to go a few rounds with me." Callahan snapped.

"OK, OK, I got the message." Woody said as he hung up.

Vic walked back down the bar, and sat down next to Tammy. He looked at her and said. "That was fun."

She stared at him and shook her head slowly. "You're crazy."

"No doubt about is it". He returned, then leaned forward and whispered. "Wanna stop by my place tomorrow?"

"See you about Two." She smiled.

Time for a Change

Vic

Vic stuck his head inside the door of Max's office. "Got a minute chief?"

"Ya, come on in. What's up Vic?" Max replied.

"It's not working. I'm gonna fuck this up. It's only a mater of time." Vic said slowly.

"It's not an easy job Vic. Cops walk a fine line, and it takes years to learn how to do it right. You've only been on the force for two years. You're doing fine." Max explained.

"Every time some ass hole tries to give me big bucks to look the other way, or some hooker offers a freebee it's all I can do to say no. If it was just a free lunch or a spiked Coke while I was on duty it would be different. But, this is big money Max at a time when my back's against the wall. You've been good to me, and you deserve better than I can give. I don't want to let you down, but it's gonna happen if I stick around. I'm sorry, very sorry." Vic told the man he respected as much as any he'd ever met.

"Are you sure?" Max questioned.

"Ya chief, I'm sure." Vic answered.

"Can you give me a few weeks? I'll get you off the street and re-assign you to the jail." Max asked.

"Absolutely, it's the least I can do." Vic agreed.

"What are you gonna do? Do you have something lined up"? Max truly wanted thing to work out.

"My Uncle Carmine wants me to start in the fitters as soon as I can. He's having a hard time finding guys he can depend on." Vic explained. "Hell, most of my family is in the trades. So, it's a natural."

"Think about this over the next two weeks." Max said. "You've made lots of enemies down town, and they lay off because you work for me. That'll change if you leave. I need reserve officers who know the strip, and how we handle things there. Stay on in reserve, and I'll make sure the schedule fits your new job."

"Thanks, I'll think about it. I'd like to make that work." Vic assured him.

Someone For Everyone

Vic cursed as he rolled out of bed and answered the phone. "Ya, what?"

"We'd like to buy you dinner ass hole, that's what." Tony growled.

"Who's up this fucking early?" The voice came from the lump under the covers in Vic's bed. He tried to remember what she looked like, then decided it really didn't mater.

"Damn it dago, not everybody is up at the crack of dawn." Vic snapped as a faint smile crossed his face.

"Most are up by the crack of noon unless they're next to the crack of hooker." Tony said softly.

"Not too loud. Annie must be close." Vic returned.

"Standing right here, smiling and shaking her head." Tony was laughing now. "Antipasto and drinks at six. Bring a friend if you want. Does she like Italian?"

"Italian what?" Vic was now laughing.

"Food. That's all they serve." Tony returned.

"I have no idea what she eats." Vic could here the laughter explode on the other phone. "OK, OK, enough. I'll see you at six."

As he turned the lump threw back the covers, and stood up. Her bare back and butt caught the sum coming through the curtains. Damn, Vic thought, that side's fantastic. She crossed the room, grabbed the cigarettes from the dresser and lit one. He decided the front side was even better than the back.

"Italian's good, but rare steak is better." Now it was her turn to smile as she watched Vic measure every inch of her nude form. "What the fuck are you staring at? You were all over every inch of my ass last night and this morning."

"You talk to your mother with that mouth?" He was now interested in more than her body.

"Well excuse the fuck out of me reverend. I didn't mean to offend." She snapped.

Vic stood, slowly shed the shorts he was wearing and crossed the room to where she was standing. His interest was back on her body.

Her gaze dropped to the area just below his waists. "Why reverend, you look inspired. Did you get used to my dirty mouth?"

"You talk too much." Vic wrapped his arms around her hips and pulled her close.

Her dark eyes locked onto his. "What's my name?"

Vic returned her dagger like stare. "Let's talk later."

"What's my name?" She demanded.

Vic relaxed and let a broad smile cross his face. "Terry Richmond. It's Terry Richmond. Can we fuck now?"

In one quick move she pushed him back, and headed for the bathroom. "Do you talk to your mother with that mouth?"

"I'll come in and wash your back." Vic said.

"You'll shit if you eat enough." She replied.

Vic watched her butt cheeks disappear behind the bathroom door as she closed and locked it. She knew how to keep him interested, and he liked the feeling more than he wanted to admit. He barely noticed her return as he banged on the old electric typewriter at the weathered desk by the window.

"What's this?" She asked from over his shoulder.

"A book, or at least the part I have done." He returned.

"Can I look?" Terry was interested too, and also liked the feeling.

"Can you read?" The chipped tooth showed as he smiles.

"Can you kiss my ass?" She snapped, but continued to look over his shoulder.

"I can't kiss your ass and type at the same time. So, go ahead and look." His smile got broader.

During the brief exchange she finished most of the page he was working on. "Where's the rest?" She inquired.

"On the night stand by the bed." He was surprised that he enjoyed her interest.

Terry crossed the room, lit another cigarette and moved to the night stand where the manuscript was stored. As Vic continued to write she began to read. After about twenty minutes noise from the old typewriter stopped. She looked up and found Vic staring at her. "Well, at least you're not laughing." She heard him say.

"This is very good Vic." Her voice was calm, and very sincere.

"You read a lot?" Her praise sent him fishing for more, but he didn't want to act anxious.

"I have a degree in literature." She said through a faint smile.

"Get the fuck outta here!" He exploded as they both burst into laughter.

As the laughter faded she replied. "Educated girls like sex too."

"Sure, but I thought it'd be limited to doctors, lawyers and blood sucking bankers." He suggested.

"They're boring stiffs, all wrapped up in their careers and stock portfolios." Her voice was sincere again.

"Would you like to have dinner with me and a couple of my old friends tonight?" Vic was amazed at how interested he'd become in her in just a few hours.

"Are you sure you want me along? You've only known me for a few hours. I could be a real bitch." She was still showing honesty.

"My friends eat bitches for breakfast. Tony and Ann are the two most honest and down to earth people I've ever met." He let his own honesty show. "So, what do you say, dinner at Gino's Place at six? I'll pick you up at five-thirty."

Terry scribbled her address and phone number on a scrap of paper and handed it to Vic. "See you at five-thirty."

Vic pulled up in front of the old house with the address that matched the one on the slip of paper. He took a minute to take in all the old place offered. The ancient wood work was freshly painted and the bushes were trimmed. The bases of the old foliage were huge indicating the age of each plant. The old place had character.

As he walked up the steps to the front door the wrap around porch reminded him of the residences of all his family that included at least fifteen uncles, all named Frank, none of whom were actually his uncles. He'd spent hours on a porch just like this one under the watchful eye of his grandmother.

He knocked and continued to study the old place until the front door opened. "Hey lover boy." Terry welcomed him with a broad smile.

"Hey girl." He replied. "Nice place."

"It belongs to my Uncle Frank. I take care of it for him when I'm in town, and whenever I can visit." She returned.

Vic burst into laughter. Then said. "No one named Richmond has an uncle Frank that owns a house like this. If your name ended in a vowel I'd believe you."

"How about Ricci? Would that do?" Terry said with a smile. "The family changed it at Ellis Island."

"Damn, you're a Wopp. I knew they're was something about you that reminded me of home." Vic's smile covered his entire face. "Let's get married, buy the place from uncle Frank, have eight kids, and make whine in the basement."

"Holy shit, paradise. I could wear me hair in a bun, get fat and scream at you all night long. Now that's what I'm talking about." They were both roaring with laughter.

"Come on. Let's go. I gotta tell Tony and Ann I finally found a girl who wants to get fat and wear her hair in a bun." Vic said through his laughter.

Gino's was full, standing room only at the bar. Terry pulled at Vic's sleeve. "This is gonna take forever. We can't even get a drink."

Gino

Before Vic could answer Gino wrapped an arm around his shoulder and said in a low voice through a broad smile. "You son-of-a-bitch, where you been so long, and what's this classy lady doin with a bum like you?"

"She likes ugly guys and good food. So, I thought I'd introduce her to you. Terry Richmond this is Gino." Vic handled the introduction through a knowing smile.

"Hi Gino." Terry said through a smile of her own. "The place is packed."

"Not for you pretty lady." Gino replied through the same smile.. "Follow me."

He led Terry through the crowded dining room, past the kitchen and into what reminded her of her grandmother's dinning room back in Boston. The room had four large tables in the center and as many booths along three walls. Tony and Ann were in the one closest to the kitchen. Ann waved and Tony stood as they approached.

"Look who I found out front." Gino announced.

"I see why you wanted to feed him in the back, but why hide his beautiful friend? Hi. I'm Tony and this is my wife Ann." Tony said as he offered her is hand.

"Hi. I'm Terry." She replied with a smile.

"And I'm......." Vic started.

"Ya, ya, sit down. The whine is on the way." Tony and Ann said in near perfect unison.

As they settled in Vic began. "Terry wants to put her hair in a bun, get fat, have eight kids and make whine in the basement."

"What the hell are you talking about?" Ann jumped in.

"Well......." Vic was cut off again.

"Shut up." Terry barked as she punched him in the arm.

"She's either Italian or Irish". Was Tony's observation.

"Italian." Terry continued. "And no bun, two kids, no weight gain, but I like the whine in the basement idea."

"She's changing her story." Vic protested.

"It's my story." Terry insisted.

"Amen sister." Ann said as they exchanged high fives.

"She's Irish." Tony pointed out as he looked at Ann who showed a satisfied smile.

157

"They're gonna have too much fun." Vic moaned.

"Ya should have left out the part about getting fat. That's what teamed them up." Tony observed.

Before the next exchange of guys versus gals, Gino appeared with antipasto, bread sticks and red whine. He loved entertaining the local Italian-American regulars, particularly Tony and Vic. They brought back memories of his boys, and family he'd left behind many years ago.

For a long while Gino's had been a second home to Tony. When Ann decided to hold their wedding reception there Gino became her unofficial Godfather. He brought the old saying to life, "when you're here you're family".

Now there was a new face in the old crowd, and Gino was going to make her welcome while gathering information at the same time. He began with. "OK kids, this will get you started. Take your time. Terry, if you want something that's not on the menu just let us know. Northern, southern, Sicilian, we do it all".

"Do you do polenta? It was my Mom's favorite." Terry said with an inquiring smile.

"Do it....it's our specialty. Don't tell a soul, but I actually got the recipe from Tony's Nona. Wanna try it?" Gino's said softly with a knowing wink.

"Sure." Terry returned.

"Make it two." Tony said. "Annie, how about you?"

"Yep, me too." Was Ann's reply.

"What about you my Sicilian piazanno, you doin lasagna?"

"Nona's sauce is the best, but I gotta stay true to my roots. Lasagna it is." Vic said.

"Don't tell a soul......" Vic shook his head. "Terry, you're the only one in town who didn't know where the sauce recipe came from, and now you're in on it too."

"Nona is..." Tony began.

"Grandma, I know." Terry jumped in while flashing the biggest smile of the night. "Mine was five feet tall, had a bun in her hair, wore nylons rolled up just below her knees, had nine kids, and yes, made whine in the basement."

"Let's make some whine in the basement. Tony, can we borrow your basement?" Vic asked.

"What are you gonna call it, police merlot?" Tony returned.

"Hey, ex-cops need hobbies too ya know." Vic snapped back.

"That was you in the night club." Terry exploded. "Now the pieces fit. You were the cop slapping the gangsters around."

"Gangsters, what gangsters?" Ann was all ears. Gino was close enough to hear, and turned to listen.

"It was in the Jolly Jester or Rapid Rabbit or something like that." Terry continued in the same surprised voice.

"The Jolly Roger." Tony helped out.

Terry was now staring at Vic. "Ya, I think so. It was my first time in town, and I stopped for a drink before calling it a day."

"OK, OK, let's get back to making whine or whatever." Vic tried to change the subject knowing there was no way that was going to happen.

"Shut up Vic. Terry is telling a story." Ann loved to pick on Vic. It was like picking on a big brother.

"Your wife just told me to shut up." Vic said to Tony in a half hearted voice.

"Better you than me Brother." Tony replied through a laugh.

"So, what happened?" Ann pressed.

Still staring at Vic, Terry continued. "I was sitting at the bar when this cop walked in. Everyone turned as he walked past like he'd come for them. He sat down next to this very cute young lady a few bar stools away from where I was sitting. All I heard before the cop swung off the bar stool was the girl say just leave it alone. He crossed the room to a table where these two gorillas were sitting with some guy in a business suit. The cop, Vic, hit Mr. Business Suit, and knocked him out of his chair. As the gorillas stood up Vic shoved a gun under their noses. That was enough for me. I headed for the door."

Ann and Terry stared at Vic as Tony leaned back and smiled.

Terry broke the silence. "It was you wasn't it?"

"Nope, it was my dumb twin brother. Now, lets get back to buns in the hair and whine in the basement." Vic replied.

Ann and Terry continued to stare, Gino continued to listen and Tony just kept smiling.

Vic finally cracked, and broke into a smile of his own as he said to Tony. "What the hell's so funny?"

"The Lone Ranger rides again. How dare you lay a hand on this school marm you low down pole cat." Tony exclaimed as he and Vic broke into laughter.

"Where the hell were you Tonto?" Vic asked Tony

"Tonto stay home with Mrs. Tonto. No get head blown off that way. Leave the bad guys to Kimosabi." Tony could hardly finish through the laughter.

Terry was smiling, but continued to stare as she said. "I just gotta ask why you hit him. Then we can go back to whine in the basement."

As the laughter died down Vic stared back at Terry and said. "The very cute young lady is a hooker. Mr. Business Suit likes to beat her up. He put her in the hospital."

"Why didn't you arrest him?" Terry pressed.

"It doesn't work that way." Vic wasn't going to go into details.

"But, you could get into trouble." Terry responded.

"It doesn't work that way either. Now, how about some whine." The message in Vic's voice said enough was enough, and this conversation was over.

The girls headed for the powder room to exchange information away from the guys. Tony and Vic dove into the whine, bread and antipasto.

"Very nice." Tony said as he nodded toward to lady's room. "You're stepping up in class".

"I figured her for a one-night-stand. But, there's a brain behind those brown eyes. Best of all, she knows when to push and when to back off. I like her." Vic admitted.

"That's good man. Life is better with someone to share it with." Tony added.

"It's too early for that. I'm still sharing with Ginger for big bucks. But, the doctor she was porkin wants to adopt the baby. Isn't that ridiculous? He's probably the natural father." Vic said softly.

"Is that what you want?" Tony asked.

"No, but it makes it better for the kid, one home, one family, you know. Maybe it'll give everybody a chance to start over." Vic said it hopefully, but didn't really believe it.

"Have you thought about trying for custody?" Tony had wondered about this for a long time.

"Sure I have. That little girl found her way into my heart the first time I saw her. But, her life won't be better living with a single father, and bouncing back and forth on the week ends. That's not what's best for her." Vic spent a long time coming to that realization.

"Well, that sucks. Guess there are no simple answers." Tony said.

"Sure there are, whine, bread and antipasto. Live in the moment, and love the one you're with. But, ya know, there's something different about Terry. She makes it easy to relax. After you called we spent half an hour in the same room while I worked on my book and she read. I can't remember the last time I was that relaxed." Vic surprised himself with what he'd said.

"Book, what book?" Now Tony was staring.

"I'm writing a book." Vic admitted.

"Get the fuck outta here. What's it about?" Tony was taken completely by surprise.

Vic leaned back and smiled a satisfied smile. "It's about baseball, you, Ann, this town, Vietnam, ass holes and the Lone Ranger and Tonto."

Before Vic provided any details the girls returned from the powder room conference. Ann was first to speak. "Hang onto to her Vic. She's a keeper."

"You can tell from one trip to the bath room?" Vic asked.

"Yep, that's all it takes." Ann assured him.

"Can I fill them in Vic?" Tony wanted Ann to know about the book.

"OK, but then we're going to talk about someone besides me." Vic insisted.

"You punched out more gangsters?" Ann jumped in.

"Vic's writing a book." Tony informed.

"Really?" Ann asked.

"Really, really." Said Vic. "But, the names haven't been changed because there are no innocent folks to protect."

"He let me read part of it. It's very good." Terry added. "In fact, it's some of the best I've read in a while. It may not have as wide an appeal as some because of the focus, but those who like it will love it."

"You sound like a publisher." Ann observed.

"I'm an editor." Terry admitted. "That's what brings me to town from time to time."

163

"Will you be here long?" Ann asked.

"Just a few weeks, then it's back to Boston. I've had fun here, but miss family and the old neighborhood." Terry explained.

Conversation was cut short as dinner arrived. The girls continued to exchange bits of information while the guys devoured the polenta and lasagna. Dinner and drinks were very enjoyable, but different than the usual friendly banter and antics. Terry brought a new feel to very old relationships. Tony and Vic talked more seriously than ever before. This evening was more relaxed and sobering than those in the past. Times were changing, and it was if all realized that they must change with the times.

Ann noticed the difference more deeply than the others. She pressed Tony for his view in the car on the way home. "So, what did you think of her." She asked.

"Who?" He returned with a smile.

Ann punched him in the arm. "Talk to me Frisano."

"She's great. I mentioned to Vic that he was stepping up in class." Tony returned.

"It's a lot more than just a new girl who can actually complete a full sentence. Terry brings out a side of Vic that he doesn't show often. He was more open and relaxed than I've ever seen him." Terry went on. "I think he's trying hard to get his life together."

"There are lots of pieces, and none of them fit worth a damn." Tony added.

"I don't see how he keeps it together. There's no one for him to lean on for support except you and me, and he'll never accept our help. I don't understand that." Ann looked at Tony, and hoped for an explanation.

"We're more like his anchor Annie. The help he gets from us amounts to something to hold onto when nothing else makes any sense. He doesn't know how to make the pieces fit. But, when he sees us he understands that they can. It keeps him trying." Tony wasn't sure how to explain it any differently.

"You make my pieces fit, and I love you." Ann smiled and settled in next to him.

"You have very nice pieces. I like to make them fit. Let's go home and fit some pieces." Tony said through soft laughter.

Ann punched him again, shook her head and said. "I give up."

Vic pulled up in front of the old house with the friendly porch. Then, shut off the engine and took a minute to take in the charm of the place. He sighed and looked at Terry who was staring back.

"Wanna come in?" She asked.

"Love to." He replied.

The home's interior provided the best of old world warmth. As Vic settled onto the couch he lifted one of the pillows with the two inch fringe around the edges. The floor squeaked a little as Terry crossed to the liquor cabinet. "Scotch and water?" She asked.

"Sure, sounds great." Vic answered.

She joined him on the couch, and watched as he studied the room. "What do you think?"

"I'm expecting my folks to come through the door followed by a gang of screaming kids." Vic said as he turned his attention to Terry.

"I know what you mean. The place almost makes me feel like I'm home again." Terry said as she placed her drink on the end table, turned and kissed him softly. She slowly settled into his arms and brushed a few strands of hair from his forehead. "Thank you for a great evening. I like your friends." She continued.

"Tony and Ann have been closer to me than my own family sense he and I got back home. Hell, they are my home." Vic confided.

"I'm flattered that you shared them with me ". Terry continued in the same soft voice. She laid her head on his chest and closed her eyes. The only sound was the beating of his heart.

Vic closed his eyes and let the world slip away. The smell of her hair and warmth of her body next to his were all he wanted to know. Something finally fit. In that moment a few of the pieces finally came together again. They both drifted off to sleep in that quiet place where each could feel comfort that can be so hard to find.

Terry was the first to wake. She allowed herself the time to look at this new man in her life, the one who slapped gangsters around and wrote books. She thought how tenderly he'd held her, and how patient he'd been at the restaurant. She marveled at the contrast between this man and the one she saw that first night in the bar, the one who was so comfortable with violence.

Vic now opened his own eyes and stared back at her. Neither said a word. He too was considering the contrast between the sides of Terry that seamed so different. This woman who could drink, fight and fuck like a hooker was also one of the most tender and understanding people he'd ever met. He slid his hand along the side of her cheek and felt her hair glide between his fingers, then gently pulled her face to his and kissed her softly. He could feel her body relax and settle in next to his.

Terry slid her hand up his chest and let it rest just under his shoulder, then settled her head back on the spot just above his heart. "I like this spot." She said.

"Then stay right there cause the spot likes you." He returned.

"I feel like I should take you to bed, but I don't want to move. Is that OK with you?" She asked.

"Making love to you is fantastic, but so is this. Stay right there." Was his reply.

After another long pause Terry asked. "What are you doing today?"

"I promised my self I'd tune up my car and spend a little time at the gym. But, I'm very flexible". He replied as a faint smile crossed his face.

She raised up just enough to free both hands and began unbuttoning his shirt. "What would it take to get you to forget about the car and gym?"

"What car?" He said as he began opening her blouse.

The trail of shoes, socks shirts, pants skirts and underwear led from the couch to the bedroom at the top of the stairs. The laughter coming from the two lumps under the covers could be heard from the street, and neither Vic nor Terry cared. But, this was different than their first night together. The passion was still there, but mixed with as much tenderness. The sharp exchanges were replaced with banter and fun.

During a brief pause in the action Terry slid over on top of Vic, wrapped her slender fingers part way around his oversized neck and said. "Make love to me big boy or you're a goner."

"Ya got at least half an hour to kill me cause that's how long it'll take for these old batteries to recharge." He said as he shook his head.

"So, what am I supposed to do for the next half hour?" She demanded.

"Choke me I guess, but ya got your hands all wrong". As he reached for her hands Terry's expression changed, and she pulled away.

"Let's find another game. Better yet, tell me about you. I wanna know more." She said as she slid along side him, and kissed him softly.

Vic took a moment to watch her carefully. He could see he'd somehow struck a nerve in spite of her smooth transition from sexy to serious. He decided to play along and go slowly. "I was a kid, then a ball player, then a soldier, then cop, and now somebody who's enjoying jumping your bones. That's it". He smiled as he finished, but continued to watch.

"Well, the editor in me's gotta tell ya, the story needs a few more details if you want your audience to stay interested." She pressed.

"Oh, I'm definitely interested in the audience. But, I gotta know a little more about their interests. How about baseball? Does the audience want to hear about that?" He wanted to keep fishing without being obvious.

"It's a start." Terry continued.

"Well, there's this little white ball called a ball, and this stick called a bat.........." He stopped as Terry punched him in the shoulder.

"OK, ass hole I assume your bat is about 32 ounces, you have trouble with off speed pitches cause you can't stay back, and your probably a middle infielder or may play a little center field. Is that close?" Terry growled.

"Get the fuck outta here. You know baseball?" She surprised him again.

"I'm from Boston, love the Sox, hate the Yankees and grew up at the ball park." she explained. "How long did you play?"

"Tony and I played until the army grabbed us. Actually, the army grabbed me. The Marines got Tony." Vic explained.

"Do you miss it?" Terry asked as she watched him closely.

"Every damned minute of every damned day." Vic went on. "The best times of my life were spent on a baseball field. It was a place to learn who I was, and what I could be. I found the best of myself there. Do you realize that a great hitter, a guy hitting three-hundred will fail seven out of ten times. So, he learns how to depend on the other guys the same as they depend on him. A baseball team is a family....."

Vic stopped, and turned his gaze back to Terry who was staring at him intently. "Don't stop. I wanna hear more." She said.

"That's the best of it. Baseball, the real game, is simple and clean. You get out of it just exactly what you put in. Life should be that way." Vic felt a knot begin to grow in his stomach. He closed his eyes and tried to get back into the moment. As he did he felt Terry's hand on his chest, but something had changed. He hated the new feeling.

"Are you OK? I didn't mean to press too hard". Terry's voice showed true concern.

Vic sighed and shook is head. "It's not you, or anything you said. It's me. I'm headed back to a place that grabs me, and I don't know why. I'm sorry. I should go." His voice held all the pain and confusion that came over him at times like this. He looked back at her as he tried to fight his way out of what was so much a part of him.

Terry looked deeply into his eyes, and what she saw sent a cold chill threw her. From the moment they met those eyes had been full of charm, strength, confidence and warmth. All that was gone now, replaced by a cold emptiness she'd never seen before. But somehow it didn't drive her away. She took his hand in hers and squeezed tightly. He started to pull

169

away, but then let their hands settle onto his chest. "I don't want you to see me this way. You're a classy lady, and I'm not what you need right now." He said in the same confused voice as he closed his eyes, and took another deep breath.

Terry said nothing. Somehow she knew there was nothing to say, but continued to hold his hand tightly as she slid as close as she could. Why didn't he let go? She asked herself. What was he keeping inside? "I don't want you to leave. It feels good here next to you. We're doing fine." She reassured him.

Vic was bouncing back and forth between the emptiness and the sound of her voice. At that moment she was what he wanted to return to, what he needed to find. He felt his hand close around hers as if he was holding onto a life line, but in that moment that's what she was. He wanted so badly to talk to her, but no words were possible. He began to feel the anger that comes from frustration. He'd lost control, and couldn't accept that.

"Vic, my hand!" Terry exclaimed. "Let go!"

Her voice startled him back into the present, and made him realize he was about to break her hand. "God Terry, I'm sorry". He said as he released her. "I'd never hurt you".

Terry was sitting up now with the covers across her legs where they'd fallen. Her nude body caught the dim light from the room. She was the most beautiful women Vic had ever seen. He sat up, and pulled her close. He could feel her soft, warm skin next to his. She melted into his arms as if every part of her was made to fit along side him.

Vic sighed again, and said. "I want to talk to you. I'd like you to understand some things, but it's tough cause I really don't understand myself."

"I started this whole talk thing, remember. So please, go ahead. I want to hear." Terry said in a reassuring voice.

As they settled back Vic began. "It's like I'm two people, the one I used to be, and some new guy who is out of control. But, this new guy is all about control. I hate the son-of-a-bitch, but at the same time feel like I can't live without him. It's like having an attack dog with me twenty-four, seven. The bastard's asleep most of the time, but wakes up at the damnedest times".

After a long pause Terry broke in. "Don't stop now."

"Go on? You want me to go on? Cause this has to sound as crazy to you as it does to me." Vic insisted.

"You were in the army, right?" Terry asked.

"And?" Vic began to feel the knot returning.

"Vietnam?" Terry pressed.

Now he was angry. "If you're headed for the shell shock thing, don't go there. I'm not one of those twitchy bastards who jumps behind the bushes when a car backfires."

Terry stopped, and let things settle down. She didn't press, but didn't pull away either. After a long pause she said. "Ever hear of Ernest Hemingway?"

"Ever hear of Donald fucking Duck"? Vic snapped.

She tried her best to hold back the laughter, but failed. It wasn't what he said, but how he said it. "You're moving too fast for me." Terry said shaking her head. "Which guy am I talking to now?"

"The one who's trying to figure out how we went from Vietnam to Hemingway." Vic was also laughing, a subtle, quiet laugh.

"Hemingway did a short story called Soldier's Home. In it there's a guy just like the one I saw a moment ago. He's not twitchy, and doesn't jump behind bushes. He's just a guy who's seen too much shit." She explained.

"So, what happens to Mr. Seen Too Much Shit?" Vic asked.

"He screamed fuck you Donald Duck, and jumped off a bridge." Terry burst into laughter, and Vic followed.

When things quieted down Vic said. "OK, Vietnam, Hemingway and Donald fucking Duck, now I understand. It's so simple. Why didn't I see it before now?" The laughter began all over again.

When things quieted again Terry pushed the hair back from Vic's forehead and said softly. "You're one special man Morretto". As she did her attention turned back to his eyes. They were the ones that she first saw, and they were taking hold of her in a way she'd never known before. This new feeling caused warmth, apprehension, fascination and concern, all at the same time.

Vic pulled her close and kissed her softly. "I think my batteries are recharged." He said.

"I noticed." She replied.

Terry was another example of the mixed bag of characters who were always a part of Vic's life. As she gave it new meaning and purpose others tested his ability to adjust and cope, none more so than the cast of characters he was about to meet in his new job as an apprentice pipe fitter.

"So, you wanna be a fitter? Tell ya what, become a piano player in a whore house. You'll get lots more respect." A quiet laugh followed the advice from Butch Clay, the journeyman who Vic would work with as he started his apprenticeship. He'd been in the trade for years, and didn't particularly like training anyone.

"I don't like the piano." Vic snapped.

"I don't like you, but I'm stuck with you. I'd love to have the piano." Butch continued.

"Look Butch, I'm here to work. The more I learn the less you have to do. So, let's make this as easy as we can. I really don't give a fat rat's ass about what you like, and I'm sure you feel the same." Vic returned.

"Why'd you decide not to be a cop? Did you think being a fitter was easy." Butch pressed.

"No, I don't think fitting pipe is easy. And, why I left the force is none of you fucking business. Can we go to work now?" Vic was determined that Butch wouldn't get to him.

"We go to work when I say so." Was the reply.

"OK you crusty old piece of shit. I gotta do a lot to get through the day, but taking a bunch of shit from you is not included. Now, what the fuck do you want me to do?" Vic made up his mind that this was either going to work or end now.

'OK, OK, take it easy. I just wanted to see what you were made of. Let's go to work." Butch said through a broad smile. "We gotta install a bunch of screwed pipe. If the threads are cut right we'll cruse through it. If not, we're gonna break our backs. Let me show you how it's done."

"Finally." Vic said shaking his head.

The process was simple, but Vic notices that even when done correctly there were still problems. "Why the hell are these threads good, and those bad? Did the dies get dull?"

"Good call rookie. It's not the dies. It's the pipe. That cheap Chinese shit has hard spots the dies can't cut. Chop off the bad threads, and try to use what's left later." Butch was beginning to like this cocky ex-cop.

"Why do they buy that cheap shit." Vic demanded.

"Come on rookie, figure it out." Butch barked.

"Cause it's cheap, and they know we'll make it work." Vic said through a smile.

"Bingo!" Butch hollered. "Welcome to the pipe trades. "

By the end of the day Vic could hardly lift his arms. The aluminum pipe wrench he'd pulled on since morning felt like it weighed a ton. His legs were like butter after nearly eight hours on a ladder. And, he was amazed at Butch who looked like he could easily work eight more.

"It gets easier as you learn not to fight the tools. Ya gotta relax and let leverage and your body weight do the work." Butch told his new apprentice.

"Some reason you didn't mention that earlier?" Vic questioned.

"I was having too much fun watching you sweat." Butch said as he laughed out loud.

"Fuck you Butch." Vic snapped.

"You can't say that. I'm a journeyman." Butch continued to laugh.

"Then fuck you Mr. Butch." Came the second snap.

"That's better kid. There's not enough respect in this world." Was the reply.

Tired as he was, Vic couldn't pass up a stop at Gino's on the way home. As he pushed through the front door and looked toward the bar his eyes fell onto an ice coved glass of beer placed in front of an empty chair. It was the most beautiful thing he'd seen all day. Half way to the bar he hollered. "I'll have one of those."

"That one's yours pipefitter." Came the reply from Gino's smiling face. "That nice lady bought it for you. Why, I'll never know."

"Hey there workin man. The first one is on me." The voice came from the end of the bar.

"Best offer I've had all day. No, best of the month. Today didn't bring that many. " Vic said as he slid onto the bar stool in front of the frosty beer.

Terry moved down the bar, and sat down beside him. "So, how was the first day?"

"They hooked me up with this crusty bastard named Butch. He hates training new guys, and let me know I was nothing but a pain in his ass. We spent the first ten minutes chipping away at one another until he finally decided we should go to work." Vic began.

"Damn, tough start." Terry replied. "Did things improve?"

"Ya know, it was crazy. I thought we'd be slugging it out by lunch. But, by the end of the day things were smooth as silk. The guy was definitely sizing me up. I think if I'd have backed down, Butch would have rode my ass until I quit. I don't think it was a macho thing either. They just don't want people they have to babysit." Vic said it all through a puzzled look.

"Is there a lot to learn?" Terry questioned. She watched Vic carefully, wondering if he'd be challenged, or just be putting in his time to make a buck.

"Tons to learn. Hell, just getting through the day takes practice, or the tools will wear you out. And, it all has to be done right, or there's no way to make up for the time lost fixing screw ups. As I talk about it I'm beginning to see why they're picky about who they train." Vic's look was now more understanding.

"Think you'll stick with it?" She asked.

Vic smiled a broad smile, the one that showed the chipped tooth. "Hell, I've never done anything other than day by day. But, I'm going back tomorrow."

"What are you doing tonight?" She asked in a low tone.

"Why Terry, are you asking me out on a date?" He questioned. "Why does the guy always have to pay?" He snapped through a smile.

"Cause the girl has to put up with all the bull-shit. I don't see you doing your hair, nails and buying new panty hose." She growled through a half smile of her own.

"I've been meaning to talk with you about those panty hose. They definitely get in the way." Now he was laughing.

"That's not the only thing that'll be in the way if you don't settle down Moretto." Now she was laughing too.

"OK, I'll go out with you." The laugh turned to a broad smile.

"Oh, it's my lucky day. I get to go out with a pipefitter who complains about picking up the check. Now I can break my date with the wino who offered to share his Thunderbird." No one was going to get the last word on Terry Richmond.

"I quit. You're too tough." Vic admitted.

She looked at him with quiet eyes and realized he'd never quit on anything in his life. She also realized that he was the kind of man who could give someone the last word before they even had a chance to take it. Her feeling of him were beginning to bother her because she'd promised herself that she'd have no serious relationships until her life was exactly where she wanted it to be. Maybe Vic was right. Maybe one day at a time was best. "Pick me up at eight?"

"I'll be there. Need a ride?" He asked.

"Nope. See you in a few pipefitter." She replied.

Vic slugged down the rest of his beer, and walked Terry to her car. He watched her drive off and wondered how he could trust or feel for anyone after the mess with Ginger. But, this was special and he had to see it through.

Their evening started with dinner back at Gino's. It was filled with the same banter interrupted by serious conversation about careers, dreams and the reality that so often gets in the way of dreamers. Each listened carefully to the other, trying to understand how two people could have so many differences, yet have so much in common.

At the end of the evening as they reached Terry's front door she asked. "Wanna come in for a drink?"

"Not tonight. I have some things to work out." He said through dark, serious eyes.

"What's wrong?" She asked quickly.

"I'm falling in love with you." He said in the same serious tone.

She stood there staring at him. For the first time Terry Richmond / Ricci was lost for words. Her mind raced as she tried to get a hold of this situation. But, the words wouldn't come. She just stood there.

Finally Vic leaned forward and kissed her. "Call you tomorrow."

The Building Trades

Vic walked into the project trailer at exactly eight o'clock, not a minute before or a minute after. The small room was filled with men pouring over drawings and others finishing cups of coffee on their way to the change shacks and job sites to line out their crews. He sat his welding hood and thermos on the closest table and asked. "Are the G.F. and shop steward around?"

"I'm the steward. Got a dispatch?" The stocky guy seated by the door asked.

"Here ya go." Vic replied.

After a minute staring at the paper work the steward said. "Says here you're a fifth year apprentice welder. So, what are you, an apprentice or a welder?"

"Both. I'm a fifth year apprentice and certified welder." I just drug up from a nuke plant where I passed four x-ray tests." Vic explained.

"Well this ain't no nuke plant, and apprentices don't weld. That's journeyman's work." The steward growled.

"Well I don't weld for apprentice wages. So, if they don't intend to pay for what they get, I'll go back to the nuke plant that I just left."

"Hang on Rudy. I need welders, and if this guy can weld, he stays." The tall man at the other end of the trailer said.

"I gotta call the hall on this one." Rudy replied.

"There's the phone." The tall general foreman said as he pointed to the desk in front of him. He turned to Vic and continued. "Why don't you wait in the shack next door while we work this out."

"Nope" Rudy jumped in. "That's the same as accepting him onto the job site. And, that's not gonna happen until I talk to a business agent."

Vic smiled his broad smile that showed his chipped tooth. "I can wait outside if you want privacy."

Rudy gave him a quick glare and headed for the phone. Jack Stroud, the general foreman, returned the smile and said. "That'll be fine. We'll get back to you in a minute."

"No problem." Vic replied. "I'm on your dime."

As he stood outside the door Vic could hear Rudy hollering into the phone. Pushing this guy's buttons would be a snap, but probably not worth the hassle. He'd learned over the past four years that it was much easier to set the boundaries, and then roll with the flow. But, he still liked a good fight now and then. And in the trades there was always a fight available.

Vic learned to weld on a power plant job he was on during the second year of his apprenticeship. A close friend of Terry Richmond was the marketing manager on the project, and Vic and Terry spent lots of time helping her with siting and permit problems. Terry was a natural at behind closed doors politics. And Vic's writing skills made them a great team.

During that time Vic learned much about what it took to make the wheels turn. Much of it was as sleazy and sorted as anything he'd seen on the police force. There were hundreds of millions of dollars at stake. And, the race for the money didn't generally go to the fastest horse.

Suddenly the door swung open and another stocky guy carrying a cup of coffee walked through and said. "I'm John Taylor. You'll be working for me. Can you weld?"

"Anything from the crack of dawn to a broken heart." Vic said through the usual broad smile.

"Ya, Ya, heard that before. We'll see". John replied.

As the morning breeze shifted Vic caught the smell of the coffee in John's cup. And, his cop's nose recognized lots more than Folgers. He nodded toward to mug and said. "Good to the last drop."

John smiled. "Want a taste?"

"No thanks. Too tough for me." Vic said.

"You're probably gonna hear more about the apprentice welding thing when the regular steward gets back. Tex Collins makes his own rules, and most of the guys at the hall don't like to cross him." John warned.

"There was a Tex Collins that played for the Cowboys". Vic recalled.

"That's the guy." John noted.

"Can he weld?" Vic asked.

"Nope. He's the guy who cracked the dawn and broke the heart along with a couple of heads." John said through a stone cold expression.

Vic laughed out loud. This will be interesting he thought.

As they approached the last change shack John said. "You can leave your stuff here, and we'll get you started."

While walking onto the job site John explained. "We have eight inch steam lines to run from the new recovery boilers to a small processing plant near the road. You won't have to test, but the plant engineer will want to see your first and second weld pass. Then you can weld the rest out. But, don't go ahead without inspection."

"They want me to weld steam mains without testing me first?" Vic questioned.

"That's right. They just want a visual. You got a problem with that?" John replied.

"Not as long as the checks don't bounce." Vic assured him.

Buy this time they were half way through the tunnel leading from the new recovery boiler to the building annex where the recovered steam would be used for several cleaning and production processes. The tunnel was small and the sections of pipe were long and very heavy. Handling them was dangerous because if one got away there was no place to run.

"Your working partner is setting up your first weld. You'll be able to turn this one, but eventually they'll have to be done in position". John explained. "Your working partner has been around a while. You may recognize him."

"Get the fuck outta here. I'm not working with this old bastard." Vic shouted as he threw his arms around his uncle. "This guy can't rig or fit pipe."

"Just you stay outta my way kid and listen. You might learn something." Vic's uncle Frank Janetta bellowed as he returned the hug.

"Where the hell ya bin old man?" Vic said as he slapped his uncle on the shoulder.

"Been splittin my time between this place, the union hall and keeping your aunt happy." Frank replied through the normal hand gestures that make up all Italian conversations.

"How's Aunt Lina, and why is she still putting up with an old fart like you?" Vic continued.

"Hey kid, she's a lucky woman." Frank added as he lit the stub of a coal black Sicilian cigar.

"Damn, you still smoking those turds?" Vic continued to jab at his uncle.

"Not always. When they get too short I chew um." Frank informed him. "Want one? I got extra. You'll never have worms after a couple of these".

"I'll take the worms." Vic decided.

The banter went on all morning and into the afternoon. It was like turning the clock back to days when things in Vic's life were simple, and family was all that was necessary to make life worthwhile. Those were the days before Vietnam, Ginger and all that he set aside while coping with a colder, harsher world.

The men in the Frisano and Moretto families were raised on principles based on strength, simplicity and a strict code of honor. But, in the world where Tony and Vic lived and loved and fought for survival honor was in short supply. In that place the lion was no match for the snake. Skill was overshadowed by deceit. Courage was unnecessary for those with the right contacts and connections.

Generations of men and women who were driven from their home land by poverty, corruption and brutality were exploited by those who rose to power believing that honor was a handicap. Those power hungry leaches saw no value in eye to eye contact followed by a firm hand shake. To

183

them anyone foolish enough to speak their mind, and commit to their beliefs was simply an easy target.

For many such a cold and petty world would have provided a reason to quit, or at least give up the principles that became more of a burden than an asset. In this world where so many rolled with the flow why should honor be cherished when it meant standing against the tide.

As Vic watched his Uncle Frank he remembered an afternoon years before when a hand full of young men began to mock Vic's Uncle Frank behind his back. One slid a cork between his teeth representing the old man's cigar and then began to chew it as he allowed a stream of drool to run down his chin. As the spit flowed the kid began to bellow incoherently to the delight of the others.

The show continued without the participants noticing as Uncle Frank walked up behind them. Vic was anxious to see the confrontation that he knew would follow. But, to his amazement Frank said nothing. Instead, he simply stood smiling at the foolishness.

When one of the gang finally noticed old Frank the mockery stopped. Each young fool waited for what was to follow. When Frank took no action the pack took this as a sign of weakness, and pressed the old man looking for even more fun.

Still, Frank took no action while the pack grew bolder. Finally the one who started the foolishness grabbed Frank by the front of his coat and said. "You are one ugly old bastard."

In the blink of an eye, and without a sound Frank drove a fist into the young man's mid-section just above his stomach. The blow caused him to collapse as he gasped for air. As he slumped one of the others stepped forward with a knife drawn, and said. "That was a big mistake old man."

Before anyone else could react Frank turned and replied. "You ready to die boy cause I am." It wasn't as much what he said as the way he said it.

The tone and calm of his voice left no doubt that this was no longer a joke. Any further action would cause serious bloodshed.

The young man stood motionless except to throw a quick glance at the one lying on the ground. Frank said no more. He simply motioned to Vic to follow him out of the area.

When they were clear Vic turned to his uncle and said. "Why did you let it go so long? Why didn't you smack the guy first thing?"

"Do you know the kind of damage those hands can do?" Frank questioned as he pointed to Vic's now clenched fists.

"They started the shit Uncle Frank, not you. You don't have to take that crap." Was Vic's reply.

"So, I put the guys' eye out or break his jaw because he was acting like a fool? Does that sound like justice to you?" Frank's voice was still calm and strong.

"But, they were making you out to be a fool. No one has the right to do that." Vic demanded.

"Vic, no one can make me a fool, or you either. The only one who can do that is me or you". Frank was now smiling as he spoke.

"But, you hit him." Vic pressed.

"After he put his hands on me, that was the difference. That gave me the reason that was missing before. That made him a threat. Do you see the difference?" Frank questioned.

"No I don't." Vic snapped."

"Sure you do. Pride is getting in your way because you don't want to see the truth. Pride is a fine thing Vic as long as it doesn't get in the way of

185

common sense and humility. Do you care what a bunch of fools like that really think cause I don't. If I did then I'd be making myself the fool." Frank's tone was much deeper now, and the smile was gone.

Vic said no more as they continued to walk toward home. Suddenly his uncle punched him in the arm hard enough to jar him off the sidewalk. "So, does that make you a threat?" Vic said with a smile.

"Told you that you understood." The old man said as his smile returned.

Vic often thought of moments like that when senior members of the family led by example rather than lectures although lectures were also part of the passage into manhood.

He practiced the things shown him by those who earned his respect throughout his formative years. He saw that the cost of honor was sacrifice, but the reward was respect. And, without respect leadership was impossible.

He also learned that following an honorable road gave no guarantee of success, at least not the kind of success that meant fortune and fame. Those rewards came through compromise with others as well as personal adjustments of values and priorities.

Time spent on the job with Uncle Frank was short. His old mentor decided it was time for a little fishing and travel with his wife, Lina. He'd promised her some quiet time, and she was holding him to his word.

The replacement, Vic's new working partner, was a middle aged man who'd spent a good deal of time in the military, and far less learning how to pull his weight in a construction site. But, he tried hard, and seemed to want to find his place on the crew. His name was Bob McCormick.

John Taylor introduced Bob to Vic on a cold, wet morning when conditions make handling heavy material even more dangerous than normal. Footing was poor and everything was slippery. Nothing could be taken for granted.

"Vic Moretto, Bob McCormick, your new fitter." John announced. "He'll be working with you on setting the steam main in the bottom of the pipe tunnel. We gotta get this done so they can start forming up the tunnel roof."

"Mornin." Vic said as he extended his hand.

"Good morning." Bob replied as they shook hands. "I brought some new cables along with me."

"Some what?" Vic asked.

"Cables." Bob repeated as he extended his arms, showing what he'd delivered.

"Oh, chokers." Vic said as he flashed a look at John Taylor.

John took a minute to sizes things up, then said. "Don't rush it. Take your time and be careful." He was looking eye to eye with Bob, and Vic could see the concern.

"We got it covered boss." Vic assured him. "Did you bring any softeners?"

"Any what?" Bob asked.

"Hang on a minute." Vic replied as he climbed down into the half constructed pipe tunnel. He returned with four short pieces of two by four wooden blocks. "See ya later boss. It's under control. Come on Bob, the stock pile is over here. Bring that new four foot choker."

Bob followed along as they headed for the pile of pipe in the laydown area. As they got there the operator fired up the thirty-ton crane they'd use to set material that day. Vic dropped to one knee as he looped the choker around the pipe, then slid two pieces of wood under the bite made by the loop. "Ya gotta use softeners on a day like this or the choker will slip." He watched Bob who was carefully watching him.

Vic raised his free hand and tapped his hard hat as he held the choker in the other. Within seconds the operator had the crane's hook directly overhead and in position. Vic hooked the load, and gave the easy up signal. Slowly the operator lifted the load. The pipe tipped slightly as it cleared the ground. Vic gave the down easy signal, and the pipe dropped to its original position. As Vic re-set the choker Bob began to give the easy up signal he'd seen Vic use. The operator immediately took his hands from the controls, and stared at Vic.

Vic stopped, gave the dog-it-off signal to the operator who nodded, and then looked coldly at Bob. "Only, and I mean only, the guy handling the load gives signals."

"Sorry Vic." Bob said slowly and sincerely.

"We're gonna do this by the numbers, one step at a time. When I get the load in the air I'll dog it off. You get a tag line on the end and wait for me to get into position. Then, walk the pipe to the tunnel opening. Neither of us gets into the tunnel until the pipe is below us. If anything doesn't work, stop and we'll figure it out." Vic said slowly. Bob nodded.

"Hey man. We'll get there. Just take it slow. If we're not on the same page then stop." Vic assured him.

The rest of the morning followed the same pattern. Vic leading step by step, and Bob following and watching intently. By lunch time things were beginning to fall into place. It wasn't a productive morning. But, progress was made, and no one was hurt.

As the pair headed to the lunch shack John Taylor approached. "Got a minute?" He asked Vic.

"Be there in a minute." Vic said to Bob as he stopped to talk with John.

"How's he doing?" Was John's obvious question.

"He tries hard, learns fast and doesn't know jack-shit." Vic replied.

"Can you make it work?" John asked.

"Guess it depends on how much you want to get done. I gotta go slow, and watch him every minute. If that works for you, I can handle it." Vic replied honestly.

"OK, let's give it a few days, and see."

A few days turned into a few months. As the job wound down the crew shrunk in size when man power needs dropped off. Vic and Bob continued plodding along as Vic lead and Bob followed. When it finally ended Vic returned to the fabrication shop, and Bob went his own way.

There was plenty of work at the shop with a new contract to fabricate a huge fire safety system for a power plant. Vic was there for over a year. One afternoon the superintendent asked if he'd go to a local paper mill to help with a project that was falling behind. Vic agreed, and liked the idea of being in the field again, and out of the shop.

As he checked in at the gate he was met by the shop steward, Bud Terry, who welcomed him with an enthusiastic. "God am I glad to see you."

"What's going on." Vic asked.

"Nothing, no material, no drawings, no help and no one who has any idea what the fuck is going on." The shop steward snapped. "This ass hole, McCormick has us running around like a bunch of fools while he spends the day covering his own miserable ass."

"Ya? I worked with a Bob McCormick about a year ago. Wonder if they're related." Vic commented, never imagining the response.

"Related hell, that's the guy." The steward replied.

"No way, a middle aged guy, kind of stocky with a little white mustache?" Vic asked.

"That's him." Came the reply.

"Hell, I spent months leading him around the job site just trying to keep him from killing himself or somebody else. "

"Well, he hasn't killed anyone here yet, but it's only Tuesday." Came the reply. "You'll be working with me on an old stainless steel product line".

As they made their way down the road that divided the north and south side of the aging plant Vic sized up the general condition of the equipment he'd be working on. Obviously, no one had spent any money modernizing it. In fact, there was little evidence of even the most basic maintenance. Broken windows dotted most of the walls. The exterior concrete was cracked and pitted. And the pot holes in the road could swallow a compact car.

Upon reaching the work site Bud pointed to a rusty gang box at one end of the pump station. "That's ours. Your welding machine is the one in back."

Vic walked over to the box, and popped it open. "You gotta be shitting me." He said as he lifted a chain hoist that was completely covered with rust. "You actually plan to lift something with this thing?"

Bud broke into laughter, then assured Vic. "Hey man, I got the good stuff. You don't even want to see what the rest of the crew is working with. "

"You still bitching about tools?" Came the voice from the other side of the pump station. Vic looked up to see the familiar face and form of Bob McCormick walking toward them. He wore the white hard hat normally reserved for supervision, a new Carhartt jacket and pants, and brand new cowboy boots.

He walked by Vic without a word of greeting or anything else, directly to Bud. "You ever gonna get these pumps hooked up?" Bob growled.

"You ever gonna get me material to hook them up with?" Bud growled back.

"There's plenty of pipe in the bone yard damn it. I showed it to you yesterday. Why haven't you used that?" Bob's voice grew louder with each word.

"It's the wrong size. I told you that yesterday." Bud's volume matched Bob's, and even topped it a bit.

"It's ten inch, just like the pumps Bud. Quit draggin ass, and get it done." Bob was screaming now.

Bud spun on his heals, and covered the distance between Bob and him in a few quick steps. "The pump size is O.D., the pipe in the bone yard is I.P.S.. The bone yard pipe won't fit. It wouldn't fit yesterday, It won't fit today. And, it won't fit tomorrow. There isn't enough welding rod in the entire world to fill the gap. Got it? Cause if you don't there's no sense in me wasting my time explaining it again."

"That's insubordination Bud. You can't talk to me like that. You saw it Vic." Bob's hands were shaking.

"Hi Bob. Long time no see." Vic allowed himself a broad smile, but held back the laugh. "Did you buy the pumps or did the plant supply them?"

"The plant bought um. Why?" Bob's volume dropped a little.

191

"Then it's there problem, not yours." Vic informed him. "Just let um know."

"What the hell do I tell them about no progress for three days?" Bob's voice was back to normal.

"Did we set the pumps." Vic questioned.

"We set them. What's that got to do with anything?" Bob pressed.

"Sorry, you have to figure that one out for yourself." Vic said as Bud shook his head.

Bob turned and disappeared through the other side of the pump room.

"That's gotta be the dumbest bastard that ever drew breath Vic." Bud noted. "And we're gonna bail his sorry ass out."

"You lookin for justice or a pay check?" Vic was a little disappointed in Bud. He'd been around long enough to know how it worked.

Vic and Bud spent the rest of the day scrounging material and fabricating pipe hangers they'd need to finish the project in the pump room. Throughout the week Bob came by to pick their brains about this problem or that process, never once showing any appreciation for the help.

One afternoon while returning from the scrap yard where they found most of what they needed they noticed a Lincoln Continental pull up in front of the project trainer. A seriously overweight, slightly bald man wiggled his way from behind the steering wheel, and was greeted immediately by Bob McCormick. The greeting was more like something one would see at a family reunion rather than a job site. The two headed off toward the plant main entrance with Bob trailing like an anxious puppy dog.

"Well that sums it up for me." Bud noted. "I wondered if he was kinfolk or just a suck ass. Looks like he's both. By the way, I ran into your Uncle Frank at the union hall the other day. He said they need a replacement on the executive board to fill an open slot between now and the next election. You interested?"

"You bet, about as interested as I am in shoving a hot welding rod up my ass. " Vic laughed.

The dented, rusted chunks of scrap Vic, Bud and the rest of the crew put together were molded into operating systems that kept the old mill running, and actually improve output. For their effort they each received a pay check and little else. Their innovation, imagination and skill were neither appreciated nor properly compensated. In fact, Bob McCormick took credit for the project that finished on time and well under budget while the same Bob blamed members of the crew for every delay and mistake.

Bud took the injustice personally, and openly objected. Vic simply smiled and moved on. But deep inside him the resentment lingered. The war, disastrous marriage to Ginger and corruption he live with on the street had taken their toll. He was becoming cold and cynical. Without realizing it he was changing. The world was teaching him that if he didn't care he wouldn't be hurt, if he expected nothing he wouldn't be disappointed. The number of people who were truly part of his life was dwindling rapidly.

Shortly after leaving the project at the old mill as Vic sat enjoying a cold beer he saw a familiar figure approaching from across the bar. "Hey, my old piazzano." Uncle Frank bellowed.

In the same tone Vic hollered. "No."

"No what? What the hell kind of a greeting is that for your old uncle?" Frank tried hard to look surprised knowing full well it wouldn't work.

"No I don't want to be on the executive board you old con man." Vic snapped.

"Damn it Vic, it's one night a month, and then one day a month with the board of trustees." Frank coaxed.

"Trustee, what's the trustee shit about?" Vic said in amazement.

"The guy on the E-board was also a trustee. Well actually he was the vise-president of the local. That meant he was chairman of the E-board and a trustee". Frank said through a broad smile. Everyone who I talked with liked the idea of you serving until the next election. It's only for six months."

"Damn it Uncle Frank, I'm tired. I just want a little time to get my shit together." Vic protested.

"How about this? There's a Health and Welfare and Pension trustees convention in New Orleans next month. If you take the trustee's job we can send you as a representative. It's all expenses paid, and you can learn all about what makes the wheels turn. When you get back we'll talk about the e-board and vice-president's job." Uncle Frank was doing his very best negotiating.

"Answer this and I'll think about it. There are dozens of guys who'd jump all over what you're offering me. I know you're making this happen, and will take heat because I'm your nephew, and you're the union president. So, why me? Why not one of the guys standing in line for a chance like this?" Vic watched closely as he waited for an answer.

"Simple. I want you because you don't want the job. You're looking at it as work, responsibility and a pain in the ass. And, it's all of that and more. You can think on your feet and don't bull shit yourself." Frank meant every word. He knew his nephew well, and was certain he'd struck a nerve.

194

As Vic handed his ticket to the flight attendant he asked himself how he'd been talked into sticking his neck out again. He wanted to help his uncle, the one who had meant so much to him. But, this was one more thing that he didn't need.

Even before the plane touched down in New Orleans Vic was lobbied by union officers and contractors alike. Few wasted time sizing up new guys, any of whom could become either an adversary or ally.

One contractor in particular took special interest in Vic. He was a long time trustee and management representative. His name was Tom Quinn, a feisty, single minded hardnosed self-made man. He owned and operated a controls specialty company he started many years before.

Tom and Vic met in the hotel's massive main lounge. It boasted a huge house shoe shaped bar backed by a pit where two guys shucked oysters as fast as drunken conventioneers could down them.

Vic was seated at the far end sipping a gin and tonic when a particularly obnoxious representative from a large east coast union offered him a plate of oysters saying. "You know what they say about oysters, and you might need some with the action in this town."

Vic smiled politely and replied. "Thanks, but I'll do fine without."

"Hey man, ya gotta at least try one." The drunk pressed.

"I did once. My throat slammed shut and said sorry, it just ain't gonna happen." Vic was still smiling, but could feel old juiced begin to flow.

The drunk grabbed a couple of freshly opened specimens in his hand, and made his way over to Vic's side. "Here, these are for you". He said as he opened his hand.

Vic turned slowly and locked onto the drunk's half closed eyes, then let his gaze drop to the open hand and shell fish remains it held. "What the hell happened to the seagull?" he asked.

"What seagull?" The drunk stammered.

"The one that shit in your hand." Vic replied.

As he did the crowd around the bar erupted in laughter as the drunk actually looked overhead for the mysterious bird.

"Get the hell outta here Butch, and let the man finish his drink. And, take that hand full of bird shit with you." Tom Quinn said as he sat down next to Vic.

"Drunks are a pain in the ass." Tom added softly.

"For a while they were my livelihood." Vic replied. "I was a cop."

"Why'd ya quit?" Tom asked.

"Too little money, and too much temptation." Was Vic's answer.

"Lots of both here, money and temptation." Tom observed.

"And that's the very reason I should be someplace else. I have an uncle who talked me into this, and I think it was a big mistake. I don't need the temptation and aggravation, and the money has too many strings."

"All money has strings." Tom was becoming more interested.

"Not the kind that comes from a pay check. That cash is all mine, no strings attached." Vic said confidently.

"Ya, but it's hard to depend on. The guys with talent enough for a regular check get pushed aside by the ones who don't mind the strings." Tom wanted badly to see how this first conversation would end.

"You one of the guys who pushes them aside?" Vic demanded. And again he felt the same old juices flowing.

"Nope. The guys with the talent cover my ass while I cover theirs. Works great. I could never figure out why more don't do it that way. Here's my card. I'm staying here. Give me a call, and I'll buy you dinner." Tom pushed a business card in front of Vic.

"How about my dinner?" The two men looked around to see a tall red head staring at Tom.

"Yep, definitely temptations here." Tom said through a broad smile.

As Vic finished his drink a familiar voice said. "Can I buy you another." It was Barbra Kelly, one of the regular office staff at the union hall that sent Vic to the convention.

"Barb, what are you doing here?" Vic asked. He was surprised, but at the same time happy to see a familiar face.

"I'm one of the reps. from the office workers local. I was hoping Frank would talk you into coming here." She explained. "If you're not ready for a drink I'll buy you dinner. This place has great steaks."

"Let's go. A couple more drinks, and they may talk me into trying the oysters." Vic said as he accepted her offer.

As they waited for menus Barb asked. "Are you going to take the vice-president's job?"

Vic took a long look at her, and tried to catch the reason for her interest. It seemed like everyone here had an agenda, and he wondered what hers was. He decided to play the game. As long as he was here he might as well see how it worked. Or, as Uncle Frank said, …..see what makes the wheels turn. "I'm taking lots of time to think about it. I honestly don't know if it's what I want."

Barb was a very attractive woman, and liked men very much. She was not only intelligent, but street smart as well. She could see Vic was fishing, and decided to play the game too. "You'd make a great union officer. The guys like and respect you. I'd like to see you spend more time around the union office."

During his time rousting the Jolly Roger Vic was hustled by the best of the best. And the look in Barb's eyes cause his bull shit meter to go off at its maximum crap point. But, he had to give her credit. Those blue eyes, big tits and her catch me come fuck me voice could momentarily distract even an old pro like Vic. "Well the office would be interesting. I'm sure there would be a lot to learn." He suddenly felt her leg brush against his.

Barb said nothing for a long moment. She was looking for a little bit of sweat to form, or to see any reaction. But, it took more than a bit of footsy to throw Vic off his game. He stared deeply into her eyes, and leaned into the table, a move that increased the leg contact.

Suddenly her leg was gone, and a girlish smile crossed her face. "Know what I think?" She asked.

"No." Vic replied returning the smile.

"I think most people come to these things to get drunk, over eat and get laid." She said through the girlish smile.

"Wow, go figure." Vic said through his own smile.

"Is that why you're here?" She asked.

"Sounds better than munching raw oysters." They both broke into laughter.

Vic decided to call the first round with Barb a draw. If she was simply looking for someone to party with he was sure she could do it well. If she had a deeper agenda she hid it well. He was anxious for round two to begin.

They took their time with dinner. The food, wine and drinks afterward were excellent, and someone else was paying for it. Round two, three and four all ended in draws, but each was interesting.

"Did you hear about the dinner party that the pipe trades international is throwing tomorrow night?" Barb asked.

"I'll be there. My Uncle put it at the top of my agenda. He wants to see how I mix with the heavy hitters." Vic informed her.

"You'll do fine". She said through a subtle smile. But, her tone was now full of sincerity. Vic was winning this round, but losing interest in the game. Once someone showed they truly cared the game no longer fit, and cheapened the relationship.

"Are you coming?" He asked.

"Yes, they're looking at me too." Her smile was still there.

"I'll save you a seat." Vic promised.

"The seats are assigned." She told him.

"Tell ya what, I'll bet you another dinner that you'll be sitting next to me." He told her through a smile of his own.

"It's a bet." She said as she stood to leave. "Thanks for a very pleasant dinner, Vic."

"My pleasure." He watched her cross the dinning room, and reminded himself that this was business, and only fools let things get out of control.

The dinning room was huge. As it began to fill with delegates Vic settled into the place where his name tag rested on the table. A tall, middle aged waiter asked. "Can I get you a drink Sir?"

"I'm a Vic, not a sir, and I'd love a gin and tonic." Vic replied.

"Cummin up. Anything else?" The waiter asked.

"Nope, that'll do it." Vic answered.

"I'll have the same". Vic heard Barb say as she sat down next to him. She stared at the name tag on the table in front of her. After a short pause she added. "OK, how'd you do it? I'm supposed to be next to some fat old bastard chewing on a cigar."

"Well, I'm about fifteen pounds overweight, and used to chew tobacco. Is that close enough?" Vic said through a quiet laugh.

"I'm not buying you dinner until you tell me." She replied through a stern smile.

"There's gonna be someone named Alice something or other sitting next to the fat bastard. It was easy. I came in early and switch the name tags." He informed her.

"How in the hell did you find mine?" She demanded. "There must be a hundred tags in here."

"I'm an ex-cop who knows how to pay off the right people. There's a busboy in here somewhere who's fifty bucks richer." Vic replied through a satisfied grin.

"Hell, for fifty bucks I'd have switched them myself." She watched for his reaction, but he stayed cool with the same satisfied grin on his face. OK, she thought. It's time to for the heavy artillery. As Vic took the first sip of his freshly delivered gin and tonic Barb leaned over, put her hand gently on his stomach and whispered softly as she gently blew in his ear. "Why don't we skip dinner? You can come to my room and I'll fuck your brains out."

Vic sputtered and choked on the sip of gin. It wasn't what she said but her delivery that caught him completely off guard. While he regained his breath and struggled for control he had to admit that this round was hers. As he looked over he saw her version of a satisfied grin. He repeated silently to himself over and over, this is business, this is business, this is business............

Barb wasn't going to loose her edge in this most recent contest, and took advantage of her victory. "Got ya big boy."

"Got me hell, you almost drowned me in gin and tonic." He had to admit. No use trying to salvage this round he thought. He'd just concede the loss with humility.

That brief surrender peaked her interest in him even more. She was used to bullies who didn't have enough confidence or courage to admit even the smallest defeat. Vic was different. He was sure enough of himself to admit loosing a small battle while staying focused on the bigger picture.

The pre-dinner speeches were filled with the kind of bullshit Barb was used to. Both union and management representatives grabbed their chances at one-up-man-ship. And, Vic and Barb picked each one of them apart quietly over several more drinks. By dinner time they'd become the life of the party at what normally was a very boring affair. During the after dinner break they slipped away to the u-shaped bar where a small band was doing covers of tunes from the fifties and sixties.

Half way through more gin and tonic the band began their second set with their rendition of Stranger On The Shore. Barb flashed her best school girl smile and said. "Are you going to ask me to dance?"

Vic replied. "Yes I am, and we better do it now cause after a few more drinks I won't even be able to walk."

The dance floor was crowded, and Vic and Barb moved to a far corner that they claimed as their own. Half way through the song Barb leaned close and ran her fingers up Vic's neck and slowly into his jet black hair. As her cheek move close to his she whispered softly. "The offer still stands."

"And, it's the best offer I've had in a long time." He replied. "But, I can't mix business with pleasure. Every time I have business suffered. As much as I'd love to I can't let that happen."

Barb pulled back, and looked deeply into his eyes. The calm, determined honesty she saw there actually scare her a bit. She wasn't offended at being turned down. She knew that he was attracted to her. But, she'd never met anyone who knew themselves as well as Vic did. Finally she said. "Then how about walking me to my door."

"Be my pleasure." He replied.

The ride up the elevator, and walk down the hall were quiet. As Barb pulled the room key from her purse she said. "Kiss me good night."

"Be my pleasure." He replied.

But, the good night kiss is where it ended. And, it was more than mixing business with pleasure. He'd found something truly special in Terry, something that demanded honesty.

Just Life

Everyone should have their own glimpse of paradise no mater how short it is. Without those few precious times there's no reason to believe, no reason to keep trying.

For Tony and Ann it was a house on a hill overlooking the river, their place and theirs alone. Helen was there with them for a while as their link with the best along with the Frisano, Riley and Morretto clans who filled that home with what only family and friends can provide.

Tony designed and built the place on his own. Very little was done by contractors. And, the few who were included worked under Tony's watchful eyes.

On one very cold morning as he balanced on roof trusses installing sheathing that would support the roofing material he was annoyed by the hammer that kept slipping from his hand. Each time he lost the tool he'd have to climb down and retrieve it. Before climbing back to his working position he'd push his hands into a pile of snow to remove the blood that flowed from his chapped skin. He used the same snow to wipe the blood from the hammer handle. Gloves were no answer because they made taking nails from his belt pouches far too slow.

It was Ann who provided a pair with two finger tips cut from the left hand that finally gave him some relief. He used them to shovel fill sand and carry all types of building materials until they finally wore through at the palms.

For Tony the thought of not finishing that project or any other was not an option. In fact it wasn't even a consideration. That approach was passed down to him from his grandfather through his father, and would be passed onto any new Frisanos who came along.

He loved the satisfaction that came with building and repairing anything and everything. But, college courses were a different challenge. It wasn't that he couldn't handle the work. He simply saw no value in it. He'd finished his apprenticeship, and graduated with honors as a journeyman electrician. His plan was then to complete all things needed to get his engineering degree.

But, so many things got in his way that graduation seemed impossible. One huge obstacle came from none other than Ann. It began on an evening as they sat on the patio and enjoyed the sunset.

"Tony." She began.

"Yes." He answered as he turned to look at her.

"I love this place. I'm glad it's so big." She continued.

"OK, glad to hear it." He said as he wondered where this was going. For whatever reason he drew a complete blank on the message that he knew was on the way.

"Well we need the space." Ann never missed a chance to keep him guessing, especially when she saw that confused look.

"Where are we going with this Annie? You have your mother's look in your eye, and that always means something is up." He watched her closely, and truly loved this game they'd played so many times.

"Well I'm gaining lots of weight even though I can't keep my breakfast down." She could no longer hold back the smile.

"We need a big house because you're getting sick and fat." He still had no clue.

"Oh, you won't believe how fat I'm gonna get." Her smile turned to laughter.

"Are you saying we need to join a health club?" He asked with the same confused look.

Her laughter turned to a roar. When she finally regained control she said. "Shit Frasino, do I have to draw you a picture? You're going to be a father."

"No shit? I mean, no shit." He exploded.

"Yep, that's what happens when you spend as much time in bed as we do." She was still laughing.

But, Tony didn't laugh. He sat looking at her as her laughter died down. He'd wondered many times about this moment and how he'd react. Was he ready? Would he be able to share his Annie with someone else? Would he be a good father, and at the same time a good husband? And, why when all these things were so important had he not picked up on her message sooner? "Wow Annie, that's incredible."

She looked back with a puzzled gaze. His reaction wasn't what she expected. "Are you OK with this? I mean is it what you want?"

He could see her concern and surprise. "Yes, it's what I want. But I'm concerned about how it will affect us. And, I wonder if we're ready."

Ann looked into his eyes during a long pause, then stood quickly and walked into the house. He followed close behind, and caught up with her at the kitchen table. She was leaning on it with her head lowered. As he gently turned her toward him he saw the tears running down her cheeks. "Annie, what's wrong? If what I said hurt you I'm sorry. Of course I'm happy that we're gonna have a baby." He pulled her close, and could feel her crying as he held her.

She finally moved back far enough for eye contact. Her crying had stopped, and her gaze was now filled with confidence and sincerity. "I've been waiting for weeks to deliver this news, and you tell me you're concerned and wonder if we're ready. Life doesn't come with a set of rules or instruction booklet Tony. We're going to make lots of mistakes along the way, but you can't be so concerned that you let worry get in the way of all the beautiful things." She broke free and headed for their bed room.

He stood alone staring down the hall where she'd been. Was he afraid, unwilling to face what life had to offer? Did he doubt the strength of their relationship? He moved toward the bed room where she'd gone.

As he walked in he saw her lying on the bed facing the windows with her back to the door. He crossed the room and sat on the bed at her feet. "Annie, I've been through war feeling at times that I'd never see you or home again. I've spent eighty hour weeks building this place while going to school. I've faced bigger, stronger, faster guys on every kind of field or court I ever heard of, and never once doubted my ability. But, all those things are nothing compare to how I see my responsibilities as a husband and father. If there was ever anything in my life I wanted to do right it would be being your husband and our children's father. And, you're right, there's no instruction book. I realize that I'm going to make mistakes, and it scares the hell out of me. But, you made me see that by feeling that way I was doubting our love and relationship, and that was wrong. I'm truly sorry, and it won't happen again."

Ann sat up and moved down by his side. "Why do you make things so hard on yourself? I've never doubted you or us, and can't understand how you can."

"It's because I care. I want us to have a chance at the good life, and don't want to settle for anything less".

She stood and then settled back onto his lap as she placed her hands on his neck. "There is no good life my darling, there is just life."

The next morning Ann found herself alone in bed. She had plans for the weekend that included work on the room where the baby would sleep,

206

general house cleaning and some shopping with her mom. She intended to start early, but it was only 6:00 am and Tony was already up.

She slipped on her favorite warm up jacket and headed down the hall where she could hear clanging and banging in the kitchen. As she walked in she saw him at the counter cutting fresh fruit. Along side him was an open carton of eggs and what looked like pancake batter. Beside that was a bowl filled with some yellow liquid.

Before she could speak he turned and said. "Good morning. Hope you're hungry. What'll ya have, pancakes, French toast, scrambled eggs or all of the above"?

"How long have you been up?" She asked.

"Which time? I was up at two, then at four and finally about an hour ago. I couldn't sleep, and didn't want to wake you. So, I sat up and read for a while." He said in words that came out in rapid fire.

"You worked ten hours, were up talking to me until eleven, and then spent most of the night reading?" She said while staring in amazement at Tony's version of the pancake house on Sunday morning.

"Yep, that's pretty much my story of last night. So, what'll you have? We're a full service establishment." He continued in the same rapid fashion.

"Well I guess I'll have a pancake, but what is that yellow stuff in the bowl?" She asked.

"It's French toast batter, but you can use it for scrambled eggs too". He told her as he described the various items on this morning's menu. "I got the idea form one of your mom's cook books."

"You were reading cook books with Sports Illustrated and Popular Mechanics on the end table?" She was trying hard to get a grasp of what she was seeing. "You're scaring me."

"What's going on?" Helen Riley asked as she entered the room.

"Mary Pippins is making breakfast. She replaced the Marine and jock that I married." Ann explained. "He spent the night reading cook books to get ready for this morning."

"You're shitting me?" Helen replied.

"Nope. I hope he doesn't break a nail while he's mixing the batter." Ann said while rolling her eyes back.

"Hey, give me a break. I'm trying to help a little with the baby on the way." Tony informed them. "I did a load of laundry. It's folded on top of the dryer."

"AAHHH, I can't handle any more." Ann hollered as she slumped into a chair.

"Tony, you're wife is pregnant, not disabled. She needs a husband, not a house keeper." Helen explained.

"Ya, but I thought it would be a good time to get in touch with my feminine side. You know, learn to be a little more sensitive to what you lady's lives are really like. I thought you'd understand." He added as he slowly lowered his head, and turned his back.

The two women stared in amazement. Neither could believe their eyes. Suddenly he turned, crossed the room in two huge steps, and flung the refrigerator door open. As he popped a beer open, slowly scratched his arm pit and farted he hollered. "Yes, got um both in the same morning."

Ann screamed. "I'll kill him!"

"Not if I get there first." Helen hollered.

Tony sprinted through the laundry room, and out through the garage yelling. "Be careful, remember you're condition. And, could one of you go back and flip the pancakes?"

"I'll flip your pancake Anthony." Helen yelled.

When Ann and Helen finally gave up on any idea of catching and punishing him the three went back into the kitchen, and settled in for breakfast. As Tony reached for the mixing spoon Ann grabbed a frying pan and growled. "You touch one more thing in my kitchen and you're dead."

Tony took a slow, deliberate step backward, crossed to the table and settled into one of the chairs. "OK, OK, I know when to back away. Sky don't have to fall on my head."

Helen tried her best to hold back a smile, but failed. As she turned toward the window he followed her eyes with his until she had no choice but to look his way. "I'd get you a cup of coffee, but she still has that frying pan in her hand." He explained.

"I'll get my own thank you Anthony. Can I get one for you?" She offered.

"Can I trust you?" He enquired.

"Not for a minute. And, remember what they say about pay-back." She warned.

Tony raised his eye brows, shook his head and replied. "I have no doubt I'm gonna pay."

The three of them made a great team, and were backed up by countless family and friends. Helen struggled through her ongoing medical problems, but seemed to gain strength with the thought of being a grandmother. Fred, Paul and Tony argued over what position the new family member would play on the baseball field. Olga and Rose hauled Ann into town nearly every week end stocking up on baby items of every description.

One afternoon as Tony came through the door he asked. "Is that Vic's car out front?"

Ann nodded and replied. "Yes it is."

"Where is he?" Tony inquired as he looked up and down the hall.

"He's in the garage cleaning paint brushes." Ann told him.

As Tony headed for the garage she stopped him and said. "Come here and look at this."

She led him to the baby's room where he saw freshly painted walls covered with every kind of animal and cartoon character imaginable. Each one was arranged methodically, and fit into its own place. "He worked on it all day. The guy ate the sandwich I made him in one hand while he painted with the other."

"It's beautiful." Tony said in amazement. "How did he put up the characters over wet paint?"

"One of the painters on a job site told him how to do it. He must have asked me a hundred times if this was OK, and if that looked alright until I finally told him to keep going. It looks fantastic. He was scared to death that he'd started something we wanted to do ourselves. He was like a kid with a new toy." She replied through a warm smile.

After a long pause Tony said. "You know where this came from don't you?"

"Yes I do." She answered, then looked back down the hall to make sure Vic was out of range. "He never even got a chance to see Ginger's baby, and stayed away to keep the peace. That woman ripped his heart out."

"Thanks for letting him do this. I know it meant a lot to him." Tony said gratefully.

"He's like a brother and our best friend. The guy is family." She admitted.

As Tony entered the garage he hollered. "What in the hell happened to the baby's room?"

Vic spun on his heals toward his friend's voice. There was a panicked look on his face that disappeared when he saw Tony laughing. "Ya got me man. You definitely got me. Hey, I hope it was OK. I don't want to......"

Tony didn't allow him to finish. "It's beautiful Vic. Honestly my Brother, it's beautiful. Annie loves it, and so do I. Come on out back. It's time for a beer."

The two men sat on the patio talking about everything and nothing. It was the kind of conversation very close friends know how to enjoy. It strengthens bonds between them, and gives each a sense of belonging. As different as they were each found a part of himself in the other.

During this exchange Vic questioned Tony about their approach to challenges. "Man, why do we do it when it's so much easier to go with the flow. Why do we seem to always swim up stream?"

Tony's answer came quickly. "Sweat, black eyes and bloody knuckles make a thing worth while. The effort makes it special and precious. Lying, cheating and stealing your way to the top makes you and your life cheap. I'd rather have one precious thing than a whole mountain of cheap."

"You definitely have something special. She's inside cooking dinner." Vic added just as quickly.

Ann watched them through the window as she prepared their meal. This was the way it was supposed to be she told herself. And, she cherished each moment as she pitied those who trade friendship for success, family for money and love for cheap entertainment.

In a while she yelled out the back door. "Would you like to call Terry, and see if wants to come over this evening Vic?"

"She's out of town. What's for dinner?" He replied.

"Irish lasagna." She informed him.

"Now there's a combination. Ya know, it just occurred to me. The baby is gonna be half Italian and half Irish. He'll either be heavy weight champion of the world or public enemy number one." He observed.

"What if it's a girl?" She countered.

"She'll either be heavy weight champion of the world or public enemy number one." He replied.

In spite of all they found in their special place the world outside still waited. And, their simple beliefs continued to throw them into the paths of those with different outlooks.

Harsh Reality

As Tony moved up through the ranks of supervision and middle management, he left the tools behind, and found himself in charge of the activities of others. The promotions came in spite his limited formal education. He was still several hours short of an engineering degree.

But, his hands on experience and ability to work under pressure more than compensated for any lack of formal training. This put him in a unique position. It allowed him to establish an excellent working relationship with the craftsman and women in his department. They understood his approach to problem solving because it was the same as theirs.

His military training and combat experience made him incredibly loyal to all those who worked for him. They covered his back while he covered theirs. All were always ready to go the extra mile for someone they knew they could depend upon.

However, Tony's approach to management and supervision was far different from those with similar responsibilities. Most had degrees in some technical field, and were proud of their educations. They looked at Tony as one who received advancement he didn't deserve. They were not ready to cover his back, but at the same time expected loyalty from him. This set the stage for conflict that came regularly.

On one particularly busy morning he got a call from his boss, the engineering manager. He ignored the first attempt at contact because of a breakdown that demanded his attention. The second call came on his cell phone, and that one couldn't be ignored.

"Tony, I need you in conference room A right away." The voice demanded.

"Can it wait? I'm in the middle of a breakdown that's costing big bucks." He replied in less than a respectful tone.

"Now." Came the second demand.

"Shit, I don't have time for this. Keep um going and call for outside help if you need it." Tony told his lead electrician.

"We got it covered. Enjoy the meeting." The craftsman told him through a sarcastic smile.

"Fuck you very much." Tony replied.

As he walked into the room all heads turned his way. The table was filled with department heads on all sides. He sat down in the only remaining chair, and was immediately confronted by the production manager. "We took a huge hit yesterday because of the CO_2 system failure, and can't afford those kinds of losses. Why didn't you file a report on the causes."

"I did. Each of you got an e-mail on the problems caused by the system valve failures." Tony calmly explained.

"What we're asking is why it took so long to get back on line. Your chief engineer spent all his time venting the system rather than repairing the valves. I want him written up for poor performance." The engineering manager instructed.

"The problem is with the valves, but not something that can be fixed by servicing them. They won't open as long as the system is over pressurized. They always fail under extreme conditions." Tony continued in the same calm voice. "The chief engineer did exactly what was necessary in a very timely manner."

"Why haven't we replaced valves we can't depend on." Was the question that the production manager asked, and the one on everyone else's mind.

"The project to replace the valves was rejected cause of cost." Tony went on.

"The project was rejected because those valves were selected by corporate engineers when the machinery was installed. Are you a CO2 systems expert now?" The engineering manager was scrambling to cover his ass.

"I'm not an expert, but the folks who sell us CO2 are. They're the ones who told me the electrically actuated valves we use have problems at high pressure because they depend on pressure difference to open. When the difference is too high they stick shut." Tony knew he'd crossed the line, and the glare from his boss confirmed it.

"I want the valves replaced now!" The production manager growled. He then stood and headed for the door followed by the rest who had gathered.

When Tony got to the door he heard. "Wait a minute. I want to talk to you." As he turned he saw the same glare he'd just faced.

"You threw me under the bus Frisano. I won't forget it." His boss was furious.

Tony felt the old juices flowing. But, he knew he had to stay under control, and not give the guy any good excuse to take justified action. "I was doing my job."

"I'll tell you what your job is, and that it includes loyalty to our department." This came from the man who did his annual review, approved pay increases and gave promotions. But. Tony knew he'd gone to far to back down.

"You ask for loyalty, but aren't willing to give it. I didn't throw you under the buss. You dove under yourself." Tony met the man's eyes with his own cold stare. He had to play this in the only way he knew. If he played their game they'd tear him apart.

As he returned to the breakdown he'd left because of the meeting he found the machinery running perfectly. The chief electrician smiled and asked. "How'd the meeting go?" Then added. "You fucked up again didn't you?"

"They flung the shit may way, but I ducked. It hit my boss dead between the eyes." Tony said shaking his head.

"As a politician you'd make a great electrician Tony. You're hopeless." The two men broke into laughter.

The rest of the day was routine with systems to check and reports to file. Before he left the production manager stopped bye, and caught Tony at his desk. "Thanks for setting things straight about the CO_2 system. I talked with our supplier and got the same information you gave us. There'll be capital money set aside for new valves. I know you took some heat over this. I want you to know your covered with the plant manager."

Tony smiled and said. "If it hadn't been that system problem it would have been something else. Heat comes with the territory."

"You handle it well, and I've got your back." He was assured.

"Thanks, I appreciate you saying so." Tony knew this man's loyalty was based on the direction of the political winds. He couldn't be trusted any more than the rest. Tony's only allies were the craft people who worked for him. Their skills and his calm leadership was the only thing he could depend on. He grew to truly hate the petty politics that made his job so difficult.

The pressure was even greater now that is son was born. Sean Fredrico Frisano was the first of the new generation. The name was a compromise between the Italian and Irish factions, and Tony was amazed that Ann went along with it. He didn't know it was actually her idea.

Within a year and a half Tony and Ann had a daughter, Angelina Maria. By this time the Irish gave up on the name game battles, and even agreed to an Italian Godmother and Godfather. Ann was overwhelmed with work and two babies. And, Helen needed more attention as her medical condition deteriorated.

One evening as Tony returned from work he found his wife in the kitchen trying to fold cloths, feed babies and answer questions on the phone from one of her former patients. He took Angelina from her arms, and crossed the room to where Sean was seated in his high chair. He took the bowl of Spaghetti-Os from him, most of which had been thrown against the adjacent window. "Kids got a great arm." He said as he pointed at the window.

As Ann hung up the phone she added. "That's because he throws everything he gets his hands on."

"You look very tired." He told her as one of the remaining Spaghetti-Os left within Sean's reach hit him in the back of his ear.

"Gee, go figure." She said as she pulled Sean from the chair and headed for the sink.

"You gonna drowned him?" Tony asked through a muffled laugh.

"No, just hold him under for a while." Ann declared.

"You need to either quit work or drowned them both". He told her. "But honestly, you should quit work, at least for now. This action day by day is too much."

"I hate to do that with the way things are for you at work. The stress is showing on you too." She told him.

"I think we need to take a chance, and lighten the load. There's a few dollars in savings, and I can always go back the tools. In fact, I got an offer from one of the contractors who's working at the plant." He reassured.

"I like the idea of being a full time mom until the kids start school." She told him honestly. "But, before we go any further tell me about work."

"I caught them in a code violation today. They wanted me to ignore it so that production could go on. I said no, and pissed em all off." He began.

"How bad was the violation?" She asked.

"Bad enough to get somebody killed." He went on.

"And they actually wanted you to ignore it?" Ann asked in amazement.

"They insisted I ignore it, and the fight was on." Tony didn't like bringing these things home to Ann. He knew she was concerned about how his job was effecting him. And, going back to work as an electrician could mean he'd have to be out of town from time to time. This was the main reason he took the management job.

"Did anyone in the plant back you up?" She asked in a tone filled with anger and contempt.

"You know how that works Annie. They have their own butts to cover, and are not about to stick their necks out for me. Most of them have no where else to go." He tried to explain, knowing what her reaction would be.

"Then why do you help them? Each time they get the chance they stab you in the back." The contempt in her voice was still there.

"I have no idea." Tony admitted. "Let's clean the kids up, grab your mom and go out for dinner. We haven't seen Gino in a while."

"Can we just stay home? The kids will be ready for bed soon, and we can have some time to ourselves." Ann proposed.

Tony looked at his son who was looking back at him. "OK buddy, I need your help tonight. Some day you'll understand just how important some time to ourselves can be. Until then trust me, it's important!"

Within an hour Sean and Angelina were asleep, and Tony and Ann had their time, a part of their lives that was much harder to set aside now. Tony tiptoed out of Sean's room and down the hall to the living room where Ann had settled in on the couch. As he sat beside her he said. "Finally, I thought he'd never drop off. The kids got energy to spare."

"He's a hand full." She added. Then looked at Tony with the same steady gaze he'd seen many times. It meant a question was coming, one that wouldn't wait. "Can I ask you something?"

"If I said no would you ask anyway?" He teased.

"Of course." She informed him then asked. "Remember that night in Gino's when the drunk asked me to dance, and you threatened him with hospitalization?"

"Yes." He replied, wondering were this was going.

"What if he hadn't backed down? What if Rocko hadn't thrown him out? Were you really going to put him in the hospital?" She watched closely as she added. "What if he was too much for you to handle?"

"It never crossed my mind. There wasn't time to consider all that." He told her in a calm and sincere voice.

"But Tony, how can you not consider all that? Even the Frisanos aren't invincible. I mean the guy was being a jerk, but hospitalization?" She pressed.

"I wasn't going to go after him just for being a jerk. And, it had nothing to do with being macho. The guy was big and drunk. He was fool enough to ignore all sense and reason. He just didn't care. That made him a threat to both you and me. My reaction caught him off guard. He didn't expect it. That stopped him. If I'd have hesitated he'd have kept pushing, and that would have made things worse." Tony tried to explain.

"Before that night at Gino's when we first met I heard about you and your family. The word was you were trouble. But, my Uncle Henry told a different story, and I had to see for myself. On that night I saw both sides of you, and it confused me. The change in you happened so fast. You went from gentleman to street fighter, and back to gentleman in the blink of an eye." Ann was trying hard to understand, but was still unsure.

"Annie, I came from a neighborhood where if you didn't fight you didn't get to play. Anyone who backed down was tormented all day, every day. Being willing to fight got you a place on the playground, in the lunch room and on the street walking home. The worse thing anyone can do is go into a fight thinking about loosing. If the other guy is bigger and tougher you can still bloody him up, and that's enough to get his respect. Once he knows taking you on is gonna hurt he'll move onto someone else." Tony truly wanted her to understand.

"Respect means a lot to you doesn't it? But, honor and respect can come at a big price. Is it worth it?" Ann was getting to what she really wanted to know.

"I can't imagine living without it. And, it's more than backing down a drunk. You went with me on our first date to a deserted parking lot. You wouldn't have done it unless you trusted me. You saw something in me that gave you that trust. You depended on your Uncle Hank's view of me because you had faith in him. If he or I did anything to violate your trust it would change the relationship forever. And, truly good relationships are far too precious to loose." Tony couldn't believe how much of himself he'd just passed onto her.

There was another reason for Ann's questions, and she already knew the answer, but wanted the perspective of the man she loved. She was looking for the difference between the world of logic, reason and compassion compared to that of survival, instinct and brutality. Tony knew both worlds, and could switch from one to the other in the blink of an eye.

She wondered how he could control these changes, how he made sure the primal side didn't interfere with things that made life worth while. She'd seen him struggle with control in some cases, and be master of it in others. She asked herself. What was the key? What made her believe he'd always make the right choices. It was suddenly clear to her. It was because he cared.

"I love you Anthony Frisano." She said as she kissed him.

Vic sat by the window sipping a gin and tonic when the door burst open and a familiar voice blared. "What in the fuck are you listening to?"

"It's Nat King Cole's version of Hoagy Charmichael's Stardust." He said in a calm, controlled voice. "And, next time try knocking. You know, knock, knock. Come in, that silly civilized shit."

"Well, it sounds like crap." Ginger snapped from across the room.

"Then put your fingers in your ears. But, first you'll have to pull your head out of your ass." He replied in the same cool tone.

"Kiss my ass and give me my money." Her voice hadn't changed either.

"Your final payment is in the account the court set up just like it's always been." His voice was now much stronger.

"It wasn't there last week." She insisted.

"Well you just discovered the difference between last week and this week. Congratulations. It sure doesn't take you long to figure things out. Oh wait. I guess you missed that one." Vic began to laugh.

"If it's not there you'll be sorry." Ginger's voice was a little confused.

"Don't let your alligator mouth overload your tadpole ass." Now get the hell outa here. You're trespassing." He'd had enough of this old game.

The door slammed as she left.

A moment later he heard a knock.

"What?" He snarled.

"Just wanted to stop by and say hi." Terry Richmond said as she opened the door and leaned in the doorway.

Vic stood shaking his head, and slowly walked to the door. "Sorry if you heard any of that. I hope it's over, and she's out of my life."

"Can I make you dinner?" She asked in an understanding tone. "How about my place at six?"

"I'll bring a bottle of Red." He told her. "It sounds great."

"I can make you feel better." She smiled. "Guaranteed."

"I know. I've been thinking about you and your feel better since you left." He slid his hands to her face and kissed her softly.

As Vic walked up the steps leading to Terry's front door he was greeted by smells that reminded him of home. The simmering marinara sauce and toasting garlic bread could not be mistaken for anything else. Before he reached the door it swung open, and Terry welcomed him with. "Your timing is perfect. Come in. Open the wine, and relax."

"Damn girl, that smells fantastic. We gotta get married, have eight kids, and grow old screaming at each other." He said in a voice similar to a kid walking through the gates of Disneyland.

She turned slowly, and looked him straight in the eye. "Be careful what you wish for."

"I know what I want Terry. It's the simple things, the ones that come naturally and last a lifetime." Vic surprised himself. It was like he was listening to someone else, or watching a forties era movie.

She turned and looked closely at him. "Wow, my spaghetti sauce never had that effect before. Pour me some wine, quick."

Vic smiled as he retrieved the opener from the table, and twisted the spiral end into the cork. As he filled their glasses Terry advised. "That bottle won't last long at the rate you pour."

"I have three more in the car". His subtle look of satisfaction was something Terry recognized, and was looking for.

She headed for the kitchen to gather and serve the various parts of their meal. As she turned with her arms full she found Vic directly behind her. "Let me do that. You did the cooking." he volunteered.

As he took bowls and serving dishes from her hands she said. "You're scaring me Vic."

"Hey, I'm getting in touch with my sensitive side. Like it?" He added with the same satisfied look she saw as he poured.

"I don't know. I never had dinner with Mr. congeniality before. Give me some time to adjust." Dinner was unusually quiet, missing much of the banter and snappy exchanges that began their relationship. Vic looked more relaxed than she'd ever seen him, but at the same time very confident, the kind of confidence that made her feel safe and out of harms way. It was a very good feeling, but at the same time unsettling.

As they finished Vic asked. "Like to take a walk? I can grab another bottle of red on the way back."

A sarcastic remark flashed through Terry's mind, but stuck in her throat. It just didn't fit the evening, or this new man she found in her dinning room. "Sure, let's go."

The night was cool, but beautiful. The moon was full, and nearly bright enough to read by. As Vic pointed to it he said through a quiet laugh. "La bella luna."

"What?" She asked as she was blind sided again.

"La bella luna. It's a line from a movie, and also something my grandfather used to say." He noted.

"I feel like your grandfather had dinner with us." She paused and quickly added. "I didn't mean you acted like......."

Vic was laughing, and interrupted. "I know what you mean, and I feel the same way."

Terry stopped and turned to him. "I saw a guy walk into a bar, knock the shit out of a gangster, and back the whole place down. That wasn't the same guy I had dinner with tonight."

"Yes it was. He was just gone for a while. I saw glimpses of him before, but he never was around for a whole evening. I think I'm tired of the hassle, and the fight. Every minute I spend pissed off is one more minute wasted. Life is too short to waste." He was surprising himself even more than he surprised Terry.

"I don't know what to say Vic, and that doesn't happen often." She stood staring at him.

"Well, hang on. I'm not done." He announced.

Terry suddenly felt very nervous, and somehow knew what was coming. As she gently put her hand over his mouth she said. "Don't Vic. I can't handle it."

He softly pushed her hand aside and said. "I'm falling in love with you." He paused and repeated. "I love you."

She froze and looked deeply into his eyes as she felt tears running down her face. "Damn you Moretto. Why now? How could you do this to me? We were friends. We were lovers. We were drinking buddies. Now you have to use the fucking L work."

He threw his arms around her, and pulled her close as she sobbed on his shoulder. After a long while he said. "Let's go get that wine."

They walked quietly back to her house. Vic grabbed a couple more bottles before escorting her inside. After setting them on the table he wiped the remaining tears and said. "It's OK. I understand. But, I had to be honest. We know each other too well, and respect one another far to much to do it any other way."

"You and your honor and respect. Why can't you just party, take advantage of me and toss me aside like I expected?" Her mind was racing, and she was angry because she could see his wasn't.

"Because I care. I can't change that any more than you can change how you feel." He told her.

"I'm not ready Vic. I wish I was. But, it wouldn't be fair to either of us to pretend. I care for you deeply. Maybe it's love. But, I don't know, and that's the problem." She was finding her own honesty.

"When it's love, and you're ready you'll know. Until then thank you for some of the best times I ever had. I see a side of myself now that I thought was lost forever. You brought it back." He kissed her, and turned toward the door.

"Will you stay and help me drink this wine?" She asked.

"That would hurt too much." He smiled and walked away.

Tony walked through the front door and asked. "Who's car in the driveway?"

"It's mine Tony. How ya doin?" Terry replied.

As he entered the kitchen he saw her and Ann seated at the kitchen table. Each had a fresh cup of coffee in front of them. He couldn't help but notice that Terry had been crying in spite of her best efforts to hide it. "I'm doing fine. How about you?"

"Good thanks". She replied.

His dark eyes locked onto hers in the Frasino fashion. "Really?"

"You guys don't miss much do you? Vic walked out last night because of how I reacted to the things he said. I feel like shit." She admitted.

"If this is girl talk I'll get outta here, and leave you two alone." He offered.

"No, I'd actually like you to stay." Terry told him. It came in the form of a request.

Tony asked the natural question. "What did he say?"

"He said he loved me." She realized how foolish it sounded the minute she said it.

"That heartless bastard." He said to confirm what she realized.

"Damn it Tony. Give her a chance." Ann snapped.

"No, no, it's OK. I know it sounds ridiculous. But, he took me by surprise. Through the whole evening he was a completely different guy, no smart remarks, no sarcasm, not even a dirty joke. It wasn't the Vic I knew, and I didn't know how to handle it. I was scared." She admitted.

"The fact that you came here tells me you care. Loving someone is easy. Building a relationship is tough. It takes lots of time, effort and commitment. Tony and I work on it every day." Ann explained.

Before anything else was said the door bell rang. "Bad timing. Let me see who it is." Tony interrupted.

As he opened it they all heard Vic's voice say. "Hey Tony. There's an opening for us at Cedars, course number two. A couple of guys want to loose some money. I really need to kick some ass right now. What da you say?"

"Wow, bad timing is right." Tony replied.

"Come on in Vic. Ann has fresh coffee." Terry invited.

Vic tipped his head back and sighed, then looked at Tony. Both men were completely out of their element and they knew it. But, in true street fashion they took the whole thing head on, and entered the kitchen side by side. Tony went to the coffee maker and asked. "Cream and sugar Vic or hot and black? I never made you coffee before."

"Whatever you're drinking man. Whatever you're drinking." Vic said as if it was the forth quarter, and his team was down by forty points.

Terry turned in her chair, and locked eyes with Vic. "Good afternoon." She said in a tone that even she'd never heard before. She was nervous and confused, but couldn't look away.

Vic sighed once more, and then relaxed completely. How are you?" He asked.

"I feel like shit, thank you. Two bottled of wine and no sleep will do that." They were still locked eye to eye.

"We need to check on the kids Tony." Ann interrupted.

"I'm right with you." Tony said as he set a cup of coffee on the counter beside Vic.

There was a long pause once Terry and Vic were alone. She was the first to speak. "There's more to say Vic. We can't just leave it like we did last night."

"We can't be pals Terry. It would drive me crazy. Seeing you with another guy would land me in jail. I can't do it. I love you totally, completely, and I'm sure of it. You don't feel that way. That doesn't leave us much room to maneuver." The words came easily because he knew exactly how he felt.

"Ann said something that's stuck in my head. Love is easy. Relationships take time. This is knew ground for me. I don't know how to handle it, and you're the reason. I don't want to let go, but I'm scared to death to hang on." As she talked her feelings began to fall into place. She was starting to understand.

"I guess I don't get the part about not knowing. When I'm in I'm in one hundred percent. When I'm out I just don't care. What I heard you say was you're in and out at the same time. I don't know how that works." Vic was frustrated, and it was beginning to show.

"Last night I told you I had deep feelings. I know now it's love, and it scares the hell out of me. I've never let myself be this vulnerable. I'm afraid to let myself love you, and then loose you." She was trying harder than she'd ever tried before.

There was another long pause as a puzzled look came over Vic's face. "You're pushing me away because you're afraid to loose me? That's what you want me to understand? That's what...."

"God damn it Moretto, shut up and listen to me". She screamed as she jumped from the chair. Tears were pouring down her face. "I love you, you stupid ass hole. Does that make is easier for you to understand. That's just one simple thing you have to wrap yourself around. Can you do that one simple thing?"

Vic crossed the short distance between them, and put his arms around her. She laid her head on his shoulder and continued to cry. In a short time she raised her head and said. "Look at me. This is all your fault."

He smiled as he wiped her face. "If you'd have said love last night I could have had some more of that wine I brought over."

"Tony, get the good glasses down while I get them some wine." Ann ordered from the hallway.

As Ann and Tony came back to the kitchen Terry said. "I feel foolish, but he's driving me crazy. Does it get easier?"

"Nope. There's nothing easy about it. But, the good stuff outweighs the bad by a bunch." Tony told them as he retrieved the glasses from the pantry.

"My man the philosopher." Ann said as she put one harm around Tony and poured with the other.

It didn't get easier for Terry and Vic. The next several months were filled with regularly occurring battles that began over things like how the toilet paper should come off the roll, in what part of the drawer the spoons should be kept and who forgot what about which.

Vic would blow up and walk out, only to return when he realized how much he missed her after only an hour or two. Terry would dig her heals in and fight like a cornered bear, only to apologize later when she realized that she couldn't remember what they were fighting about. But, neither could let go of what they'd found in each other.

As time went on Vic began to soften first. He wasn't weakening, but rather beginning to understand that there was much more to loose than gain in the war of the ridiculous. He began matching anger with indifference. This whatever approach infuriated Terry.

On an evening as they traveled to a family get-together Terry challenged with. "Where are you going?"

"South." He replied.

"But, why this way?" She pressed.

"Because I'm going this way." He knew where this was headed, and that there was no way to avoid the inevitable.

"It's gonna take longer damn it." Her voice was becoming stronger and more challenging.

"OK, exactly what fucking way do you want me to go?" The what fucking way part slipped out reflexively.

"Well sure as hell not this way. What are you thinking?" She pressed.

He let the moment develop, and calmly said. "I'm thinking I don't give a fat rat's ass."

Her response came so fast and furious that Vic couldn't understand much of what she screamed. The fact that he didn't respond in kind made Terry even more angry. The rest of the evening was spent in a deafening silence.

By morning both were still angry, and neither could understand why. The mood had to run its course because each one was far to defensive for peace talks. Yet, by afternoon they managed guarded conversation, and evening brought back the good times.

It began with Terry. "I'm sorry about last night. I guess I overreacted, and don't understand why."

A thought flashed through his mind that started with the response, overreacted, you lost your mind. But, small gems of wisdom were creeping into his makeup. Winning wasn't as much fun if it included a ruined evening, and miserable day. So instead he said. "We both pushed way too far."

"When Tony said it was tough I had no idea how tough it could be. I really am very sorry. I was a bitch." She admitted.

"We have a long way to go, but have already covered lots of ground. In the past few months neither of us has tried to kill the other. That's gotta count for something. But seriously, we're going to keep making mistakes. This is all learn as we go." He said as once again his dark eyes met hers.

She continued to look deeply into his eyes, then said. "You surprise me every day Moretto."

Continuing Struggles

The changes and surprises not only continued, but grew in both intensity and frequency. There was much more to Vic's wisdom and patience than even he imagined. It took all he had to deal with what life threw his way.

Hanging on to Terry was the best choice of his life, and she proved to be his greatest source of support. The foolish battles over insignificant issues went on, but they were put with other small set backs that became routine.

Tony and Ann were tested with as much as any two should have to endure. One by one the things that meant so much to them were taken away. The first great loss was Helen. All knew how serious her health problems were, but none imagined that such a strong and wise woman would finally loose her battles with illness.

Ann was crushed. As they made their way home after the funeral she said nothing. She didn't loose control or even cry, but simply stared out the car window noticing nothing that passed by. Her eyes were glazed and showed no emotion.

When they were home she set about her tasks in a robot like manner with the same cold, impersonal process that began as she made arrangements for her mother's funeral. Tony, Sean and Angelina were treated with efficiency that she'd practiced as a nurse. But, none were allowed inside the protective shell she built around herself.

Tony watched for days, and became more concerned as each one passed. His many attempts to comfort her were politely ignored as she marched through the hours completely detached. He was at a loss for words or actions.

One evening after the kids were asleep he walked into their bed room, and found Ann staring at a small piece of costume jewelry that she played with as a child. "She gave this to me. I should have put it with her. Why didn't I put this with her? Why didn't I put this with her Tony?" Her hands began to shake, and then she started to tremble all over. "God damn it, why? Why her?"

By the time he reached her she'd burst into tear, and cried hysterically. Tony held her for what seamed an eternity. He picked her up as he felt her legs begin to buckle, and placed her on the bed. As she continued to cry more softly he covered her with a small blanket, and laid down beside her. She continued to clutch the piece of jewelry until she finally fell asleep.

During the night he checked on her and the kids often, and found some comfort each time he saw them resting. Like Vic, he admitted to himself that there were things he couldn't fix, things that just had to be accepted. He knew he'd always continue to try, but would focus on what he could effect and improve.

Their second crisis came one summer as Sean began to limp badly on his left leg. Ann could find nothing to cause the problem, no apparent strain or injury. Their family physician could also find nothing, and referred him to a local orthopedic surgeon, Dr. Robert Cummings. As luck would have it, he was one of the best in his field, and had years of experience with complex problems.

Following a thorough examination he called Ann and Tony in to discuss the results. "Your son has A.V. fistulas that are starving parts of his leg of proper blood flow."

Ann interrupted with. "Isn't that usually found in old people. How can it happen to someone so young?"

"I've never seen or heard of it in someone his age. But, both the cardiovascular specialist and I agree that that's the problem."

"So, what do we do about it?" This time Tony interrupted.

"Surgery is our only chance to save his leg." Dr. Cummings told them.

"There's a chance he could loose it?" Tony asked in horror and amazement.

"Yes, there's that chance. We're pretty sure we can take care of the blood flow issues, But, there's a big chance of serious infection because of the large area we have to work on.

"Can antibiotics take care of it?" Ann asked. She was trying to understand as a nurse, and keep her mother's emotions under control.

"We'll be using them in huge quantities. He's young and tough. That gives him an advantage."

"When?" Tony asked.

"As soon as possible. I have him scheduled for tomorrow afternoon. We'll put together one of the best teams in the country. He'll have the finest care possible." He was reassuring, but painfully honest.

"We'll see you in the morning." Ann told him.

Late that night when the family was asleep Tony walked out onto the patio, and stood looking into the darkness. Suddenly he dropped to his knees and looked skyward. "I've never asked for much old man, but I'm asking now. Please, please give my son, Sean, every chance to pull through this. I know this isn't your standard prayer, but it's more sincere than any I said in the past." Tears ran down his face as he continued. "If I could give him both my legs I would. But, we both know that's not how it works. All I can do is stay by him however this works out. But, you can do more. Stay with the doctors tomorrow, and let them use all their skills to help my boy."

Ann watched through the patio doors. She'd followed him as he left the bedroom, and saw him praying. In all the years they'd been together he never looked so helpless and afraid. As he stood she returned to the bedroom.

The next afternoon was the longest of their lives. Every time someone passed by the waiting room Tony would turn toward the door in anticipation. Finally Ann said. "This is gonna take some time. Why don't you get us some coffee. I'll come get you if the doctors come in."

Reluctantly, he headed to the cafeteria, and all but sprinted back with cups in hand. "That must be a record for service in this hospital or any other." She said as she hugged him and took the cup.

It took four more hours before they got the word. Dr. Cummings came slowly through the door as Tony jumped to his feet. Ann stared deeply into the doctors eyes, ready to take in every bit of information. "He's doing fine, and I gotta tell you, someday he'll probably play in the Rose Bowl. His bones are huge. He'll be well over six feet and two hundred pounds." The doctor said through a broad smile. "You can go back and see him. He's just waking up."

As Tony and Ann stood quietly beside his bed Sean's six year old eyes rolled open. "Hi Pop". Am I all better?"

"Hi buddy. Yep, you're all better. We just have to give you some time to heal up". Tony choked back the tears. "Mom's here."

Sean reached out for his mother's hand. As she took it she gently brushed back the hair from his eyes. He squeezed her hand as if he'd never let go, and asked. "Where's Angie?"

"Your sister is with Aunt Terry. You'll see her tomorrow." She reassured him.

"Can I go home tomorrow?" He asked with his weak, sleepy voice.

"Probably not tomorrow, but soon." She promised.

He continued to look at his mother, then said in the same six year old voice. "Don't worry anymore mom, I'm gonna be fine."

That was more than Ann could handle. In spite of her best efforts to stay in control the tears began to flow. "I know sweet heart. I know." She managed to say.

"She doesn't have to cry pop." Sean told his father.

"Sometimes people cry when they're happy buddy." Tony told him.

"Are you crying cause you're happy mom?" He asked as he fought to stay awake.

"Yes, I'm crying because I'm happy. Now go to sleep. We'll be here when you wake up." Her tears still flowed.

Sean's stay in the hospital lasted for a week, and included medication pumped into his small body through every possible source. Late one night Ann left his bedside for just a moment, returning as fast as she could. As she passed by her favorite warm up jacket she'd left hanging by his bed she saw his tiny hand clutching the jacket sleeve. As she sat down he opened his eyes and said. "I wanted to make sure no one took it mom."

"Thank you sweet heart. I know I can depend on you." She told him as she took his hand, and held it while he fell asleep.

The next morning when Tony came in to give Ann a break he found them both sleeping, and still holding hands. As he walked around the bed Sean woke and said. "Hi pop. Mom is very tired."

"I know buddy. Thanks for taking good care of her." He said as Ann woke.

"Do I have to have more shots today? They really hurt, but I'm not gonna cry." Even at the age of six he wanted his father's respect.

"It's OK to cry when it hurts." Tony reassured his son. "I'm very proud of you for being so brave. But, it's OK to cry. Mom and I are gonna step out into the hall for a minute, but we'll be right back."

Once outside the room Tony asked. "How's he doing?"

"Still no sign of infection, and he's resting well. The poor little guy is pumped full of meds. that he needs, but it's very hard on him. Try to get him to eat as much breakfast as he can, and call me after the doctors come in." She asked.

"You need to get home and get some rest. But, I need to talk to you one more time before you leave." He told her as they went back into Sean's room.

As they reached his bedside Paul and Vic walked in carrying an electric race car and model plane. "Hey buddy, how ya doin?" Vic asked. They'd become very close. Vic spent hours with the kids, and he and Terry were their favorite baby sitters.

"Hi Uncle Vic. Is that for me?" Sean asked as he looked at the gifts through wide eyes.

"Yep. Aunt Terry said I had to bring them this morning before I wore them out." Vic admitted.

"Hi papa." Sean said as he waved to Paul.

"Good morning buddy." Paul responded to his grandson through a loving smile.

He then turned his attention to Ann and Tony. As Vic and Sean inspected the toys Paul asked them. "How you holdin up?"

"Fine, just tired." Ann assured him.

"Lets go out in the hall and talk while the boys play." He said to her as he and Tony exchanged knowing glances, and made plans without saying a word.

Ann looked a little puzzled as she followed him. Once in the hall and out of ear shot Paul said. "This is a terrible time, but I didn't want you to find out the way Tony did." Ann felt a sickening feeling. She watched her father-in-law closely as he continued. "Olga has cancer. She's on the next floor here at the hospital for more tests. She wants to come down to see Sean this afternoon when they're finished. I'm so sorry to have to tell you now."

She stood looking at him in disbelief. Once she gathered herself she asked. "How did Tony find out?"

"He overheard the staff talking, did some checking and forced them to tell him all they knew. It all happened this morning." Paul explained.

"No wonder he came in late, and no wonder I couldn't get in touch with her yesterday. How did you find out?" She questioned.

"Olga called me as soon as they told her. I met her so we could talk. But actually, the doctor called me before he told her. He's an old friend, and wanted family ready when Og. got the news. She put me down as first contact." He explained.

"But, you guys split up." Ann was trying to make the pieces fit.

"A little paper work doesn't wipe out thirty years together. I was glad I was there for her." Paul went on.

"Our lives are turning into a soap opera. What the hell is next?" Her tone had changed from amazement to anger.

"Don't worry about what's next. Don't even think about it. Just deal with right now." Paul advised as he gave a fatherly hug and kissed her on the forehead.

As Ann entered the room she put her arm around Tony, and pulled him close. "I have a stop to make upstairs before I go home."

"She'll like that." He said as he hugged back.

As the half closed door to Sean's room swung the rest of the way open all heard. "Hey my buddy. How they treatin you? Aunt Joan brought you some donuts in case the food here isn't that good."

"Hi Aunt Joan. Look what papa and Uncle Vic brought me." Sean pointed to his new toys.

"Hey, great. But, make Uncle Vic give you a turn too." Joan instructed.

Tony's cousin Joan had been more like a sister throughout their years together growing up. Joan's sister, Nancy, was the youngest of the trio who'd been very close throughout their lives.

Nan entered shaking her head, and snapped at Joan saying. "This is a hospital Joanne, and I think the people three floors up heard about your donuts. Your Aunt Joan is crazy Sean. She got hit in the head."

"Grandma says papa has a crooked nose because he got hit. Did the same one hit you Aunt Joan?" Sean asked.

Ann jumped in saying. "I hate to break up this riot, but the room won't hold anymore people, and the doctors might want to stop bye soon." She looked both of Tony's cousins in the eye and continued. "Let's go out into the hall, and give Sean a break. Uncle Vic will stay here for a minute."

The cousin's eyes turned her way. Then Joan, Nan and Paul headed for the door led by Ann. Vic watched closely as they left.

Once in the hallway they continued to look closely at Ann. All family members and most close friends had the Frisano ability to read body language as clearly as the written word. It was as much a curse as a benefit. Sometime too much information was exchanged when a little secrecy would have served better.

Paul was the one to break the groups focus. "Olga is in the hospital. They're treating her for lung cancer. She'll get the best care, but there's not a lot they can do."

Joanne and Nancy stood for a long while in stunned silence. Olga was nearly as close to them as their mother, Rose. Then Joan reacted the way all knew she would. "This isn't the only hospital. If they can't help we'll find someone who can."

"Ya, I'm sure there's more that can be done." Nan said as she turned and walked down the hall.

"Where are you going?" Joan demanded.

"I need some coffee." Nan snapped back.

"Let her go Joan". Paul said in the commanding voice he inherited from his father. "She needs some time to get a handle on all this."

Joan's reaction was lightening fast. "We don't have time. She needs help, and needs to get it now. I'm not gonna sit by............."

Tony cut her off as he put his arm around her and pulled her close. "Listen to me Cuz. She'll get help, and we'll talk with the doctors as soon as possible. But, all of us, especially mom, need a few hours to let this soak in. It's too big a chunk to bight off in one gulp."

She looked up at him, and he could see the anxiety that was overtaking her as she said. "But, we have to move fast Tony. This can't wait."

He continued to hold her close, and could feel her tighten. "Stop." He said in a tone that was as comforting as it was firm. "She'll be busy all day with tests. As soon as she gets a break she's gonna come down to see Sean. Let her set the pace. Believe me, mom will let us know what she needs and when. We just need to stay close right now, and wait for her to start giving orders. You know that's what's coming."

"Where the hell is Nan. She doesn't need any God damned coffee." Joan growled.

"Come on, let's go find her." Ann stepped in and took over for Tony.

As the two women headed down the hallway Tony turned to his father. "Son-of-a-bitch Pop, I can't deal with this shit."

"You just did. Now listen to me. Take the advise you gave Joan. Do it one step at a time. You can't fix this buddy. All you can do is deal with it." Paul half slapped and half patted Tony on the back. "I'm very proud of you."

"Thanks Pop, and thanks for being here." Tony said as he headed back to Sean's room.

Paul watched his son disappear through the doorway, and yearned for the days when they played catch in the back yard. Times were simple then, and he was sorry he didn't appreciate them more while he could still enjoy them. He felt the time slipping through his fingers. Things were changing so fast, and seamed so out of control.

His free and loose life style began to change when he lost his father and mother. They'd been so strong throughout his life that loosing them never entered his mind. Fred's health deteriorated a couple of years after he retired. A stroke and long bought with cancer had done what bootleggers, corrupt police, the coal mines and the depression couldn't. They sapped his immense strength and will. Paul watched his father hopelessly fight the battle that none can win, and it broke his heart.

His mother's death was just as painful, but hit in a very different way. She'd been on her way to Mass with Joan when a massive heart attack took her life. She was the anchor that held the family together through every storm, the rock they built their lives upon. The family was crushed, and Paul's life was torn apart.

For a time after he and Olga divorced he was completely lost. The week end flings didn't mean much when there was no one to come home to. He looked desperately for something or someone to fill the void.

Vic was still looking toward to door when Tony came back in. His heart sank as he looked into his friend's eyes. Then both men changed gears the way they'd done so many times before. While with Sean they would turn their backs on pain, and fill the time with all the joy they could provide. Paul soon joined them, and the four partied until the hospital staff demanded things tone down.

"I'll be here for a while if you and Vic want to go for a cup of coffee." Paul told his son.

"Thanks Pop. We'll be back in a few, and bring you a cup." Tony told his father. He and Vic stepped out into the hall with no intention of going as far as the cafeteria.

Instead, they each grabbed a cup from the nearby nurse's station, and settled in for an exchange of information. Vic stared intently as Tony began. "Mon has lung cancer. She's here now for tests, and some preliminary treatment. I haven't talked to her yet, but she knows what's going on."

"God damn it man. When is enough enough?" Vic said followed by a deep sigh. "That lady doesn't deserve that shit."

"Deserve has nothing to do with it my Brother." Tony paused in his own deep sigh. "It is what it is."

"It's bull shit, that's what it is." Then Vic stopped, and looked closely at Tony. "What can I do? Should I go see her while you and Pop stay with Sean?"

"No, not right now. There'll be plenty to do in the next few weeks, and she'll be happy to see you and Terry. Let's grab a cup for Pop. Can you stay for a while after the doctors check on Sean? They should be here any time." Tony knew Vic would be great for his son, and also how much he wanted to help.

"Sure I can." Vic assured him. As they headed back down the hall the day shift doctor and nurses were just entering Sean's room."

"Hey little man. How are you doing? You sure are a big boy." The resident physician said without looking up from his chart.

"How do you know how big I am? You're looking the other way." Sean told the doctor. The nurse directly behind him lowered her head and covered her mouth to muffle her laughter.

"I'm your doctor. I know everything about you." The young physician replied, still looking at the chart.

"My doctor is a big guy with red hair. He made my leg better. He's great." Sean informed him. It was more than the nurse could handle, and she didn't even try to hold back. Everyone in the room was laughing except Sean and the doctor who finally looked up.

"Dr. Cummings is a friend of mine. He said I could take care of you today if it was all right with you. What do you say? Can I give it a try?" The young doctor said through a smile.

"Sure, if it's OK with my mom. She's a nurse, and is real smart." Sean said in a stern six year old voice.

"We know your mom, and she is smart. We work with her all the time. I'll check to make sure it's OK." The nurse told him while still smiling. "I need to check a couple of things right now though, but I'm sure it'll be OK with her."

"Are you gonna give me a shot in the butt?" Sean asked.

"Yes, I'm afraid I have to. But, I'll be as careful as I can." She told him.

"Can you do it on this side? The other one is still pretty sore." Sean asked as he pointed to his left hip.

"I'll give it anywhere you like." She agreed

"Then, can you give it to him?" He asked through a smile of his own as he pointed to the young doctor, and the laughter began again.

Sean took his morning injection in true Frisano fashion as he choked back the tears. He was tough like his father and grandfather before him, but like them, sometimes too tough. He reserved his softer side for his mother, grandmother and sister. Both Tony and Ann knew how hard loosing Olga would be for him.

Her room was quiet, but very bright as the afternoon sun flooded through the windows. It gave the area a warm, peaceful feeling like a summer Sunday afternoon. Olga sat on the bed with her arms around her knees and head turned into the sunlight. Her face showed a calm focus as if she was miles from the hospital room and those who had just delivered the horrible news.

The silence was broken by the resident priest as he entered, and said in his deepest comforting voice. "Good afternoon. I'm Father Noonan. How are you doing?"

Olga turned toward him and stared coldly into his eyes as she said in a voice that matched her stare. "I'm dying, how are you?"

"I heard your bad news, and wanted to stop by. Would you like to pray with me?" He asked in the same comforting tone.

"No." She snapped.

"Prayer can help. God always listens. He's there for us always." The priest replied.

"Well I'll let you know if I need someone to relay a message to God for me. But, for now I'll do my own talking. Thanks just the same." She growled locked in the same cold stare.

The priest said nothing as he left the room. Olga turned back to her window and the sunlight. There was comfort there that allowed her time away from all she now had to face. She was more angry than afraid. So, if God was waiting for a humble prayer he'd just have to wait. And she had absolutely no time for the priest and his tender, loving bullshit.

"Hi Ma." Tony said as he passed the priest at the doorway.

"Hi. How's Sean? Are they still pumping him full of meds.?" Her grandson could easily take her away from the window and her sunshine.

"Still no sign as infection. The doctors are very happy with his progress. He hates the shots, but won't shed a tear." Tony passed on. He was anxious to see what was on her mind, and was not surprised that her first concern was for Sean. He knew he'd have to wait for her signal to talk about her condition, but decided to try a gentle prod. "Did you have something to eat?"

"They're not giving me much until the tests are complete. I've been waiting for hours for them to get things done. I'm not going to wait much longer. They'll have to find me in Sean's room if they don't get in here." She told him. "And I'm not going there dressed like this."

"Let me see what I can find out." Tony volunteered. "Do you have something to change into?"

"There's cloths in the closet. I need you to take some dirty laundry with you. I'm running out of socks and underwear. I also want you to go ever to Swanson's funeral center, and make arrangements." Her voice was calm and firm with no difference between dirty socks and funeral plans.

Tony stood staring in amazement. His mother had been the source of many surprises throughout his life. But, this was beyond anything he'd seen or could imagine. "Now? You want to see Swanson's now?"

"I want this all settled, no loose ends. I also need you and I to be on the same page with my most recent husband, Jake. I made him sign a pre-nuptial agreement before we got married. Everything goes to you, Ann and the kids. That includes my retirement. Here's the name of the lady to see about transferring the funds." Her tone was still the same.

"Anything else?" He asked in a mildly frustrated tone.

Her mood quickly changed as she allowed herself a brief moment of emotion. "I need you to do this for me Tony. I'm not trying to add to what you and Ann are already dealing with. But, this is very important to me, and I know I can depend on you to take care of it."

"I'll get it done. But please, no more for now." He asked.

"OK, no more for now." She smiled and allowed herself a sigh. "I can see you watching me, and want you to know it'll be all right. I don't understand why or how, but who the fuck does."

"Who the fuck, you said fuck? Why mother, I'm shocked." He replied through a boyish smile.

"Ya, stick around kid. You ain't seen anything yet." She replied through a smile of her own.

"You can bet there's lots more." Tony heard his father say as he came into the room.

"Hi Paul." Olga said as she looked past her son toward her first husband.

"You look great there in the sunshine." Paul said in his most cavalier voice.

"And, you're as full of shit as ever Frisano." She added.

Tony watched as his parents bantered in ways he'd seen all his life. They brought out the best in each other in a style few could see and fewer understood. The chemistry between them was as incredible as it was powerful. Yet, it wasn't enough to keep them together.

Olga could forgive but never forget. The years of drinking, infidelity and inconsideration pushed her to a point where she decided to take no more. She never once doubted Paul's love for her. She simply asked for more than he was willing to give.

Paul never felt for any woman what he felt for Olga. There were others, but never a relationship like the one with her. Even after the divorce he kept a special place in his heart for her. He took responsibility for all his actions. As much as he regretted his mistakes he knew he would never change, and took responsibility for that too.

Sean was picking at his food when Olga walked in. She'd taken great pains to clean and dress to hide any sign of the disease that racked her body. The sight of her grandson closed off that part of her life like nothing else could. For now there was no cancer, no pain, no fear of death. "Hey Sweetheart, what's for dinner?"

247

"Hi Grandma. It's some brown stuff and some yellow stuff. It doesn't taste very good. I don't think hospitals know how to cook stuff." Sean observed.

"Well, they have to cook for lots of people, and don't have much time to do it all." She explained knowing there was more to come.

"Why don't they get more cooks? And, why can't I have a hamburger? Hamburgers are easy. You showed me how. Remember?" He loved these exchanges with Olga. She always listened, and was completely honest with him.

"Well, I'll talk to them about hamburgers, and see what they say. That sounds good to me too." Now she had a campaign, hamburgers for Sean.

"I heard them say you were in the hospital too Grandma. Did they fix you yet? My doctor is real good. I can talk to him about you if you want." He was now watching her closely through those Frisano eyes that allowed no bullshit to pass unnoticed. There were many things he couldn't possibly understand at six yours old, but few things important to him were ever ignored.

Olga allowed herself a long pause to gather her thoughts. An answer like, I'll be fine, was out of the question. He deserved more than that, and his trust in her demanded honesty. But, how could she keep it honest, and at the same time give him something he could understand. "I have some very good doctors who have already helped a lot. We're gonna give them some time to do all the work they need to do. Some things are not easy to fix. So, we have to give the people taking care of us the time they need to do their work."

Sean continued to watch his grandmother closely. Neither said anything for a time as they simply sat quietly, each giving the other some space and time. He wasn't satisfied with the answer she gave, but would accept it for now. Having her there all to himself satisfied his immediate needs.

Olga's efforts to be so honest with one so young would seem foolish to many who would take neither the time nor effort that she did. But, it was the basis of all her relationships. That approach also meant she had to be completely honest with herself. And, that caused her to face her illness with all the fear and pain it would bring.

Ann broke the temporary silence as she entered the room from the hallway where she'd been listening. Her previous night had been long, and the day even longer as she questioned every staff member who had any knowledge of treatment given to either Sean or Olga. Shortly after lunch she grabbed a couple hours sleep in the nurse's lounge, and was planning to stay another night with Sean. "How's dinner?" She asked.

"Not too good mom. Grandma's gonna get us some hamburgers if she can." He told her.

"Wow, that sounds great. Can she get me one too?" She asked.

"Grandma can do it mom." There was much more to that statement of faith than hamburgers. Both women knew what they'd soon have to face, but neither would allow anything to spoil precious moments.

Facing Change And Pain

Terry stood at the kitchen counter editing a client's manuscript as she prepared dinner. Angelina was settled in her play pen, methodically inspecting each component of the plastic entertainment center that Vic bought for her the day before. He continued to amaze Terry with his interest and devotion to Sean and his sister. It appeared so out of character for someone who once rousted gangster bars, but at the same time somehow fit this complicated man she was trying so hard to understand.

She'd learned to accept those in her life at face value, expecting no more than what they had to offer at the time. But, Vic was very different. There was always much more than he allowed others to see. She wondered if she'd ever see the whole Vic, and at the same time wasn't sure she wanted to.

"Hi girls." Vic said as he came through the front door, moved down the hall and into the kitchen to a place behind Terry. He put his arms around her and pulled her close as he kissed her neck just below her ear.

"Ah, I kind of have my hands full right now." She said as she smiled and tipped her head to expose more of her neck.

"I have my hands full too." He replied.

"I noticed. And, it's having an effect on both of us, especially you big boy." She chuckled.

"Wanna play a little before dinner?" He asked through a chuckle of his own.

By now Angelina was standing at the side of her play pen, and laughing as she watched the antics at the kitchen counter.

"We have company. So slow down, and go see your little girlfriend while I finish dinner." She directed.

"Hey Little Sugar. What have you and your Aunt Terry been doing all day?" He said as he crossed to the play pen.

Angie bounced quickly, then kicked her feet as Vic pulled her from the play area. With one smooth motion he twisted, rolled to the floor, and finished with her sitting on his chest. He then raised her in his hands so that his arms were fully extended, released her, and caught her just above his chest.

Angie squealed with glee, and Terry moaned in horror each time Vic repeated the process. "How are you going to explain to Ann and Tony that you killed their daughter?" Terry asked while shaking her head.

"Aunt Terry is getting old Angie. She doesn't recognize fun anymore. She just edits and cooks and cooks and edits. Poor old thing." Vic knew that would get a reaction, and he was right.

Before he could utter one more word Terry was on top of him with the fingers of her right hand encircling his balls. "Watch Aunt Terry Angie. She's gonna make Uncle Vic screams like a Porky the Pig."

"Hey girl, I said fun. That's not fun." He stammered.

"Depends on who's doing the squeezing and who's being squeezed." She replied.

"OK, OK Aunt Terry is fun, fun, fun." He conceded as he gently placed Angie on the floor beside them. As Terry released her grip he kicked out from under her, and the wrestling match began with all three involved in the action.

Finally Terry interrupted. "All right, my sauce is burning, and I need you to fill me in on what's going on at the hospital."

251

The change in Vic was immediate. He raised himself from the floor slowly, picked Angelina up and placed her back in her play area. After settling her in with her favorite toy he turned to Terry and said. "It's a mess. Sean is doing well, even better than expected, but Olga's there being treated for lung cancer. It doesn't look good."

She dropped the spoon she'd used to stir the sauce, lowed her head and leaned on the counter. "My God, what's next?"

"Don't even ask. I don't want to know what hits next in this shit storm." Vic began to show the anger and frustration he'd pushed aside during the day.

"How's everyone holding up?" She questioned.

"Too well." He said with a sigh. "Tony and Ann are moving in all directions at once. Both are exhausted, and neither will slow down. Paul is doing all he can to support the family, and Olga is being Olga. She's too strong to let go at a time when she needs to let go."

"What do you mean? Is she pushing everyone away?" She questioned.

"Not at all. She's as tough and determined as ever. But, it's putting pressure on everyone else. Hell, she has Tony making funeral arrangements, and reporting back to her so that she knows everything is taken care of." The more he talked the more his frustration showed.

Terry turned the stove off and crossed the room to where he was standing. She put her arms around him, and laid her head on his shoulder. "Is there something we can do?" She asked.

"Thanks." He said as he held her close.

She raised her head, and looked deeply into his eyes. "For what?"

"For being you, and being here." He told her.

A few miles away in their home at the end of a long driveway Joan dashed through the kitchen setting out all the elements for the evening meal as she talked with her sister, Nancy, about who needed to be where at what time, and how long they'd be. For her the ducks not only had to be in a row, but also on time and dressed appropriately. On the other end of that call Nancy sat politely listening even though she cared little about how the ducks marched, much less about how they were dressed.

"I have to go now Joan. I have papers to grade and............. Oh my God, what in the world is that?" Nancy exclaimed.

"What is what? What the hell is going on now?" Joan was frustrated at her sister's lack of interest, knowing Nan's ducks were scattered in all directions.

"There's something on the steps, and feathers are scattered all over the place." Nan screamed in a panic.

"Feathers, what feathers?" Joan reacted with some concern, but more frustration.

"Is jack there? Let me talk to Jack." Nancy demanded.

"What does my husband have to do with feathers? Damn it, what the hell is going on?" Joan replied.

Jack sat at the kitchen table watching what he'd seen so many times before. He knew from experience that the best plan was to simply wait until he was drawn into the action, and adjust as needed.

"Jack?" Joan heard Nan say into the phone.

"Here, I give up." Joan snapped as she passed the phone to her smiling husband.

"And how are you today?" Jack aksed in a tone he was sure didn't match the situation.

"It's dead Jack. The poor little thing is dead, and almost all its feathers are gone." Nancy shrieked.

"So, we're talking about a naked bird? How do you know he's dead?" Jack said calmly through the same broad smile.

"His head is gone. The poor thing doesn't have a head." Nan replied in a very solemn voice.

"Well that'll do it. Yep, he's probably dead." Jack was holding back the laughter building up inside.

"The cat did it again. I just fed him. Why is he killing birds? He can't be hungry." Nan questioned.

"He's returning the favor by bringing dinner to you. He'd probably appreciate it if you took a little bite of that bird. It would make him feel needed." Jack could no longer hold back the laughter.

"Damn it Jack, can you come over and pick up the little bird? I'll clean up the feathers." Nancy pleaded.

"I'll be right there." He reassured. "Be back soon." He told Joan as he headed to the garage.

"Do I want to know?" Joan asked.

"Nah." Jack replied.

By the time he reached the scene of the recent carnage the mess was already cleaned up including the body of the departed bird. Nan was

254

seated at the kitchen table with her mom, Tony's Aunt Rose, and two of Nancy's closest friends.

The conversation was far more serious than what the cat dragged in. The news of Olga's condition spread quickly, and all wanted an update. Nan was the only one present with firsthand information. Jack only knew what Joan had passed on after returning from the hospital.

"Are you sure it's lung cancer?" Jack heard Rose ask as he came in.

"I'm sure mom. Uncle Paul was positive about it." Nancy assured her.

"She's right mom." Jack told his mother-in-law. "Joan was sure that's what Paul said. Tony and Ann talked with the doctors too. There's no doubt."

"But, how can it happen to someone so young?" The stunned look on Rose's face told Jack that she simply couldn't cope with the news. She and Olga were like sisters for years.

The family had its own way of dealing with tragedy. Each member faced desperation in their own good time. The strong took care of business until the others could cope. Then the ones first to adapt were relieved by those now able to manage things. And, the roles changed through each passing of desperate times.

There was a standing unspoken rule not to dwell on a problem no matter how serious. Difficulties were not avoided or ignored. Rather, they were included with whatever time and effort was required, and then set aside until they demanded more attention. In the meantime life included laughter over headless birds, and wrestling matches in the kitchen.

Olga's time with Sean was her way of winning a battle with her disease knowing she couldn't win the war. But, winning those daily battles made life worth living no matter how bleak the long term outcome might be.

255

Sean would soon learn these lessons the way all had learned before him. It was the glue that held them all together. It was the meaning of family to them all.

Tony picked Angelina up late in the afternoon, and declined Terry's invitation for dinner. After bringing them up to speed on the day's hospital news he headed for home for some quiet time with his daughter. As usual, Ann stayed at the hospital with Sean for what they hoped would be his last night there.

After waving goodbye to Tony Terry turned to find Vic directly behind her. As the front door slammed shut he wrapped his arms around her, and pulled her so close that it seemed she could feel his heart beating. She placed her hand on the back of his neck she asked. "Are you all right?"

"No." He answered in a low, tired voice.

"Lockup and turn of the lights, and I'll see you upstairs." She said softly.

By the time Vic entered their bed room she was already in bed. When he pulled back the covers to join her he saw she was already undressed, looking as seductive as she did loving and understanding.

"Can you read my mind?" He asked

"Sometime you're an open book. Other times you amaze me with something completely new and unexpected." She told him.

"Right now I just want to hold you for a while. I think I need that." He told her as he pulled her close.

In the months that passed the family laughed whenever they could, and cried when the pain of it all built to the breaking point. Each of them in their own way found that special something that made life precious no matter how difficult it became.

Olga would load up on pain pills, and clean and dress for Sunday dinner. Rose and Joan would do her hair as they talked endlessly about nothing at all.

During the gatherings Sean watched his grandmother closely. All the makeup and hair spray in the world couldn't hide the changes in her. One afternoon when all the guests finally left he turned to Tony and asked. "Why can't the doctors fix grandma? They fixed my leg."

Tony felt a huge knot build in his throat as his mind raced for an answer he thought his son might understand. He turned slowly, sat down in the nearest chair and said. "Come here buddy."

As Sean climbed on his lap he decided that honesty was essential, but in a form his son could handle. He knew he had to go slowly. "Some things are very hard to fix. Some time they have to fix just a little bit at a time cause the problem is so big."

"Is grandma gonna die dad?" Sean looked deeply into his father's eyes as the tears began to run down his cheeks.

"Not today buddy. We'll get to see her some more." Tony felt his own tears flow as he pulled his son close.

"It's OK for us to cry now isn't it dad?" Sean observed.

"Yes son. We'll cry a little together." Tony said as he held Sean tightly.

As the months passed the family watched Olga grow weaker. She would rally and fight until her energy and spirit failed, then rally again. One afternoon as Tony sat by her side as she dosed he began to feel frustration and anger well up inside. Watching her needless suffering was becoming more than he could bear.

Somehow feeling his despair she opened her eyes and looked deeply into his. "Don't son. It's alright." She said in a calm, reassuring voice.

257

"No ma, it's not alright. You deserve better than this." He tried to choke back his anger.

"I've watched you come a long way, but you still have a long way to go. Don't make it any harder than it has to be." Her voice was still calm, and now also tender.

"It's just not right." He said as he shook his head.

"Listen to me now Anthony. Sometime you have to let life go in order to get the most from it. It was never intended to last forever, and never supposed to be easy. Holding on to the past too tightly keeps you from the best of the future. It's time to move on. And, if that means letting go then you have to let go." She reached out, took his hand and squeezed it gently.

"I wish we had more time. You and I have lots more to talk about." He said as he took her hand in both of his.

"Go home son. Ann and the kids need you, and I need to rest." Her words somehow released him, and allowed him to leave her. Once again this amazing woman showed him the way.

After Tony left, and her room was dark and quiet she allowed herself time to let go. Her first reaction was panic mixed with terror over what she could neither understand nor control. The disease that would soon take her life was beyond what her strength and courage could handle.

Suddenly she realized the solution to this overwhelming condition. She didn't have to control or understand any of it. There was nothing to fix, nothing to explain or understand. It was all the natural order of things, just another part of life.

She began to understand the true meaning of faith, and realized how powerful it could be when strength and courage were not enough. It was

258

the answer to all questions that had no answers. It gave her peace that she hadn't known for as long as she could remember.

The Family Moves On

Tony sat on the patio looking out toward the river, but seeing little of what surrounded him. His mind took him back to places that meant so much in the years when life was simple. He could almost feel the heat on his neck as he struggled through a double-header in August, and smell the grass in the fall as football practice ground through daily doubles.

He closed his eyes and thought of Annie, and evenings in the vacant parking lot by the river. He remembered the fragrance of her hair as it brushed across his face, the softness of her skin and the warmth of her laughter. There was so much then that was new and stimulating. Even the struggles were rewarding as they brought new challenges. These places and times allowed him to test himself and grow.

But, now challenges became burdens in a work environment where money was king, and creativity and dedication were only measured on the bottom line of a balance sheet. He was secure in this place where he didn't fit only because of his own skill and his relationship with those who could make machinery do what few others could. He stayed only because of responsibilities to those he loved.

His dream world was shattered by a voice coming from the kitchen door. "Hey pop, hit me a few grounders before supper?" He heard Sean request.

"OK, grab some extra balls, and get me my bat. Stay loose. Remember? Ya gotta feel it." He smiled as he remembered sessions in the back yard with his own father.

Ann watched through the window, but only for a few moments. Angie needed help with a school project, and dinner was only half prepared. There was laundry to finish, and a check book to balance. And, she would not rest until these things were complete, and all was ready for the next day.

Following backyard baseball practice Tony and Sean washed for dinner, and entered the kitchen where Ann was darting from table to stove to refrigerator and back again. "Can we help?" Tony asked. Then realized both the question and his timing were wrong.

"It's done. Can you tell Angie to come and eat?" She snapped.

As Tony turned toward the hall and Angie's room he saw Sean hug his mother and say. "Smells great. Love you mom."

"Love you too. Go sit down." She replied in a matter of fact tone.

"Dinner's ready girl. Come and eat." Tony said to his daughter through her bedroom door.

"Can I eat later dad? I have so much to do." She asked.

Tony crossed the room to the desk where she sat, pulled the pencil from behind her ear and used it for a marker as he closed her book. "No." He said as he kissed her on top of the head.

She smiled, and followed him to the table where Sean was sampling bacon bits from the salad. "Get your fingers out of my food mister." Ann said in the same matter of fact tone.

Tony, Sean and Angie chatted through their meal about events of the day that included bits of information on new friends, old enemies, their homework load and who got in trouble for what. From time to time Ann looked up from her checkbook and calculator with a question, observation or advice. Tony watched in amazement at her ability to stay on top of the conversation, balance accounts and slice pork roast all at the same time.

After dinner as Ann began to reach for dirty dishes and cups Tony said. "Sean and I got this. You take Angie back to her room and ancient

Egypt. Her place in the history book is marked with a pencil that has teeth marks chewed half way through it."

"Hey pop, I have home work too." Sean objected halfheartedly.

"That's right, and it includes dirty dishes." Tony informed him.

By eight o'clock the Egyptian empire was concurred and Sean's math problems solved. Tony settled back in his favorite chair with the latest Sports Illustrated as Sean flipped through the TV channels. The girls came in with a small basket of brushes ribbons and various gadgetry necessary for proper hair care.

Suddenly Angie took the basket from her mother, crossed the room and jumped into her father's lap. "Remember how I used to make you beautiful when I was little dad?" She asked through a subtle laugh.

"Yes I do, and still have scars in my scalp dug by the hair pins." Tony recalled.

"I think you need to be beautiful again." She said as she captured a handful of his hair with a spring loaded comb, then laughed loudly at the ridiculous form his head now took. As she leaned forward to attach another Tony poked her under her arm causing the second comb to fly through the air and bounce off the nearest wall.

"I can't do this if you poke me father." She protested.

"I know daughter." He informed her.

"Mom, he won't hold still." Angie told her mother.

In a flash Ann had hold of both of Tony's ears and ordered. "Get him girl. He's all yours."

In the same instant Sean grabbed both his mother's ankles, and began to pull her to the center of the room. In seconds all four were on the floor in a pile of magazines, hair pins and pillows. As the hair pin battle continued the guys strength and quickness failed them both because of their laughter.

This was Tony's and Ann's world now, and it held little time for the past. The good was set aside along with the bad to make room for so many things that were new and needed attention. They both found great satisfaction in their family and friends, and controlled their places at work with all the energy and determination that their jobs required.

Vic's and Terry's lives had taken the most dramatic turns. He took on his chosen trade as a steamfitter with passion and determination that no other craftsman showed. In a trade where specialization was the general approach, Vic took on all the various specialties, and was proficient in each one. But, his broad knowledge base was coupled with an approach that left no room for politics or compromise. Many of the fitters with whom he worked considered him a threat to their job security, and many contractors viewed him as a huge pain in the ass. But, he worked steadily and was in demand because when Vic finished his work rework was never necessary.

Terry too had carved out a new place for herself. She managed a small local bakery that produced cookies, cupcakes and bread in huge quantities in spite of the size of the facility. Vic and Tony helped with improvements and provided considerable technical support. But, it was Terry who kept the daily operation humming, and a difficult work force moving in the same direction. She had a remarkable ability to bring control back from chaos, and manipulate people without making them feel manipulated.

Their lives were also filled with family responsibilities that included two children of their own, a son and daughter they adopted shortly after they were married. Both came from troubled homes, and needed a combination of love, special attention and control that took all the energy and creativity that Vic and Terry could provide.

Late one evening as Vic came through the door after a particularly long day he found Terry in the kitchen finishing a phone call. "Who was on the phone?" He asked.

"I was talking to Ann". She told him as she leaned against the counter and watched Vic closely.

"How they doin? I haven't seen either of them in a while. We should get together soon." He too was now watching closely, knowing by her body language that something was up.

"I called to ask her about Bupropion. There's a bottle of it in the medicine cabinet with your name on the label." Her arms were folded and her gaze was fixed.

"Why didn't you ask me." He questioned.

"You weren't here, and I wanted a nurse's input. She says the dosage is pretty high, and that it's an anti-depressant. Talk to me Vic. What's going on, and why didn't you tell to me about this?"

He took a long, deep breath, and gave himself a moment to gather his thoughts. The anger was building quickly, and he had no idea why. "The dosage is high particularly since I'm taking three a day. That's about enough to make a pit-bull think he's a fucking butterfly."

Terry said nothing, but continued to watch him closely knowing he needed time. He was always able to master the moment when issues were important.

"I'm seeing a shrink, and have been for a few weeks. An old G.I. buddy recommended him. The drugs are to get my system back in balance.

Basically, there are some things that kick me into high gear, and I have a tough time calming down." He said as he fought to stay in control.

"Does it bother you to talk to me about it?" She asked.

"No." He tried to reassure her.

"Come on Vic. This is me. Be honest." She demanded.

Vic now felt the rage building from deep inside. He fought with all he had to stay in control. Who the hell was she to demand anything? He didn't owe an explanation to her or anyone else. Fuck her and this whole shit for nothing world. His mind raced from one hateful thought to another. "Slow down Terry." He managed to say.

The look on his face sent a cold chill through her. The change in him was so sudden and dramatic that she now needed a moment of her own. "Are you OK?" She finally managed to ask.

"No I'm not. You want honesty? Be careful what you ask for. The reality that goes along with it sucks. There's a side of me you don't want to see. I'm doing all I can to deal with it while I keep the best for you and the kids. That's the best way I can explain it." He was glad to get that much out as he fought the demons inside.

"I had no idea. I don't know what to say except I love you. What can I do?" She asked in a concerned and uncertain voice that was totally unnatural for someone as strong and independent as she.

He took time for another long pause, then said. "You're already doing it, and have been for a long time. I depend on you more than I can say. You're my contact with a world where I want to be, a place away from a part of me that's dark and miserable."

Terry suddenly turned her gaze down the hall to where their daughter, Katie, was standing. She'd come through the door unnoticed during the intense kitchen conversation. Vic followed Terry's gaze and greeted his daughter with. "Hey, Sweetheart. Welcome home." He moved quickly down the hall to add a hug and kiss to the greeting.

"Butch needs a ride home from practice. Actually, he's at Bobby Turner's place. He said he checked with you, and it was all OK." Katie told him. Both she and her brother were very good at handling the complicated process of who was where, and what was needed. Neither took advantage of the opportunities that the complexities presented. They both earned the trust that Vic and Terry gave them.

"OK, I'm on my way. I'll be right back with the kid and a pizza. Love ya both." Vic said as he headed out the front door.

Katie headed down the hall to join her mother who was still leaning on the kitchen counter. After a short pause she asked. "What's wrong with dad?"

Now it was Terry's turn for a long sigh. She knew she must be honest. But, how much was too much for her twelve year old daughter to understand, particularly when there was so much she, herself, didn't understand. "There's nothing wrong that will keep him from loving us and being there for us. Your father is a very strong man Katie, sometimes too strong. He has a lot on his plate now, and sometimes it catches up with him." She stopped there and waited for a reaction.

Although Katie understood there was still a deep feeling of insecurity that came any time things at home weren't just right. She had a very close relationship with both her parents, and depended on them deeply. "He looks very tired mom. Is he working too hard?" She asked.

Terry put her arm around her daughter, and hugged her tightly. "Ya, he's working too hard, and he's come a long way over the years. Sometimes those years add up and make things tougher."

"What can I do mom? He does so much for us." She asked in a tone much older than her twelve years should produce.

"Give him a hug, and a little time out of your day. You'll be amazed at how much that can help." Terry felt good about that bit of honesty.

Butch bolted through the front door of his friend's house as Vic pulled up in front. He stumbled a little as he made his way down the steps, a move he often repeated as he tried hard to deal with all that a fourteen year old boy must face as his body changes rapidly. His growth rate exploded over the past year, and mastering the new bulk and strength was often more than he could handle. "Hi pop." He said as he opened the passenger side door.

"Hi buddy. How was your day?"

"I made the team, but just barely. I'm third string". He watched closely at his father's reaction to the news of his limited success.

"We talked about this before. But, I guess it's time for a review. The sun don't shine on the same dog's ass every day. Remember?" Vic told him in a way that showed both honesty and sincerity.

"Well, this dog's ass hasn't seen the sun in quite a while." Butch said solemnly.

"Careful with the dog's ass thing. You're gonna slip in front of your mom, and we'll both be in trouble." Vic said through a half smile.

"Honestly pop, I worked my butt off at practice, harder than any of the guys who made first team. When is it my turn?" Butch's frustration was beginning to show.

"Listen Butch. All you can control is what you do and how you do it. You're growing son, faster than you can handle right now. But, you're learning at the same time. And, the more you learn about yourself the

267

better you'll be at whatever you try. That's what sports is all about, learning who you are and what you can be." Vic understood the hard lessons that growing up brings, and was determined to pass all he could onto his son.

"By the end of practice I was stumbling all over myself dad. The guys make me look like a fool." The hurt was showing deeply in Butch, and Vic could see it all.

"Son, no one can make you a fool. Only you can do that. Each time you stumble you have two choices. You can either get up or stay down. In all the years I've known you I've never seen you stay down. That makes me very proud of you." Vic said it in a way that let Butch know he was being totally honest and sincere.

Vic's response struck a nerve and Butch's tone showed it. But, he continued to press. "Wouldn't you rather have a starter for a son?"

"No, I'd rather have a son who'd help decide what kind of pizza to order." He replied.

"Thin crust combination." Was the immediate response.

By the end of dinner both extra -large pizzas were gone, and Butch was responsible for finishing most of one himself along with nearly a full quart of milk. As he stood with the rest of the family to leave the table he managed to tip his chair over backward while kicking the nearest table leg hard enough to spill what was left of the milk. His sister wasn't about to let this go by without some comment. "Mom, can he leave the table before us from now on? That way we can each hold onto something before it hits the floor."

"Thank you for making me feel even more like a klutz sis." Butch half snarled.

"Love you brother." She replied "Can you take care of my part of doing dishes tonight? I have lots of homework?" She added. Then without waiting for a reply she turned toward the hall and stairway to her room.

Before she made the turn at the corner of the kitchen a wet dish cloth hit her in the middle of the back, stuck for a moment and then dropped to the floor. "If that leaves a stain on this blouse you idiot I'll kill you." She screamed as she grabbed the wet cloth and dashed toward him.

As soon as she was within reach Butch grabbed both her wrists, pushed her to arm's length and shuffled to avoid her kicking feet. He was in total control until he turned to his parents and said. "Look mom, we're dancing, we're dancing."

The brief lapse in concentration was all Katie needed to plant the toe of her shoe directly onto her brother's shin bone. But, the satisfaction was limited because there was more damage done to her foot than his leg. "You big gorilla, you broke my toe." She exclaimed.

"OK, let big brother see your toe zee woe zee." He said through a satisfied laugh.

"He's an animal mom. We need to get him a cage. In the last half an hour he ate enough to feed Africa, drank more milk than a whole herd of cows can produce in a month, smashed the dinette and broke my toe." She exclaimed.

"Ya, I know. Ya gotta love him." Terry replied. "And, stick around until the dishes are done. You have the rest of the evening to finish homework. We'll help with it if you have trouble."

"It's OK mom. I got it covered. Hit the books sis, and take care of your toe zee." Butch volunteered.

"Thanks big brother. I owe you." Katie said as she punched him in the arm.

Later that night after dishes, homework and the last half of an old movie Butch had seen dozens of times he leaned through the open door of Katie's room. "Got a minute to talk?" He asked.

"Sure, come on in." She replied.

After checking that both Vic and Terry were out of ear shot he found a place close enough for quiet conversation. "I'm worried about dad sis. He's a lot more serious about everything, and not his regular self. I mean he's always there, but different. It's like there's something wrong."

"When I came home from school he and mom were talking in the kitchen about some medicine he's taking. I think it's supposed to calm him down. As soon as they saw me they stopped talking. Then he took off to bring you home." She said showing her own concern.

"We had a talk this afternoon, and he was the same old dad. The things he told me helped a lot. But, last week end while we were watching the game he was just staring at the TV like he didn't even see what was going on. It was weird." He told Katie as he watched closely for her reaction.

She returned his solemn gaze with one of her own. "I'm scared Butch. I don't know what's going on, and I'm scared. If anything happened to mom or dad I don't know what I'd do." She said as she choked back her tears.

"We need to talk to mom. We need to know what's going on." He decided.

"No, we can't do that. What if it makes everything worse? What if she gets mad at him or something just cause of us?" Her voice was louder, and the tears began to show.

"Not so loud Katie. They'll here you." He said as he tried to calm her. Finally he slid close, put his arm around her, and held her tight.

"We gotta be careful Butch. We can't make things worse for mom and dad. No problems at school. No trouble with the family. We gotta be extra good." Katie was finding some satisfaction in this plan to help. It was her way of taking some kind of control over something she couldn't possibly understand. "Will you help me?"

Both of them shared memories of the misery that filled their lives before Vic and Terry became their parents. The thought of losing this new life was more that either could bear. This fear was leading them to a place where no child should go, a place where they grow too fast and turn away from being a child far too soon. And, to make things worse they would hide the whole thing from those who could help them most.

It only took another year for Butch to begin to find himself physically. And, by age sixteen he was six feet two and two-hundred-thirty-five pounds of mostly muscle and bone. What's more, that bulk was doing exactly what he asked of it.

But, he struggled with two nagging problems. Walking the straight and narrow with Katie was becoming more than he wanted to handle. And, while things of interest came easy for him, he had little tolerance for routine tasks. Classes like philosophy and social studies he viewed as a complete waste of time, but excelled at math and science.

His personal life followed a similar pattern. He chose his few friends carefully, and was close to each of them. By contrast he had no time for casual relationships or high school's social activities. He was viewed by many his age as a loner who was callous and insensitive.

One winter afternoon as Butch and his close friend Bob were driving home Bob mentioned. "Linda Turner and Craig broke up, so she doesn't have a date for the Snowball Dance. Why don't you ask her? She's a knock out man."

271

"I sit next to her in English Lit., and she never so much as gives me the time of day." Butch replied in a mildly annoyed tone.

"She thinks you're stuck up. Lots of people do. You need to work on it." Bob informed cautiously.

"She thinks I'm what? Are you kidding me?" Butch replied in amazement.

"Hey man, I'm not trying to make you mad, just help. I know it's not true, but most times it's how you come across to anyone who doesn't know you." Only Bob and a very few others could have this kind of conversation with Butch.

"I can't believe this shit. All I want is to be left alone. Maybe the problem is I don't really give a shit what people think. If they want to judge me then judge away. Who the fuck cares anyway?" The fury in his voice even surprised Butch.

After a long pause Bob asked. "You OK man?"

"Ya, but, I don't have time for the petty bullshit. Too much of the day is full of who said what to who, and how this one feels about this, that and the other. The rest of it is a pissing match to see who gets the last word. And, God help anyone who can't hold their own. I've had it." Butch was no longer talking to his friend. Instead, he was attacking his whole world. There was relief in letting his feelings out. It made things clearer in his own mind.

Neither said anything during the rest of the ride home. As Bob stopped the car in front of the driveway he said slowly. "I'm sorry that I said anything Butch. I had no idea it would make you that mad."

"No big deal. It's not you or anything you said. It's me, and I can deal with it, and all the rest of the shit." He said as he slid from the passenger

272

seat, slammed the car door behind him, and neither waited for a reply or looked back.

As he walked through the front door a sense of uneasiness came over him. His mother and father were across from one another with the kitchen island separating them. It was obvious that their conversation stopped because of him.

Vic swung around the end of the island, and greeted his son. "Hey buddy, how was your day?"

His voice was slurred and walk down the hall unsteady. As he reached Butch the smell of booze and stale cigarette smoke was almost overpowering. He leaned heavily on his son as they made their way into the kitchen. Butch said nothing as he looked in his mother's direction for some indication of what was going on.

Vic slid into one of the kitchen chairs and said. "Sit down buddy. I want to talk to you. You see these?" He said as he pointed to Butch's hands. "Never be afraid to use these cause you don't have to back away from anything."

Butch's gaze jumped from Terry to Vic and back to his mother again as he tried to take in and make some sense of what was happening around him. It was like he was looking at two people he didn't know, neither of whom fit those who'd been so much of a part of his life. He said nothing as he turned away from the kitchen, and headed for his room.

He could feel as much as hear his father following him as his mother said in a deep, angry voice. "Leave him alone." At that same moment Vic pushed past him, and walked out the front door.

Butch tossed his jacket on the floor, and flopped onto his bed. As he did his mother came in and sat beside him.

"We need to talk about your dad." She said in a calm and caring voice.

"No we don't. You married him. That makes him your problem, not mine." He growled.

Terry sat in disbelief as her son's words ripped into her heart. In her entire life she'd never been this confused, frightened and at a total loss for words or actions.

Across town Ann hurried through the kitchen door leading from the garage. The phone was ringing, and had been since she pulled in. She reached it just before the answering machine kicked on. As she picked up she heard Terry say. "You got time to talk Ann."

"Sure, what's going on?" She replied in a concerned tone. Terry sounded shaken in a way totally unlike her.

"I'd like to do this face to face if we can." Her voice sounded a little more hopeful.

"Wanna come over here. I'll put the pot on, and we have a little something to add to the coffee if you like." Ann assured her.

"I'll be there in a half an hour." Terry said as she headed back up stairs.

When she reached Butch's room she found him still laying on his bed, blindly staring at the ceiling. "I want to talk to Aunt Ann for a while, but I need to know you're OK for now. I don't have any answers for all this, but I'm going to find some. Can you give me some time?" Her voice was now controlled, and her focus totally on Butch's reaction.

"Take all the time you need." He snapped.

Terry crossed the room to the foot of his bed. She was now back to the woman who set confusion and despair aside for reason and action. "Listen to me Butch. I know you're angry and confused. So am I." Her tone included confidence and sincerity to a level that got his full attention. "I need you to hang on while I have time to sort this out. Can you do that for me?"

Butch looked her straight in the eye as he said. "I've had it mom. Don't you get it? I'm burned out. I don't have anything left. If that makes me weak, then OK, call me weak. If that disappoints you, then I guess you'll have to live with it."

"I don't think you're weak, and I'm not disappointed in you. But, I think you're letting your anger and frustration take over for the strength and reason I know you have. I'm asking you to help me son because I need your help right now. Can you be here for your sister when she gets home? " She asked with all the sincerity her heart could provide.

"Why ma? What did we do to deserve more crap? Answer me that and I'll do anything you ask." He matched her sincerity with his own.

She sat down beside him and took his hand. "I wish I had answers for you. I wish I could explain it. I wish for your sake and mine I could make the pieces fit. But, I can't. All I can do is promise I'll find a way to make things better. Can you be here for your sister while I work on it."

"Do what you have to do. I'll be here for Katie. What do I do if dad comes home?" His tone told her she could depend on him, at least for now.

"Wait til his back is turned, and hit him with a bat." She said as she stood and left his room.

As promised Ann had coffee on, and a bottle of bourbon uncorked in the center of the kitchen table. "Come on in. Tony took the kids out for pizza. So, we have the place to ourselves." She told her friend as Terry came through the front door.

"Thanks. I'm sorry if you felt you had to chase the family away because of me. How did you know I was looking for a little privacy?" Terry asked.

"Tony and I have known Vic for a long time. He reads like an open book, and so do you. You guys are family, as close as any we have." She reassured, then went on. "I know things have been tough for a while, and wasn't surprised when you called. Is he back on medication?" Ann inquired.

"No, and he's not doing counseling anymore either. But, he's drinking every week end, and doing it around the kids. Today was the first time I've seen him drunk during the week. It really surprised me." Terry admitted.

"Is he giving you a hard time when he's drunk?" Ann asked.

"He's not abusive. In fact, he's usually more of a party animal. But, he goes way overboard, and it gets to be embarrassing. Katie tolerates it, but Butch hates it. He's always put Vic up on a pedestal, and it tears him apart to see his dad act like a fool." As Terry described the situation it was clear that she had an accurate picture of the pieces of this puzzle, but just as clear that she couldn't make the pieces fit.

"Does he just keep sliding farther downhill?" Ann was trying to find a pattern to the problem.

"It's crazy. Today he'll be all the way at the bottom of the hill, and tomorrow he'll be the same guy I fell in love with. Honestly, it's a classic Dr. Jekyll and Mr. Hyde. I never know who the hell will come walking through my door." Her answer showed her deep confusion and frustration. "He's a good man. The best I've ever known. Whatever's got a hold on him is very powerful." She added.

"How are you and the kids holding up?" Ann asked still trying to find a pattern, and understand how much pressure they were under.

"It's one day at a time. But, even when things are good I can see the kids are very nervous about when things will turn to shit again. And, I react the same way. It's pushing us farther and farther away from him. I know he can see it. And, I know it bothers him a lot." For the first time Terry admitted to herself that things had to change. She and the kids couldn't go on like this.

Ann was beginning to understand their situation, and saw that their conversation was making things clearer to Terry. "What are you going to do?" She asked.

"I have no idea Ann. I love him more than I thought it was possible to love anyone. I feel him slipping away. I don't understand why, and don't know how to stop it. Never in my life have I felt so helpless." The look of desperation on Terry's face said more than all the words they'd exchanged.

Their conversation went on for another hour, and included lots of old fashioned girl talk intended to provide some relief for Terry. Suddenly they heard Angie say. "Hi Aunt Terry. We brought you a pizza. Are Katie and Butch here?"

"No sweetheart. They're at home getting a jump on homework. Thank you for pizza. It smells great." Terry answered.

"Bring um over next time, OK?" Angie asked.

"I promise." Terry assured.

"You guys need to get a jump on your own stuff". Tony ordered as his kids headed for their rooms. When they were out of range Tony turned to Terry. "You want me to find him?" He asked.

"He has to find himself Tony." She said. Then, after a long pause added. "Yes, just for tonight I'd like you to find him."

He walked slowly around the table and kissed Ann. "I'll be back as soon as I can." He assured her. When he passed by Terry he gave her a hug, and added. "I'll get him back home tonight. Tomorrow we'll deal with tomorrow."

There was a night club in the center of town where the saying "what happens here stays here" fit perfectly. Tony found his friend there, alone at the end of the bar nursing a scotch and soda. "Just a tonic water." He told the bar tender as he sat down next to Vic.

After an unusually long time Vic asked. "Did she send you to find me?"

"Oh fuck no. I come here every night to stare at the wall and drink tonic water." Tony said still looking straight ahead.

After an equally long time Vic told Tony. "I can't stop. I'm ruining my life, losing the woman I love and hurting my kids, and I can't stop."

"I know." Tony said.

"So what the hell do I do now? Even when I'm OK everyone is waiting for me to fuck up. I'm waiting for me to fuck up." Vic admitted.

After a long sigh Tony said. "Well, the answer is not here. I don't have an answer, and don't even know where to start looking. But, I guaran-God-damned-tee it's not here."

"What happens if I can't find an answer?" Vic was now staring directly at his friend.

"Oh, I dun no. You could die in an alley, blow your brains out, drown in your own puke, any number of things are possible." Now Tony turned and looked directly into Vic's eyes. "It starts here man, right here, right now. You don't look back cause you can't change the past. You don't look ahead cause you can't control the future. You take care of business right now cause now is the only place you can make a difference."

A puzzled look came over Vic's face as he asked. "Where did all that come from?"

"How the hell do you think I make it through the day, each and every day? You know how many times I want to just crawl into a bottle and drink myself to death? I got a story for you Brother. The last time I was in the hospital for knee surgery this nurse in admitting asked if I had any thoughts of harming myself or anyone else. I thought to myself, ya sister every fucking day, and every miserable night. But, I was sure if I was honest I'd never get out of the psych. ward and into surgery. So, I took control, lied to her, and got my knee done. I did that in the moment, and set the past with all its bullshit aside. That's just one little example of how I do it. You're gonna have to find your own way." Tony stopped, and let things sink in.

Vic sat in amazement for a long moment. "So, maybe I start by going home?"

"That's a start. On the way you're gonna think of a thousand reasons to turn around, and come back here. You gotta make that trip home yourself. On the way keep in mind that what you want is there, not here." As he finished Tony knew how hard the trip was going to be.

"What if I don't make it?" There was fear in Vic's voice.

"Listen to me Vic. You'll make it home tonight. That's not a guarantee you'll make it every night. But, don't beat yourself up over it. The key is to keep trying." Tony knew he had to take things slowly. There wasn't much more to say tonight. But, he added. "You can't do this alone. I can't either. Call me tomorrow."

As Vic walked through the front door he saw Butch and Katie in the kitchen. Their conversation stopped as soon as he walked in. "You guys OK?" He asked.

"We're fine dad." Katie assured him.

He said no more as he climbed the stairs. When in the bed room he dropped his coat on the closet floor, and rolled onto the bed still fully dressed. In a few short minutes Katie stuck her head through the doorway and asked. "Are you OK?"

"I'm good, just very tired. Thanks for asking." He said.

Somehow Katie knew her father needed time and space now. Even a hug and goodnight kiss would be out of place. Where this insight and wisdom comes from in one so young no one can explain. Sometime the greatest of things have no explanation. She knew at that moment the night would be OK, and passed her relief onto her brother.

A few minutes later Terry came home and found Butch and Katie at the table finishing off the TV dinners Katie prepared. "I brought tacos, but it looks like I'm a little late". She said as she set the bag of food down.

"I'll have one". Butch replied as he pulled the bag open.

Katie leveled a stare at her brother and shook her head as she said. "You're a bottomless pit."

"Hey, they don't make frozen dinners for real people. They're designed for little girls." Butch replied. "Did you get something mom?" He asked.

"I had something at Aunt Ann's place. Thanks for holding down the fort." She told him as she included a quick hug.

"Dad's home, but he was out of reach before I could get the bat." He told her through a subtle smile.

"I'll take care of it tonight." She replied through a smile of her own.

She found her husband on the bed in the dark with his hands behind his head still staring at the ceiling. As she sat beside him she said. "Glad to have you home."

"Tony got me headed in this direction. But then, you already know that." He told her as he reached out and took her hand.

"He's a good man, but so are you. Maybe you forget that sometime, but we don't." She was now looking directly into his deep, dark eyes trying to gather all she could from this very complicated man she loved.

"I've never felt so much like a fool. I've never been so disgusted with myself." He began.

"I know……" She tried to add, but he cut her off.

As he squeezed her hand he continued. "I did a lot of thinking on the way home, and wish I could say I come up with answers. But honestly, I just found lots more questions. The hardest thing to face is the fact that I can't make this right on my own. Before I started home Tony told me about sessions he went through at the V.A. They were lots more intense than my sessions. I'm going to talk to them tomorrow."

"Tony was in therapy?" She questioned in amazement.

"For six solid months. He said it was one of the hardest things he's done, but it got him on the right track. The thing he told me that stuck with me most is that it was only the beginning."

"Tony is as solid as they come. I've never seen him out of control." She was still trying to make some sense of what she heard.

"You see of Tony what he allows you to see. It's really him, but just one small part." As Vic went on he was beginning to understand more about himself as a few more pieces began to fit. Then Terry remembered her comment to Ann about Jekyll and Hyde. But, she still couldn't come to grips with what could cause such a huge change to happen so quickly.

"So what's happening with you is happening with Tony too?" She asked. "Is it because of Vietnam?"

"I don't know. Hell, the war was over for both of us years ago. Why would it cause problems now? That's the part that doesn't make sense." He was beginning to feel pressure, frustration and anger again, and each was building quickly. Each beat of his heart was like a pounding hammer. Sweat was forming on his forehead. As he sat up in bed he felt the room closing in on him.

Before either could say another word the doorbell rang. In a few seconds Katie hollered up the stairs. "Uncle Tony is here mom."

In what seemed like only a few seconds Tony was in the bedroom doorway looking directly at Vic. In an even shorter time he was standing in front of them. In a calm, but very commanding voice he said. "Take a deep breath."

Vic simply stared up at him. Terry's focus jumped from one man to the other.

In the same voice Tony demanded. "Breath God-damn-it." As Vic took a breath Tony continued. "Keep breathing, and listen to your breath. If you lose focus don't worry about it. Just get back to it one breath at a time." After a few more breaths Vic's eyes began to wander around the room, and Tony jumped in again. "Your breath, just your breath and nothing else."

The process went on for five more minutes. Vic didn't seem to be much better, but wasn't any worse. Finally in anger and frustration he said. "You plan to stay the night watching me breath?"

"Did they give you any meds. when you were at the V.A.?"

"I'm not taking that shit. I'm no junkie." Vic demanded.

"Where is it?" Tony snapped back.

After a long, hateful stare Vic said. "On the top shelf of the closet."

In a flash Terry retrieved the poorly hidden bottle of pills. After reading the label she said. "He can't take them with alcohol."

"I told you I'm not letting a bottle of pills run my life. I don't need that shit I said." He told them.

"This isn't the rest of your life. It's now, one night, one minute of one evening. Remember what I said about the past and future. You have no place in either. Now is the only time you can control. If the pills help get you control then start them in the morning. Don't worry about how long you need them. Use them as just one more tool." Tony's voice was still calm, and now had an honest tone.

Vic looked at Terry and then back at Tony. "I still don't get it. Why now? It doesn't make any sense." He said in an almost beaten voice.

"Look at it this way my Brother. You took two huge steps tonight. The most important one was realizing you have a huge problem that needs attention. The second was trying something to help yourself when you thought nothing would help. There'll be lots more steps. But those will come in their own time." Tony assured him.

"When does this shit end man?" Vic asked in the same beaten tone.

"What did we just do for five minutes? What did I tell you about the what, when, why and how? Get back in the present Vic. You can do that. You just did." Tony reminded him.

Vic shook his head, closed his eyes and began to breath. As he did Tony said just loud enough for Terry to hear. "A walk, a run, a cold shower, a good work out also work. Try them all. But, above all remember that the worst will pass. It never stays. The trick is to hang on, and get through it. You can do this man."

Tony stood slowly, and walked from the room. Terry followed. As they reached the bottom of the stairs she took his arm and said. "Thanks you." Then questioned. "How did you know you should come over?"

"Getting him home was just the first step. I knew he'd have problems tonight. There are ways to deal with this. But, it takes lots of time, effort and help." Tony said as he tried to fill in some of the blanks.

"But, when DOES it end Tony?" She asked in a desperate voice.

He looked her squarely in the eye and said. "It doesn't, not for the rest of his life." Then assured her. "You can still have a life with him, a good one. But, you both need to know that dealing with the demons has to be his number one priority. Get him back to the V.A. as soon as you can. If they are too busy to see him again try the local Vet Center. They work much faster."

"What do I tell the kids?" She asked.

"Tell them the truth. Their dad was wounded, and the wound needs treatment." Then he pointed down the hall where Butch and Katie were standing, and watching intently. "Somehow I think they already know." He added.

"Thank you again, and thank Ann for me. You guys are the best." She said with complete sincerity.

After closing the door behind Tony Terry headed down the hall where Butch and Katie were still standing. Once by their side she put an arm around each and asked. "You guys OK?"

"I don't understand all this, but feel better than I did. What happens now?" Katie asked.

"We get ready for tomorrow, and go to bed." Terry told her daughter, then turned to Butch. "How are you doing?" She asked.

"I think I should still hit him with the bat." He replied.

When Terry returned to their bed room she found Vic still seated on the bed slumped slightly with his elbows on his knees. As she sat down beside him she ordered through a subtle smile. "Breath!"

"Fuck you and Tony, you breath." He replied through an understanding smile of his own.

She leaned against him, and rested her head on his shoulder, then wrapped her hands around his upper arm. Most of the muscle tension was gone, but she still felt his anxiety . She knew she only had hold of part of him, but it was more than she had a short time before. There was still enough left of the man she loved to keep her hanging on and struggling for more.

Vic's mind was racing from one unrelated item to another. He felt there were countless things he had to do, but had no clear picture of any of them. He clung to Tony's reassurance that it will pass, and focused on surviving until it did.

He was up and down countless times that night. The few hours sleep he managed were filled with dreams and memories he could only vaguely recall the next morning. They were more moods than images, but the feelings they left behind took him back to the day before. He wondered how long he had to hang on, then remembered Tony's advice about things to try.

After calling in sick he pulled on a ragged set of sweats, and headed for the garage. Hanging from the ceiling was a heavy punching bag that he picked up from a gym that closed a few years before. He slipped on an old pair of lightweight boxing gloves and began to hit the bag. The work out started with a few short jabs followed by a short right cross and left hook. He increased the intensity as he dug deeper into the bag with every blow.

The sweat began to flow, and his heart began to pound. But, this time the changes were caused by something other than anxiety. The burning muscles and determined focus took him back to a better time when his adversary was human, and stood right in front of him. In the midst of this physical explosion his demons would rest, and leave him for a while.

The shaking, bouncing punching bag sent a low rumble through the house, and woke the rest of the family. All three converged at the top of the stairs at the same time, and headed down to investigate. Katie was first to reach the garage door. As she slowly opened it Butch and Terry looked over her shoulder.

Each stared at Vic as he continued to relentlessly pound away at the shaking bag. By now he was soaked in sweat, and even from a distance they could see the veins bulging from his neck and forearms. Butch was first to speak, and said in a low tone. "I don't think the bat would slow him down much right now."

Terry pushed the door close, and signaled them toward the kitchen. Once there she said. "Why don't you get ready for school, and I'll make some breakfast."

Katie asked. "Is he better now?"

"He's different, and that's better. Let's stay with that for now, and see what happens." Her answer carried reassurance even if only for now.

By the time pancakes and eggs hit the kitchen table the pounding stopped, and the kids settled down for breakfast. Vic walked in from the garage, and all three looked his way to see a man that each remembered, one who brought them love, purpose and security. "Ready for some breakfast dad?" Katie asked.

"I think I need a shower first sweetheart." He told her. As he passed the table he smiled at all three, and headed upstairs.

"It's gonna take a while isn't it mom?" Butch asked.

Terry nodded her head yes, and added. "Your dad is the bravest, toughest man I ever met. All he needs from us is a little time, and lots of love. He'll do the rest."

By the time Vic finished his shower and made his way to the breakfast table the kids were gone, and Terry was working on the finances for one of the bakeries. He grabbed a cup of coffee, and sat down beside her. As he did she greeted him with. "Good morning. You were up early."

"I was up late, early and everything between. The work out helped. Tony was right." He told her.

"So, that's something you can do when things stack up?" She asked.

"I have no idea. It worked this morning. I have to keep looking for what works next time." He was trying to explain bits and pieces of what he didn't understand himself.

"Does it bother you to talk about it?" Terry didn't know if she should press, but desperately wanted to understand as much as possible.

"Not this morning. But, sometimes just thinking about it pisses me off. Last time at the V.A. they told us about triggers, things that cause reactions and trouble. There're like reflexes. Ya can't stop um, and can't block um out. They come from extreme situations." He was amazed that he was able to say that much.

"What kind of situations." She was even more nervous about questioning further, but wanted all he could provide.

Vic sat for a long moment, and the pause put her on edge. But, he showed no sign of anger or frustration, only deliberation. Finally he said. "Do you remember the news footage during the war, the cop shooting the guy in the head, and the little girl running naked down the road?"

"I remember. They plaid that stuff almost every night." She recalled.

"Do you remember how shocked people were over it?" He questioned.

"Sure. It was a driving force for the protests." She recalled.

"Well, that's war, not just Vietnam but all war. No one stopped the cop from shooting the guy. No one wrapped the little girl in a blanket. In another time or another place they would have. But, war changed them. It blocked out the things that mattered to them once." Vic felt like he was listening to someone else rather than saying it himself.

"Do they change back?" She was terrified of the answer and sorry she asked.

His reply hit hard. Vic looked at his wife through sad eyes as he said. "No they don't. Once a warrior, always a warrior. The only thing that gives me any hope at all is something an old Marine said during one of the V.A. sessions. The things that mattered before aren't gone. We just set them aside. But, they're very hard to find, and each day we have to look for them all over again."

"I don't understand why they're so hard to hang onto. Don't they mean as much anymore?" What he said hurt her, and it showed.

"They're reflexes Terry. That's the best way I can explain it. It's not that you and the kids don't matter. Hell, you're the most important things in my life. But, believe what I said. I can't control the reflexes, and can't stop them." He watched closely for some sign that she understood.

Terry sat quietly, and continued to look at him. She was trying desperately to allow all this to soak in. She said nothing.

"Think about this". He went on. "When I left I was a good old boy. I played ball, drank beer and partied til dawn. I came home a stone cold killer. I took lives with the same emotion as stepping on a bug. The reflexes that allowed me to do that also kept me alive. They're a part of me, and I can't let them go. But, I'll make a place for you and the kids because you're what makes life worthwhile. Without you nothing would matter. You're my reason to keep trying."

"So, what does it feel like when the reflexes take over?" Terry decided there was no point in stopping as long as Vic was willing to talk. Much of what he already said was more than she could process. Never the less she wanted to know more.

"The demons come in different forms. There are times I wake up and am furious, and have no idea why. Crowds make me nervous because I can't keep track of what's going on around me. Sometime I feel nothing at all. I'm completely empty. There are weeks at a time when I can't relax. Sleep finally comes when I'm too exhausted to keep going." He stopped even though he could have gone on much longer.

"Demons?" She asked. Somehow that made sense. She remembered thinking it was almost like he was possessed.

"Demons!" He repeated. "I can't get rid of them. But, there must be ways to cope with them. I need to learn those ways."

The waiting room wasn't as crowded as Vic expected. The two guys behind the desk had things moving smoothly. The one on the right looked much more like a bouncer than V.A. receptionist. As Vic approached he asked. "Name and last four of your social security."

"Morretto, 6040." I have an appointment with Karen Erickson at three." He replied.

"I'll let her know you're here." He assured Vic.

Within a few minutes an attractive lady in her early forties rounded the corner of the reception area, and announced in a calm, confident voice. "Vic Morretto?"

"Right here." He returned as he stood and headed in her direction.

"Good afternoon. I'm Karen. How are you?" The question was much more than a greeting. His response, and most all of the things he said were part of the evaluation process.

"Today's about fifty-fifty. I'm workin hard on the down side." He replied.

Karen said nothing else until they were in her office behind closed doors. Once there she inquired. "Tell me a little about yourself, and your service. And, thank you for that service."

Vic gave her the short version of his family, his past and a brief overview of his tour in Vietnam. He was sure she'd ask for whatever additional details she needed. Half way through the first hour he felt comfortable, but was confused by the questions she asked, and observations she made.

Then she dropped the first bomb as she told him. "I'm recommending you go through a series of sessions with me, but there are some things you need to understand before we start. Don't tell me anything that may incriminate you for illegal acts. Don't make treats or talked about actions that may harm you or someone else. If you do I have to report them."

Vic watched her closely as he simply said. "OK."

Then the second bomb. "Of the people who go through this about half don't finish. Of those who do only half benefit from it. I'm simply a coach. You have to do the work, and the process is very difficult. That's why so many don't finish."

"If I don't try I damned sure won't get anything from it. Things have to change. I'm losing my family and myself." He announced.

Vic went once a week. Each session was more difficult than the one before. After talking over which treatment might fit him best they decided on Cognitive Process Therapy, a method that allows suffers to view how they react to given situations, and to see how the view of those situations can be modified to minimize damaging results.

He learned ways to identify stressful conditions, determine possible causes and view contributing factors in ways that were less likely to upset him. The process was simple, but completely unnatural. It required practice many times every day. He found it very frustrating, but was determined to make it work.

The worst of the program game in the sixth week. Karen had Vic hand write a description of his worst experience during his combat tour. She insisted he include every detail, and attach side comments about how he felt while writing the account. The process was controlled, but none the less devastating as she made him read his account out loud.

Here's what he wrote:

We set up as usual in the evening for what looked like a routine night. Ambushes were out, and communications established. We were in range of artillery support, and air cover was available if needed.

I feel a little tense now. My heart is pounding. He added as a side note.

Just before one in the morning the ambush between us and the river reported movement to the south. Immediately after they began taking fire. Within seconds our perimeter was hit on two sided.

My shoulders and neck are very tight. My heart's about to blow out of my chest. He added in his second note.

The M-60s have opened up, and flares are in the air. The guys have popped Claymores, and took out a bunch of NVA. Damn, those things tear um up. My buddy, Ben, and I have no trouble picking out targets, but they just keep coming. In the dim light I see something flying through the air and holler. "Incoming".

I FEEL SICK. He wrote in the margin in large capital letters.

A blast spins me around and knocks me to the ground. As my ears clear I hear the Gooks screaming as they pound through the brush. Ben is screaming too. Then he is not screaming anymore.

There's an NVA directly in front of me, but he looks past as if I'm not there. I fire three shots that hit him directly in the chest, and he falls back. I have to move now, and keep moving.

My hands are shaking, and it's hard to keep writing. Still feel sick. He added to the previous side notes.

By this time it took all Vic's effort to continue reading his account. He forced each word as streams of tears flowed down his face, and he sobbed between words. He didn't look up, and forgot Karen was there. He continued:

I'm not going to make it. Our Father who art in Heaven……………………
Another Gook steps from behind a tree, and I shoot him in the face. I
gotta keep moving.

As another flare pops I see NVA taking fire from a spot just east of me.
Some of my guys are still there. I gotta move now, fast and low. They're
just a few yards away now. "Hey guys I'm coming out". I yell in their
direction. They watch as I move to them.

Damn, the words are all running together. He'd scrawled in a note off to
the side.

A few more join us, and we move back toward our original position.
We're not taking fire now, and the NVA we find are dead or wounded.
One of the guys yells. "That sapper is still alive". As I look directly
ahead I see the Gook in black pajamas trying to get to his feet, and I
shoot him in the back of the head. He drops instantly.

On the way we pick up a couple of our guys who were hit, and carry
them to a spot where the choppers can land. Once the wounded are
loaded three of us look for Ben, and find him at the spot where we were
separated.

I gotta stop for a minute. Was his last note in the margin. He finished
with:

The blast didn't kill Ben. His flack jacket was open, and I could see stab
wounds all over his chest and stomach. We carried him to the LZ, and
laid him with the rest of our dead.

Vic tossed his hand written account on the table in front of him, took a
deep breath and wiped his face with his handkerchief.

As he looked up Karen said. "Wow."

When Vic regained control he looked at her and said. "I'm sorry. I don't know what happened to me. I've never lost it like that before."

In her most sincere and professional voice Karen told him. "Don't be sorry. You just told me about a horrifying experience that would upset anyone. You're supposed to be upset. And, you're supposed to cry. It's a release that's necessary."

"I lost control, and can't do that. I have to stay in control." He insisted.

"God, I hate this stoic approach they program into you guys. It's OK to let go here. We're in this room alone, and the door is locked. If you can't let go here then where?" She challenged.

He looked at her for a long moment, and said nothing.

Karen continued. "Think about the work we've done, and consider another way to look at letting go. Do you understand that it's necessary?"

"I believe I have to do something, and trust you to help me find that something." He conceded.

"OK, that's a start. Keep going. You have to take that next step." She pressed.

"Well, if I can't keep it bottled up inside then I guess I have to let go." He admitted.

"Good." She reassured, and then stared at him waiting for more.

Vic sighed and shook his head. "This stuff is so simple, and yet so hard for me to see. I feel like a fool."

"Don't do that." She insisted.

"Do what?" He questioned in a mildly irritated voice.

"What do all you guys do, over and over again?" She asked as she tapped herself on the forehead repeatedly.

Vic looked at her with an expression to showed total confusion.

She smiled and said. "Stop beating yourself up. You're going to make mistakes. You're going to fall short. You're human. Accept that."

He smiled at her and leaned back, allowing himself to relax for the first time in a long time. "Do you ever get tired of spending time with wacked out GIs like me?"

"No." She said honestly. "See you next week, same time, same place."

During the drive home Vic felt the numbness that he experienced so many times before. He was spent. But, now he began to understand how complex and difficult his situation really was. Even more important, he was admitting that he had limits, and must adjust and work within them.

Terry was waiting at the coffee shop where they often met when their schedules crossed paths. She was anxious to hear about his session at the VA. After each grabbed a cup of their favorite they settled into a quiet corner, and she asked. "How did it go?"

Vic took a deep breath and tried to decide how to explain what was so difficult for him to understand. "This one was very tough. It's hard for me to admit that I broke down and cried like a fool. But, that's just what happened. Then the therapist tells me that's exactly what I'm supposed to do. Honestly, it's like I don't even know who I am anymore."

"I know who you are. This is just a part of you that's new to both of us." She observed.

"I don't know if I trust this new part." He said in a concerned voice.

"I do. And, I love this part because you're willing to try to recognize it." She reassured him.

Tony was also back in rehab. at the local Vet. Center. His councilor was and ex-Army Ranger who'd served in several conflicts. This was Tony's third try at counseling, and it was very hard for him to admit help was still necessary.

Ann no longer faced the fact that the man she viewed with such great respect could be so vulnerable. Tony didn't talk with her anymore about his service related problems because it was easier to keep them to himself.

Ann's denial reminded him of the time after her mother passed away, when she shut herself off from so many things. If this was her way of dealing with problems that needed time to accept, then he would give her the time she needed. But, he couldn't shake the fact that his problems came between them. There were still many, many things that made their relationship special and rewarding. His many years dealing with combat related stress showed him ways to make the most of what he had.

Every day he would include things that often felt unnatural, insignificant or uncomfortable. He tried in each case to find something of value or interest, and accepted the fact that often his efforts made little difference. The fact that he found a few things worthwhile kept him looking for more, and believing there was much more to find.

Summer brought on some of the most difficult times, particularly the Forth-of-July. He began preparing himself for the long week end weeks before. He paid special attention to arrangements for the barbeque that was an annual tradition at the Frisano house. Their place was big, and yard even bigger with plenty of room for celebrations.

It wasn't that Tony didn't like the company of those close to him. But, this large group was still a crowd even though it included friends and family. He learned to focus on individuals, one at a time. But, even after years of parties maintaining focus still took lots of concentration.

On one particular Independence Day the back yard was full, and Tony was involved with a neighbor who had a new truck he was anxious to describe to all who'd listen. His attention quickly shifted to one of the guys he'd played ball with many years before. He was accompanied by two friends who'd obviously been celebrating long before they arrived at the Frisano's.

The first thing Tony heard from the most intoxicated companion was. "Nice place with plenty of fucking beer".

That was enough to cause intervention. Tony crossed the yard, and was quickly in front of all three. His ball playing friend was first to speak. "This is Tony Frisano, the guy who bought the beer".

"Hey, nice fucking place Tony". The drunk exclaimed in a voice loud enough to be heard by all in attendance. His half smile said he planned to do and say whatever he pleased.

Tony struggled for control, and simply smiled and nodded to the delight of the drunk. As attention from the rest of the crowd in the back yard shifted away from them Tony put his arm around the obnoxious intruded and whispered softly. "You say fuck one more time and I'm gonna use your stupid ass as a bottle opener." As the drunk looked up Tony continued. "No really, I'm gonna shove a beer up your ass, twist quick, and leave the cap behind."

By this time Vic joined them, and added in an equally soft voice. "I can't find an opener. You suppose this ass hole can help?"

The drunk found his way to a lawn chair, and quietly nursed a drink. Ann approached Tony and Vic with a concerned look that neither could ignore. "Was that really necessary, or would a little reason work better?" She asked in an angry tone.

"Drunks don't reason, and I don't plan for these kids to listen to a jerk like that." He snapped back.

"What if things would have gone wrong? What if he wouldn't have backed down? Did you and Vic plan to slap him around in front of the kids?" She demanded.

"Can we do this later?" He asked.

Ann walked away without saying anything else.

The exchange with her stuck with him through the rest of the day, and into the evening. They'd always had enough respect for one another to allow them to agree to disagree. But, it was happening far more often now than ever before. It was something he didn't want to ignore, but he would wait for the right time and place to talk with her.

Vic, Terry, Butch and Katie stayed long after the rest were gone. The kids found plenty to keep them occupied in the basement game room while the adults munched leftovers in the kitchen, and talked and laughed about old times.

The mood suddenly changed when Terry asked. "Did anyone see the article in the paper about the problems the VA is having with funding and staffing? Is it that bad where you guys go?"

"The Vet. Center is running pretty smoothly, but the VA is always jammed up. Ya have to be patient and wait your turn." Tony told her. Ann said nothing.

"Do you think it affects the care they give?" Terry continued.

"The lady I'm working with has my bases covered. In fact, she goes to extremes to make sure I do things right." Vic replied.

"How about you Tony? They treating you right?" Terry inquired.

"I'm at the Vet. Center. It's part of the VA, but separate at the same time. My councilor is an ex-grunt, and is also very thorough. But, at the same time it's more like talking to one of the guys." Tony added. Ann still sat quietly.

"So, do they tell you how long you have to stay with the treatment? Is it the same for everyone, or does it change depending on your problems?" Terry pressed.

Tony became more thoughtful as he said. "There's no cure for what we have. The changes in us last forever. But, we learn how to deal with it. It doesn't get easier. We just get better at it."

Ann suddenly stood, and headed for the stairs. "I'm gonna check on the kids." She announced.

As she disappeared into the basement Terry asked. "Did I go too far, or ask too much?" Her voice showed her concern.

"She needs time for all this to soak in. It's nothing you said. In fact, it's good that we talked about it." Tony assured her.

"We should go. It's late, and we have a full day tomorrow." Terry said as she stood, and headed for the basement. The guys followed.

As they entered the room each carefully stepped over nearly every manner of entertainment device available at the time. All four kids were gathered around Ann as they pleaded in unison. "Can we stay here? Ya, can they stay?"

"Ya Aunt Terry. Let um stay. We'll even clean up the mess. Honest!" Sean added.

Ann stood in the midst of it all with a broad smile as she nodded approval. "It's fine. Let um stay. Besides, it's the first time ours have volunteered to clean this place up."

Terry looked in amazement at the change in her friend. In less than a minute she saw the woman who she first met so long ago. Tony was right she hoped. Ann just needs time.

On the way home she turned to Vic, and asked. "Did I ask too many questions?"

"Ya, you did. She'll never speak to you again." He replied through a subtle smile.

She punched him in the arm. "Answer me damn it."

He allowed a moment for the mood to change, and then replied. "Tony told me she had a hard time with the idea of his therapy. I didn't know it was that big a problem until now."

"Why do you think it's so hard for her to understand and accept?" She questioned.

"Tony has always been a rock. He's the guy everyone depends on to make things work. She can't accept the fact that he's struggling so hard with this. It scares the hell out of her." He tried to explain.

"I thought she'd have more faith in him." Terry said, thinking out loud.

Her reply irritated Vic. He gave himself time to try to see her perspective before answering. Then he said. "She's very scared Terry. She loves the guy, and is afraid of what this might do to him."

"I thought she was tougher than that." She continued.

"You're being judgmental. Give her some time damn it " His voice was firm, but showed no anger.

His stern reply surprised her a little, and make her shift her view if only slightly. To break the mood she said. "Judgmental huh? Big word."

"Been waiting months to sneak it in." He replied.

Back at the Frisano house, Tony and Ann left the debris cluttered basement to the kids, and settled in upstairs on the couch.

After a relaxed pause Ann said. "It's not that I don't care Tony." As she did she felt a lump form in her throat.

"I know." He reassured, and put his arm around her in the same way he had so often before.

"Are you OK?" She force while choking back the tears.

"What I have is something I need to deal with so that we can have a Forth-of-July party, and sit on this couch. It's not an easy thing, but I'll never give up. I'm gonna make mistakes Annie, and there'll be times when I have to work things out. But, I promise that you and I and our couch will always be there." Somehow he believed he'd helped her understand.

"Do I need to help. Do you need me to................?" The tears kept her from finishing.

He pulled her close and said. "You help me each and every day. You're my anchor, the one who shows me who I want to be, and why I want to keep trying. You're the one who makes the pieces fit."

There comes a time for all of us when we must face life anew, a time to separate dreams from memories. Memories are to cherish and treasure. Dreams are ours to motivate and inspire.

But, the present is where we build our lives. It's the only place we can make a difference. The past is gone forever, and the future is full of variables that are beyond our control. We can adjust and plan for it, but can never put it above the present because how we handle the present is our only opportunity for a better future.

Tony continued in his roll as the rock who provided a foundation for so many who were close to him. He accepted the burden associated with this roll because it helped those he loved. He struggled for the rest of his life with the demons Vietnam created because once war made him a warrior, a warrior is what he would always be.

Ann was there for him through all their challenges. She would falter as she had in the past, and then recover to provide love and happiness. This combination of frailty and resilience made Tony treasure her all the more.

Vic battled alcohol and depression every day for the rest of his life. But, when a situation demanded courage and decisive action he was always there. That was the easy part for him. His real challenge came at the end of the day when there were no more battles to win or action to take. In the quiet and the dark he would feel the room close in as his heart began to pound. His eyes would race from side to side as the warrior in his sole searched for the enemy who would never come.

Terry's strength in the face of a complicated and heartless world was amazing. She was tough beyond belief, but could provide a special kind of tenderness to those close to her.

Life took its toll on all four as the years passed. Strength and courage fade in all of us as time and trouble chip away. But, as Tony, Vic, Ann and Terry weakened Sean, Angie, Butch and Katie came into their own. Their story was yet to come.